It Should've Been Me

ReShonda Tate Billingsley
Victoria Christopher Murray

Houston, Texas * Washington, D.C. * Raleigh/Durham, NC

Brown Girls Books LLC
www.BrownGirlsBooks.com
ISBN: 978-1-944359-51-5 (ebook)
ISBN: 978-1-944359-50-8 (print)

First Brown Girls Publishing LLC trade printing

Manufactured and Printed in the United States of America

Chapter 1

Tamara Collins

In my last film, I'd played a psychotic woman who stabbed her husband in the stomach thirty-two times with a Swiss Army knife. Now, looking at the man who'd just stepped into this huge conference room made me curl my hand into a fist as if I were holding that knife again.

"This cannot be happening," I mumbled, as I stepped to the other side of the room that had been set up in the Renaissance Hotel for our first rehearsal. I pivoted, so that he wouldn't see me and I could get my face together in a few seconds.

I was already upset because this jacked-up, twenty-degrees warmer than normal Atlanta temperature had turned my Brazilian Blowout into a Philippine Poof. Now I had to deal with this, too?

Clearly, I was being punished for something I had done, maybe in a previous life. I didn't believe in reincarnation, but that was the only way I could explain why I hadn't had a movie role in two years. Or maybe it wasn't punishment. Maybe it was because my name wasn't Cameron Diaz or Jennifer Anniston or that my skin wasn't the color of mashed potatoes.

Yes! That was it. That was the reason why I was in this room, an A actor (okay, maybe an A minus or at worst, a B plus) on the play circuit.

Now, don't get me wrong, I loved theater, always had, always would. Some of the greats—James Earl Jones, Cicely Tyson, Vanessa Williams, even Denzel Washington—had all slayed the stage. And August Wilson's "Fences"—now that Pulitzer Prize winning play was one of my all-time favorites. Having a role in "Fences," on the Great White Way, in the magnificent city of New York, would have been as much of a coup as just about any big screen movie.

But this wasn't "Fences" nor was it "Aida" or "Fela." And this wasn't Broadway. This wasn't even off-Broadway, it wasn't two blocks over from Broadway. This was down the street, around the corner, across the river, and almost nine hundred miles away from Broadway.

And once we began touring, we'd leave Atlanta and go deep into the 'Chitlin Circuit,' probably visiting cities I'd never heard of and towns that sounded like the butt end of jokes.

I did have a little secret, though. One that I would deny if anyone ever asked me—I liked these off, off, off, off, off Broadway plays. Over the years, I'd attended quite a few if I happened to be in the city where one was playing. Of course, I made sure I was unrecognizable, always wearing huge sunglasses, always wearing a hat *and* a scarf, always keeping my head low so that no one would know that, I, Tamara Collins, the classically trained actor, laughed at all the off-center jokes, swayed to all the off-key songs, then stood with the audience at the end, giving all a standing ovation.

So while the title and some of the scenes ruffled my classical Yale University School of Drama sensibilities, I couldn't knock the thousands and thousands of fans who enjoyed these plays and the thousands and thousands of dollars that I was being paid to bring my talents to the stage.

Glancing over my shoulder, I checked to see if I'd been spotted yet. But *he* was still talking to Gwen Tanner, the creator, writer, director and producer of this play. After taking another moment and a deep breath, I sat in one of the chairs lined up against the wall. When I was ready, I raised my eyes and stared. Because him seeing me, and our having to speak to each other, was inevitable.

This made me once again ask myself what was I doing here? It had started just about a month ago. My agent, Maury had received the script from Gwen. I already knew her name. She was new on the play circuit and she was the first female to have massive success. Two plays, two NAACP Image Awards, and lots of buzz for the uplifting messages that followed the slapstick comedy. After I'd read the script, I was even more impressed. Yeah, it had the typical female-on-female hatin', female-on-male drama, but at the end, there was a powerful message of never allowing anyone's voice to be louder than God's.

So with Gwen's reputation, the ten thousand dollars per week they were paying me for the ten-week run, plus two weeks for rehearsals, and the sad fact that I had no other offers, I'd signed on, knowing it was the right thing to do.

That was what I believed when I signed the contract two weeks ago. Heck, that was what I believed yesterday, this morning, five minutes ago. That was what I believed until Donovan had walked into this room.

Donovan Dobbs, the hot R&B singer and a heartthrob who'd been commanding the stage and stealing hearts for twenty years, ever since he was sixteen years old. He could even act a little, but his major talent—he was fine. It was like God decided to toss Michael Ealy, Blair Underwood and Idris Elba into a blender, hit start, and see what came out. Yep. Donovan was the personification of brown and beautiful.

And he was a low down dirty dog.

"Well, well, well..."

My plan had been to keep my eyes on him. But I guess as I'd taken that little jaunt down that lane filled with bad memories, Donovan had spotted me.

"If it isn't the love of my life." His tone sounded like he wasn't surprised to see me.

He was still several feet away when he'd said those words, and I could feel the others in the room pause, then stop and watch as Donovan walked my way with his signature strut; he had swagger before the word had even been invented. He had swagger and that smile. The whole time he kept that smile that I loved. That smile that I hated.

"So, when did you get in?" he asked when he stopped in front of me. He opened his arms, then reached for me as if he was crazy enough to expect some kind of hug.

I wanted to hug him all right. And if I'd had that knife from my last movie, I would have—hugged him and stabbed him straight in his back. Instead, I glared and hoped that my stare was filled with the heat that I felt. I hoped my stare set him on fire, and I swear, if I saw a single flame, I wouldn't even spit on him to save him.

Standing, I didn't part my lips as I moved away. I heard his chuckles as I stomped by, but though I wanted to stop and swing on him, I kept marching until I was right in front of Gwen.

It didn't matter that she was chatting with one of the other actors. We hadn't all been introduced yet, so I had no idea what role the tall, svelte, with a tan that made her one-degree above white, woman was playing. I didn't care. There was only one piece of business on my mind and Gwen needed to handle this now. "I need to speak with you." It was a demand, not a request.

"Yeah, what's up?" Gwen replied, giving me just a quick glance.

"Privately," I said.

The actor, who I pegged as a newcomer since I didn't recognize her, gave me a smirk with a little attitude. But before I could roll my neck back at her, Gwen said, "Camille, give us a minute," and the woman did a moonwalk away from us.

As soon as she was out of earshot, I hissed, "What is he doing here?" I jabbed a finger in Donovan's direction.

When Gwen and I looked his way, Donovan winked.

Gwen grinned and I wanted to puke.

By the time she turned back to me, her expression was stiff with seriousness. "Who? Donovan?" She gave a little shrug, and then with a wave of her hand that made the dozen of wooden bangles on her arm jingle, she announced, "He's in the play."

My glance took in the woman who was really quite striking in the floor-length West African print duster that she wore. Her sister locs were swept up on top of her head and wrapped in a matching band. But right now, I didn't care that she stood in front of me like she was some kind of African Queen. I was the star of this play, and she needed to address the problem I had with this.

"I assumed that he was here because he was in the play," I snapped. "What role is he playing?"

I guess that was the question she was waiting for me to ask and the one she wanted to answer. Her grin was back when she said, "He's playing your love interest."

My nostrils flared and my fingers began that search again for that knife. But I stayed calm, remained professional, though not even my Yale training could hide the fury in my voice. "I thought Jamal was my leading man."

Jamal Brown was the R & B singer turned reality star, who didn't have the voice or the looks of Donovan. But what he did have was my approval. Seriously, my contract said that I had approval of the man who would be starring opposite me.

"Oh, yeah. Well, he had to drop out at the last minute," she said as if that fact were not a big deal. "He got a movie deal."

Wait! Stop! What? My thoughts did a little rewind. A movie deal? For a moment, I wanted to keep the button pressed on pause and ask, 'What movie deal?' because this was the problem. This was why actors, like me, couldn't get roles. Singers and reality stars and everyone who couldn't act were landing contracts and taking parts that rightfully belonged to those of us who'd been trained.

But I had to come down from that mental soapbox and stay focused on what was in front of me.

"So, Jamal left and you're telling me that you couldn't find anyone else?"

Gwen tilted her head a little, frowned and stared at me as if my words had put her into a state of confusion.

Clearly, she had no acting training. Or maybe it was just that no matter what she said or did, I knew what this was all about. Everyone in these United States of America knew about my drama with Donovan—it had been covered by every gossip blog, played out in every major tabloid, and dissected on every entertainment show. So Gwen casting Donovan in this role was no mistake. She was trying to take my drama and my pain all the way to her bank.

"Tamara, I'm sorry if you have a problem with Donovan, but the show opens in two weeks." Her tone was saccharine sweet, leaving a bad aftertaste in my ears. "I'm grateful that Donovan was even available on such short notice."

"Well, I'm not about to be in this play with him." I folded my arms and raised an eyebrow. She needed to know I was serious about this.

There was no way Gwen would ever be able to convince me that this was a coincidence. First of all, my mother had always told me there was no such thing as a coincidence. And secondly, I was just supposed to believe that she'd written a script about a woman who'd been left at the altar and now I was to play opposite the man who'd left me right there?

Oh no! I wasn't about to become fodder for the tabloids and the blogs and the shows again.

"Now, Tam," Gwen said, her sweet tone still in place.

"It's Tamara." I snuggled my arms tighter across my chest.

"*Tamara.*" All of that sweetness was gone when she said, "I know you're upset, and I'm sorry I didn't realize this before...."

Yeah, right. She must think I'm BooBoo the fool.

"But I know you wouldn't want Entertainment Tonight, Access Hollywood, Black Voices and every other entertainment outlet to know that your ex ran you off from a professional production, would you?"

I was not impressed because whatever they said about me leaving wouldn't be nearly as bad as what they'd say if I stayed.

I kept my stance and that made Gwen add, "And, if that isn't important to you, just remember, you have a contract."

"And?" I smirked.

"And, you know contracts are binding."

That made me stand up straight, lower my arms, and stare at her as if her brain had just fallen out of her head. Was this heffa threatening to sue me? Over a freakin' stageplay? A Chitlin' Circuit stageplay?

"Look," Gwen said, taking a deep breath before returning to a more natural smile. "I don't want any disgruntled actors, but I have a show to put on and I know you're a professional. You're one of the few talented black actresses out there," she added, I guess believing that flattery never hurt. "I have all the confidence in the world that you'll be able to handle this." Then, she leaned in and lowered her voice as if she were about to share something with me like we were just girls. "Don't let him get to you."

I wanted to tell her first, that true thespians of the female persuasion preferred to be called actors. And then, *don't let him get to me?* How would she handle this situation?

I knew I was trapped, but while I would never admit it, I wanted her to admit one thing. "You did this on purpose, right?"

"Oh, you give me too much credit," Gwen said, making her bangles jingle again.

Yup, she'd never taken an acting lesson a day in her life.

"Look, while this play bears *some* resemblance to your life, trust me, it wasn't done on purpose. Besides if you think about it, it's not really that close to your story. You never made it to the altar, remember?"

My fingers began that clutching thing again.

"Is there a problem, ladies?" Donovan asked over my shoulder. I didn't even turn to face him, not acknowledging him in any manner. Well, at least not on the outside. Inside, I felt a little flutter, and I cursed that right out of me.

But while I tried to do nothing, Gwen flashed a smile. "And why in the world would there be any problem?" she said, her glance settling over my right shoulder. "I was just going over some last minute script changes with Tamara."

"I'm looking forward to working with you, Tammie-Poo," Donovan said.

I whipped around. No, this fool didn't call me by the pet name he'd given me when we'd first met.

"Whatever," I said, shoving my way past him.

He scurried after me. "Hey, hey, hey, I've been looking forward to this, baby. What's the problem?" he asked, taking my hand and stopping me.

I looked down to where he still held me, then my gaze inched up until I met his eyes. I snatched my hand away and hissed, "You're my problem."

Stepping closer to me, he said, "Please don't be like that. There's a lot you don't know. So much that we have to talk about."

I blinked. Inside his voice, I heard something—like truth, like love.

He moved in what felt like the slowest of motions: His hand raised, he reached toward me, his fingertips grazed my cheek.

And a wave rolled through my center.

Inside, I cursed again. This time I cursed my libido and Donovan. Squeezing my legs together, I wondered why my own body would betray me like this? I hated him and I needed every part of my body to remember that.

His hand lingered on my cheek for too long, and I slapped him away. "Look, Donovan." My tone was as sharp as the edge of steel. "We're both here now, so we'll do our jobs and get this over with."

"Great." He exhaled as if somehow my words had given him relief. As if he'd been concerned that I'd walk out the door. "I was hoping you would stay and now, I hope this means that we can hook up...."

"What?" I exclaimed.

"For a drink. Tonight. I just want to talk."

Hook up? A drink? To talk? After I let the gall of his request settle in my mind, I said, "Donovan, you want to talk?"

He grinned and bobbed his head up and down like a puppy.

This time, I was the one who leaned in closer. "Then go home and talk to your wife."

He blinked.

I added, "Your wife, remember? The woman you left me for."

I did one of those moves that I'd learned in freshman drama—a half-turn pivot, before my arm swooped down into the chair where I grabbed my hobo, swung it over my shoulder, and then I did a slow, hip swaying strut right out the door.

Chapter 2

Gwen Tanner Weinstein

I was trying not to watch, or at least pretend that I didn't see what was happening. But, I wanted to lift my head and gawk the way everyone else in this room was doing.

What a coup! What a coup!

If I could jump up and give myself a high-five, I would. But for appearances purposes, all I did was keep my eyes on my tablet as if I were checking for last minute script changes. As if my ears didn't hear the fury burning inside Tamara. As if I didn't realize the money I was about to make from bringing Tamara and Donovan together.

Still, I kept my eyes down until Tamara slammed the door on her way out of the conference room.

Then as if the sound startled me, I looked up, looked around, looked confused as I took in everyone in the room. The expressions were many but they all added up to one thing—that I had a zinger of a winner. This little blow-up proved that my calculation had been correct. All around the country people would come out to see Donomara, the younger, sexier, more beautiful African-American version of Bradgelina, but this couple had never made it close to anybody's altar.

Forget about the roof, ticket sales would bust heaven wide open.

"Okay, everyone," I said, keeping my voice even as if I hadn't seen what had just gone down. "Let's get started in fifteen. Donovan, it'll be you and Tamara. I want to start with the third scene." I paused and glanced around as if I were in search of my star. "Where's Tamara?"

No one said a word.

"I'll find her," I said with exasperation all through my tone. "Everyone, go over your lines, we have a lot of work to do to be ready in two weeks and I don't have time for all of this." I stopped again and this time, steadied my stare on Donovan. "If everyone does their part, this show is going to be epic."

He gave me a grin as if he appreciated the major move I made and again, I wanted to do that high-five thing. Instead, I shook my head in pretend annoyance and stepped out of the room. The moment the door closed behind me, I pulled my cell from my pocket, hit the message icon and typed:

She's all the way in, the rest of your money is on the way.

After I pressed Send, I counted in my head and before I got to five:

I told you. Thank you for the bonus.

My response:

No problem, just make sure that Tam is all the way in. I don't want any surprises. I can't afford any substitutions, I need her to make this work.

His response:

No worries. I made sure that this was the only job on her horizon.

He could have saved the effort his fingers made with that text. Of course, there would be no worries. I'd paid Maury Koster a ten thousand dollar bonus to make sure he delivered his client. Agents were supposed to look out for their people, but this business, like the rest of entertainment, was scandalous. It was always about your own come-up and what you could put into your own bank account.

Glancing at my watch, I had ten minutes to get to my room and pay Maury the rest of his money. Of course, I could have done it from the app on my phone, but I never handled money this way—always only on my computer.

As I rushed to the elevator, I caught a glimpse of Tamara in the second floor atrium, with her cell pressed against her ear. Her hands moved with urgency as she spoke, and for a moment, I wondered if I should go to her, console her a bit. But then, I chose to go to my room and finish the transaction that had delivered her as the star in my play. I didn't really want Tamara calmed down. She needed to stay fired up and ready to go at Donovan each and every time they shared the stage. My challenge would be to keep all of that emotional animosity between the two through the entire tour. The key was to keep her emotionally on edge, which wouldn't be that difficult—she was an actress, one of those pretty girls, who had meltdowns when life didn't go their way.

The moment I stepped into my hotel room, though, my thoughts shifted from my star to the man who'd delivered her. Rushing to the desk, I sat at my computer and within minutes, the transfer was complete. I wondered if Maury had any idea how much I made on these plays. I was certain he didn't because if he'd done any kind of research or calculations, he would have charged me five times that amount, with what I expected the box office to pull with Tamara Collins and Donovan Dobbs as the headliners on the marquis.

I clapped my hands, excited by my brilliance. My plays had already brought me many awards, but I'd never been after that kind of recognition. It was never about fame, I couldn't spend that. I didn't mind admitting that my self-esteem was tied up in the fortune I wanted.

And not just for spending sake, money was much more than that. It was the measure of success—at least that's what my husband had taught me.

Swiveling in the chair, I turned until my eyes were on the framed photo of my husband. Standing, I moved toward the nightstand and lifted the picture that I always brought with me on the road.

Even four years later, Eli still looked so distinguished to me, sexy in that older white male aristocratic kind of way. With the tip of my finger, I traced the outline of his beard that was almost all gray now, appropriate for a man who was already on the other side of fifty.

I tossed the photo onto the bed before I grabbed my phone from my bag and clicked on 'favorites'. I pushed the phone to my ear right away, just so I wouldn't change my mind.

When he answered the phone, "This is Eli Weinstein," I wanted to hang up. That's how he greeted his wife? He had Caller ID; he knew who was on the other end.

Still I said, "Hi, sweetheart."

"You made it to Atlanta safely," was the way he returned my hello.

"Yeah, I'm sorry I didn't call when I landed. The plane was delayed at LaGuardia." It was an easy lie since I didn't have to worry about him spending the time to check. "I got to the hotel after midnight and didn't want to disturb you."

"Well, I'm glad you're safe."

"I am. And thank you again, Eli, for the money to do this."

He grunted. "Yeah, well, I hope this play pays off better than your last one."

I closed my eyes remembering that big check that I'd had to write that ate up a good part of my profits from my last play. It had been a hush-hush kind of thing, so quiet that not even my husband knew why my second play had achieved acclaim, but made no money. "It will," I finally said, telling my first truth of our conversation. "This play will make money. I'm working hard to make sure that it does."

"I know you are."

I wanted to stay in this moment, wanted to savor his softer tone, imagining that this was the way he talked to me all the time. The same way he'd talked to me when we'd met at that Entrepreneurial Winner's Workshop eight years ago. The same way he talked to me for the year of our courtship.

"Well, I have to get going." His tone was back to stone. "I have a full day in front of me while you're out hobbying." He chuckled just a bit at the term that he'd made up just for me. "I have to make that money since you don't, right?"

My hand tightened around my cell. Helping me financially had been his promise that he'd offered without my asking. But sometimes, it seemed like he'd forgotten. "Okay, I just wanted to say hello," I said, deciding not to address his dig at me. "And...."

I paused. There was a time when I said, 'I love you,' every chance I had. But I stopped about four months after Eli had stopped saying the same to me.

"Have a good day," he said as if he'd already checked out. And then the way he hung up showed me that he had.

I looked down at my cell just to make sure that the call had been ended, even though it wasn't the phone that had disconnected us. With the back of my hands, I wiped away tears that used to be there. But just as quickly, I stuffed my cell back into my purse.

There was no way I wanted to sit here and analyze the misery that was my marriage. What it had been, wasn't what it was now, and I just needed to accept the reality of the present. I'd exchanged vows with a wealthy man, who was willing to finance my 'hobbying.' Being married to a rich man whose only mistress was his father's company wasn't that bad a place to be.

At least that's what I told myself as I stepped out of my hotel room and strolled down the hall to the elevator. I just had to remember there were women who were in worse positions than mine—and my mother had been one of them.

Then, the elevator doors opened.

And right away, I smiled.

"Hi, Ms. Tanner."

I found it a little challenging to walk, even though I'd only had to take a few steps to enter the elevator. But it was hard to keep my balance with this pretty specimen whom I'd hired to handle the merchandising for me. I'd checked out his application when he first came to me; the kid was only twenty-three and had no experience. But he was fine to look at and he kept me imagining that if I were twenty, twenty-one, twenty-two years younger, I would rock baby boy's world.

"Hello, J-J…." I stuttered. Dang. I could remember his age but not this boy's name.

"Justin," he said, saving me the embarrassment (for him) of me having to ask.

"Where are you coming from?" I asked him.

"Uh…I have a friend who's in the hotel."

I frowned because one thing my psychology degree from Brooklyn College taught me was that people didn't stutter unless they were stutterers. So, what was his deal? Who was his friend? It certainly wasn't anyone in or working with the play. I'd put everyone up in the Embassy Suites which saved me a little over one hundred dollars a night on each of the rooms.

He offered, "One of my friends from high school went away to college and he's back home visiting."

My eyes narrowed slightly, something I always did when my radar went off. "He's home visiting and not staying with his family?"

"Uh, no."

When he lowered his eyes, my radar screamed louder.

He said, "He's here…with…the football team." Now, he looked directly at me. "Yeah, he's here with his team."

"Unh-huh," I hummed. But I didn't ask him a thing. I just decided I'd keep both of my eyes on him, which wouldn't be a problem at all.

"Ms. Tanner?"

I didn't even realize that the elevator doors had parted, and Justin was holding the door open for me. "Thank you," I said, then stepped in front of him.

"You're welcome and I'll see you around."

"Oh, you can count on it," I shot over my shoulder.

"That's what I'm hopin'."

I stopped, turned around and looked at him. Was he flirting with me?

He gave me a grin and a wave, then headed toward the front of the lobby. That little boy had better stop playing. Because I was one of those desperate housewives who more than wanted attention, I craved it.

I watched Justin's tight butt strut to the revolving hotel door. Right before he pushed his way through, he stopped, turned and... was that a wink? Then he walked out of my view.

I released a sigh, then a short laugh. Oh, yeah, that little boy better stop playing. Because he didn't want to mess with me. He had no idea how long it had been and if I ever got him into bed, we just might never get out.

Chapter 3

Camille Woods

The name my mama gave me was AnnaMae, the same as my grandmama who was the most beautiful woman I'd ever seen. People used to say she looked just like Lena Horne. I never knew who Lena Horne was, but if she looked anything like my grandmama, then she was a pretty lady.

But my grandmama was more than gorgeous, she was smart, too. It didn't matter that she never finished the sixth grade; she used to always say, "AnnaMae, you don't need school to be smart, you need sense to be smart."

That was how she used to teach me things, but giving me sayings that I would always remember. And one of her sayings was, "What goes up, must come down."

Grandmama was always right, and that was why I knew Tamara Collin's star was about to come down. And I was gonna make sure that it came down not only fast, but so hard that she'd break her freakin' neck!

I'd been thinking about this for six long years now, but my plan just started really coming together a little more than a month ago. I was finally going to be able to make Tamara's life so miserable that she'd want to die; I was finally going to be able to destroy her completely.

It was like the Revenge Gods were truly on my side because when I'd walked in here this morning and found out that Donovan Dobbs was going to be playing the lead, I was stunned. Gwen hadn't told me about that until right before Tamara got here, and I couldn't believe she'd kept that from me. Not that Gwen knew about my connection to Tamara, but I was the reason why Tamara was even here. I'd made that suggestion to Gwen when she was crying in that Houston hotel's lobby bar on the last night of her last play last year.

October 1, 2015

"What am I going to do?" Gwen asked and I swear a couple of tears dropped into her martini glass.

I felt so sorry for her. This was only her second play and this scandal could have cost her everything. "Think about it this way," I began. "You made the problem go away, right? This isn't going to be a stain on you, or your plays, or your reputation."

"Yeah, the problem is gone, but at what cost?" She shook her head. "How am I going to explain this to Eli?" She downed her martini. "Will he believe that after eight weeks on tour I made no money at all?" Then she raised her hand to the bartender and told him to bring her two more.

I wished there was something I could do for the woman who'd given me so much.

"You don't have to stay with me," Gwen slurred. "You need to get up to your room and go on to bed. Don't you have an early flight tomorrow?" She didn't give me a chance to tell her that I wasn't going anywhere before she said, "I can take care of myself."

It didn't matter what she said, I was going to stay. And so, I joined her, though I ordered only a ginger ale knowing that I might have to carry Gwen up to her room.

I let her slobber and cry over a few more drinks as a plan fixed in my mind. Finally I said, "I think you need to put this behind you and move onto the next play. Do you have anything in mind?"

To anyone else, I probably sounded like I was just trying to come to the aid of a friend. And it was true, that's how I saw Gwen. She'd given me the opportunity to be in both of her plays.

It had happened after she auditioned in a couple of small towns: Bitter End, Tennessee, Knob Lick, Missouri, and the place where I'd been born and raised, Itta Bena, Mississippi. I did not believe it when Ms. Evans, who owned Ms. Evans School of Acting and Modeling, had called with the news."

"AnnaMae, I just had to let my star student know. A big time New York City producer is holding auditions right here in town for her first play. You'd be perfect."

"Oh, my God," I'd said before the woman, who'd been my acting and modeling coach all through high school, went on to tell the specifics of the event that would be held in the auditorium of Mississippi Valley State University.

I'd been the first in line that Wednesday morning, calling in sick to my cashier's job at Betty Bea's Beauty Supply. I'd prayed the whole time that I'd get some part in the play—I didn't care what...I'd play a tree if they were paying me more than the four dollars and eighty-five cents an hour I was earning at Betty Bea's and if it would give me a chance to get away from the horror that had been my life in the last year.

Every prayer I'd prayed had been answered. I'd been cast in

a secondary role as the star's personal assistant. But that was a big chance! A thousand dollars a week for ten weeks, and I'd be staying in hotels in cities that I'd only seen on TV: Chicago, Baltimore, Washington, DC.

I later learned that in other plays actresses would have been paid two, even three times what I'd earned. It had been Gwen's husband's idea to go to real small towns where people were thirsty. But that was fine with me 'cause I was beyond thirty; I was so dehydrated, she could have paid me a nickel and I would have said yes to my chance of becoming a star!

I'd worked hard to not only perform well, but I made it my goal to get close to Gwen...and it worked. She'd cast me in this play, too, and the way things had been going, I had no doubt that I was going to be one of her actresses that she'd call all the time.

But my future was in jeopardy now. I had to talk her into making a comeback, something big that would help her to mentally get past this scandal. Because not only did I need these gigs for the opportunity, but I needed them because I knew, I just knew that being in the same industry as Tamara would get me close to her. I never really had a plan to pay her back. Not until I sat with Gwen that night, not until I suggested that she hit the road again, with a new play and a bigger star—someone like Tamara Collins.

Even now, I remembered the way Gwen had looked at me that night when I said that. Her eyes were glazed, her stare was a bit shaky as she tried to focus her glance on me. But behind all that drunkenness, there was hope in her eyes.

I wasn't privy to the details, but when Gwen had called ten months later and told me that she had another role for me in this, her third play starring—Tamara Collins—I actually got down on my knees and thanked the Lord for giving me this chance for revenge.

I wish I were more patient, I wish I could last through the ten weeks of this play and just torture Tamara, every single day. I could do it with all the chances I'd have to put my arms around (and maybe even talk Gwen into writing in a few kisses) with the man that I was sure Tamara still loved. I could do it with lots of other little things—finding a way to contact Donovan's wife and after she showed up in one city, I could then set up chance encounters with the many jump offs Donovan was rumored to have in all the other cities.

But the problem was, I couldn't wait. Just seeing Tamara made me hungry for that sweet taste of revenge. I had something planned that would make the national humiliation she'd experienced when Donovan had left her seem like a day at the beach. Because after what she'd done to me, she deserved it. I was sure that she hadn't cried enough, her heart hadn't hurt enough. I wanted her to have the kind of pain that would leave her crying every night. I wanted her to have a pain that she'd never be able to forget.

When the door to the conference room opened and Tamara came back in, I moved to the other side of the large room, though I watched her the entire time. My chest ached from the way my heart banged. And my hands stung from the way my nails pressed into the skin of my palms.

I hated everything about her as she strutted like she was better than the rest of us. She sat down in the opposite corner, away from everyone and I had to push down my desire to walk right up to her and punch her in her face.

I hadn't been sure how this was gonna go down this morning. I hadn't been sure if Tamara would see me and run over to greet me like we were old friends, or if now that she was this big time actress, she would be aloof and just say hello.

But that heffa hadn't done either one of those things. She acted like she didn't even know me. As if I looked that different after eleven years. Granted, the last time she'd laid her eyes on me, right before she traipsed off to return to Yale, I was fourteen, still in braces and pigtails and with legs as thin as twigs (hence my nickname, Twiggy.) But even with the green contact lenses that I wore and my twenty-eight inch honey-blond Malaysian weave, I didn't look all that different. And even though no one called me AnnaMae Wilson anymore (since that didn't really sound like the name of a star), she had to know who I was. But if she was going to play this game, then, I would play it, too. It wasn't important that she remembered me. That had nothing to do with what I had planned for her tonight.

As she sat, and I stared, I felt my patience waning. I just had to do something. Had to make my first move.

I stood and did one of those strolls that I'd learned back home in Ms. Evans's school. Tamara never looked up as I made my way to her. She didn't even look up when I stopped right in front of her. Nor when I stood there for a good thirty seconds. This coon-face never...looked...up.

My fingernails dug deeper into my palms, but I was an actress so I kept my tone cool. "How ya doin'?"

She kinda sighed. "I'm fine," she said as she finally made eye contact. There was not a hint of recognition. Like she'd met so many people in the eleven years since she'd last seen me that there was no way for her to remember all the way back to when she'd been at my house almost every day. Then she said, "How are you?"

Her enunciation was so proper, so crisp, missing that Mississippi drawl that I worked so hard to hide. The way she spoke, I wondered if she was clownin' me and if she was, the price for the debt she had to pay just went up.

I let a couple of moments pass and right when she gave me a dismissive half-smile, then looked down at her script again, I crossed my arms and said, "So, you're really gonna act like you don't remember me?"

This time, when she looked up, one of her eyebrows was raised. "Excuse me?"

I laughed, then did one of her moves. I tossed my hair over my shoulder before I told her, "Bitches like you always frontin'."

She blinked and blinked and blinked. And I glared and glared and glared. Finally, she said, "What did you just say?"

My response was quick, since I was ready and itchin' for this fight. If she didn't watch out, I would take care of her humiliation myself. "You heard me," I said. "I didn't stutter." My words were covered with every bit of the pain I'd felt since 2010.

She moved slowly, first, putting her script next to her purse on the chair beside her, then she rose up like she was really about to do something. I didn't back up and I had to hold back or else

I was gonna pop off. But I dropped my hands to my side because if this heffa came for me, I was gonna give everyone in this room a show that would be better than anything we were about to take on the road.

"Sweetheart," she began in a tone that was all sugary-sweet. "I do not know who you think I am, but let me tell you who I am not. I am not someone who will let you call me out of my name. So if you do not...."

"I know who you are, Miss Collins," I said, cutting her off. "I know very well, who and what you are." I lowered my voice to a whisper when I added, "I also know what you did."

She did that blinking thing again. "What in the world are you talking about?"

I wanted to tell her, I wanted to tell her so bad. But another thing that my grandmama always said—there was a time and a place for everything. And this was not the time and tonight would be a better place.

So, I gave her a smirk and just a few words. "In due time, boo." Then, I pulled one of her numbers—I did the same thing she'd just done to Donovan. I turned, put some serious switch in my hips—something else I'd learned from Ms. Evans—and made my way right out of that conference room, slamming the door for extra effect.

Chapter 4

Tamara

"Ouch!"

Donovan palmed his cheek as if that would lessen the burn. I knew his skin was stinging. Because my hand was tingling with pain from the way I'd just tried to slap every tooth out of his mouth.

"This is a rehearsal." His palm remained in place, over his jaw, though his voice was muffled, sounding like his mouth was stuffed with cotton. "And we're just acting!"

"That. Was. Incredible!" Gwen said, her grin so wide the ends of her lips almost touched her ears. "The chemistry between you two is amazing."

It must have been our matching glares that made her switch lanes.

"I...mean," she stuttered. "All right. Maybe we should do this one more time just to make sure we get it right."

"Okay." I shrugged.

"The hell I will!" Donovan exclaimed. Then, I guess because he didn't want to look like a complete punk, he added, "I think we got this scene down, right, Tammie?"

"Tamara," I corrected, then twisted to face Gwen. "And I don't mind doing it again." Now, I turned back to Donovan. "I want to keep at it until I get it right." That's what I said, but inside my words were different—I want to keep at it until I knock his ass to the ground.

"We got it," Donovan said to Gwen, though his eyes were on me.

Gwen's glance shifted from me to Donovan, back to me, then to him. "All right," she said, her disappointment apparent. She tapped her tablet screen. "Let's do the scene right before this one."

I'd already memorized the play—yes, the entire play, not just my lines. I'd been trained to learn everyone's lines, so I knew the scene that Gwen referenced was Donovan with the woman who'd just come at me.

I still couldn't figure out what that was about.

As I moved to the other side of the room, the woman did that walk that she had to have been practicing for days. I glared at her, but she didn't move her eyes toward me. She strutted past me as if I weren't there at all.

Shaking my head, I returned to where I'd been sitting and then watched what played out across the room. Though I'd wanted to burn Donovan with my stare, my glance stayed on her—Camille Woods was her name.

I'd been used to all of the competition and jealousy in this industry. And honestly, it was all understandable. There weren't enough roles to keep all women working, so that meant there definitely weren't enough opportunities for women of color. That was why I understood the hate and that was probably why this Camille woman came at me the way she did. But her hate—it felt a little different, it felt more personal than professional and

I wondered why. But then, I shook my head and thoughts of her away. She was a nobody and I didn't need to waste another brain cell thinking about her.

So, I shifted my glance to Donovan. I was disappointed that Gwen hadn't let us do that scene again. At least one more time. I wanted just one more shot at smacking the hell out of that man. Now that I thought of it, next time, I'd use my fist. That was what I really wanted to do. Just a single right hook followed by a power side kick that dropped him straight to the floor. Then maybe if he were hurting, some of my pain would go away.

Maybe I would do that. Maybe I would take a shot like that in one of the thirty-six cities. *That* would make the 10:00 news.

As Donovan and Camille read through their lines, he still massaged his cheek, which pleased me, and now I hoped that my glare would ignite, and set him on fire. For just a milli-moment I felt silly, but then, I dropkicked that thought because that man deserved every bit of hurt that I could serve him. And no matter what I did to him over the course of this play, it wouldn't come close to what he'd done to me.

The more I watched Donovan, the more my eyes zoomed in on him, the more he stayed in the center of my focus, the more I drifted back, back, back...four years to the day that had started one of the best years of my life....

March 20, 2012

This wasn't my first film; I almost felt like a veteran with two movies behind me. But this was certainly my most important. A big budget movie where I'd be playing the younger sister of my idol, Angela Bassett.

She was the reason why I was an actor, making that decision when I was only seven years old. It was the day my mother dragged me to the movies and told me to tell the people that I was twelve years old, if they asked, which they didn't. I didn't even want to be there; I would've rather been home finishing my book, *Are You There, God? It's Me, Margaret*. I'd tried to bring my book with me, but Mama had snatched it out of my hand, saying that the only thing I ever did was read. Mama always liked that I was reading all the time, but I knew she was just mad this time 'cause the babysitter hadn't shown up and now, she had to take me with her.

So there I was, sitting in this movie, that I didn't want to see, as mad as Mama. I was too young to know a thing about fate, but being there was where I was meant to be. After watching "Boyz N the Hood" that day in the theatre, I'd watched it at least one thousand and one times since, learning every line spoken by the lady that I wanted to grow up to be. She was the most beautiful woman I'd ever seen, even prettier than my mama. And as I got older, I bought all of the magazines that had articles about her. And then, when I was fourteen and we got computers in school, I waited for hours to use one of the four desktops after classes were over, so that I could see everything about Angela Bassett on the world wide web.

From that day in the movies, I set out to follow every footstep she'd taken. She was the reason I'd attended Yale, first four years in their undergraduate program and after that, another three years in the prestigious Yale School of Drama, though making that happen had been much more challenging financially.

I was absolutely sure that once I graduated with that bachelors and masters, there would be nothing but success in my future. Well, the success wasn't immediate, and it wasn't yet massive, but how could I complain? Four years out, three gigs in, Honda, Cherrios, and Activia commercials in-between that paid sweet residuals...I was on my way. Especially now that I would be in a movie with...Angela Bassett!

I waved my hands in front of my face to calm myself right before the elevator doors parted. I had a seven o' clock call time, and my car would be picking me up at six-thirty. As I stepped through the Marriott's lobby, I glanced at my watch. I'd set it for Toronto time, three hours in front of where I lived in Los Angeles, the same zone as New York, which was apropos since the story took place in the city, but was being filmed in Toronto for the tax breaks.

"Ms. Collins?"

I looked up at the man who was dressed in a dark suit, white shirt and black tie.

I nodded and he led me to the car that waited in front of the hotel. As I stepped into the car as if being chauffeured was just a part of my life, I remembered my first movie and how I didn't know what to do when the limousine came. I kept opening the door until the driver told me, "You can wait for me, Ms. Collins."

I'd felt like my Itta Bena, Mississippi roots were showing, but that was back then; I was all LA now, the big city movie star. That didn't stop me, though, from almost pressing my nose against the window as the car maneuvered through the streets of downtown Toronto. I may have been in a different country, but Canada looked no different than Los Angeles. So after just a few moments, I sat back and took the time to calm myself so that I wouldn't gush like a newbie when I met Angela.

Hardly ten minutes went by before the driver pulled in through the gates of Pinewood Studios and then, slowed the car next to another stretch limo near one of the stages on the back lot.

Before my driver got out of his car, I held my breath. Had I just pulled up next to Angela? Oh, my God! I wasn't quite ready. But the driver was at my door, and I had to make my move. So I did. I stepped out, looked up, and into the eyes of the person getting out of the other car...Donovan Dobbs!

It was only God's mercy, grace, *and* favor that held my legs steady enough to walk.

"Hey," he said to me.

I knew my voice would only come out in a squeak, so I made one of those sophisticated moves—I nodded my hello. And then I put all of my concentration on walking in the direction where the driver had pointed me. What was Donovan Dobbs doing here? Was he in Toronto, too? Filming a movie at this same studio?

"So," he said as he walked beside me. "Are you an actor or one of the production people?"

At any other time, I may have taken offense. But this was Donovan Dobbs...speaking to me! Why was he doing that? Didn't he know that there was no way I could respond to him and walk at the same time? I was shocked that I was able to still breathe while being in such close proximity to the guy that I'd told my best friend, Maxine Harris, I was going to marry. I was only fourteen at the time, but still.

"I'm an actor." I finally managed to speak.

"Oh, yeah? Are you in *The Best is Yet to Come*?"

Again, since I wasn't real sure of my voice, I nodded.

"Oh yeah? That's great, I am, too."

Oh. My. God. He was in the same movie? I wondered if we'd have any scenes together. Because if we did, I needed to start talking to God right now about how He was gonna keep me and give me strength so that I didn't faint!

He asked, "What part are you playing?"

God was still looking out for me because this time, I was able to speak without sounding like that fourteen-year-old who'd been in love with Donovan, the superstar. "I'm Jada. I'll be playing Angela's, I mean, Sophia's sister."

"Oh, yeah?" he said again as if those were two of his favorite words. He took a couple of quick steps to get in front of me. "Well, hey, sis. I'm your brother, Nelson, Sophia's younger brother. But my real name is Donovan." He stopped moving and I did too, when he held out his hand. "Donovan Dobbs."

As if I didn't know! As if any girl on this planet didn't know. But I was an actor, so I stepped into the role of the aloof, accomplished woman who'd never (or maybe hardly ever) heard his name.

"I'm Tamara Collins." I gave his hands three shakes, then released him. "Nice to meet you."

He grinned, a kinda smirk that said that I could act if I wanted to, but he knew that I was one of those women who'd had his life size poster hanging in her bedroom when I was a girl.

Then, he released me from his stare when he turned around and we continued our walk. We didn't speak another word except for the, "Thank you," I gave him when he opened the door to the stage and we stepped into the world of the Queens, New York family who were learning to live without their patriarch after he'd been murdered by a gang for testifying at a trial.

Inside, I did a quick calculation of the space; it was about fifteen to eighteen thousand feet, already set up with various interior sets: a living room, kitchen, and even the front of a brownstone. I knew we'd be filming outside of the studio as well: at a church and then, in a courtroom.

"This is cool, right?"

I had no idea how I'd done it, but for a moment, I'd forgotten that Donovan was there. And now, I had to talk to him again. But God (once again) stepped in and I was rescued by one of the production assistants who took me back to hair and makeup. That gave me sweet relief; the time and space to comprehend what just happened. I was going to be in a movie with Angela Bassett and Donovan Dobbs? And, according to the schedule, the first scene to be filmed was going to be with the two of them. There was no way in heaven that life could get better on earth.

My plan had been to walk onto that set and be the professional that I was trained to be. And I got it half right.

Two hours later, when I was finally called to the set, I greeted Angela with a proper, "Hello, Ms. Bassett. It's my pleasure to work with you."

She was kind and so sweet, but all of that missed me because in the first run-through when Donovan hugged me and gave me a brotherly kiss on the cheek, I wanted to commit incest right there.

It took only six days for that to happen. A brother and a sister by day, friends and serious lovers by night. At first, I was a little bothered. In ethics, that was one of the things we'd been taught and I'd never wanted to be one of those actors who fell into bed with another actor. It was so cliché and I certainly didn't want to get that reputation.

But what was I supposed to do? When Donovan Dobbs had taken me out to dinner, filled me with wine, and looked at me with those brown eyes that were meant for the bedroom, my panties fell off.

Well, it wasn't like that totally. From the first day, Donovan had been into me as much as I was into him. First he told me so (words were my primary love language) and then every day my trailer was flooded with flowers and fruit baskets and bottles and bottles of wine (gifts were my secondary love language). By the time he left a charm bracelet in my makeup chair with a card that said—*It's been amazing working with you. No one has ever stimulated my heart and soul in such a short time the way you have*—you tell me, what else was I supposed to do after a dinner of arugula salad and oysters, filet mignon with potatoes au gratin, and then the closing of the three courses with chocolate covered strawberries and bananas? How was I supposed to fight that arsenal of aphrodisiacs?

I was totally caught up in that love rapture and was ascending willingly. And Donovan was right there with me. It wasn't just a film fling. When we returned to Los Angeles (me, a week before him), he moved into my two-bedroom condo in Burbank.

When I asked him if he thought we were moving too fast, he said, "People in their twenties move fast, folks in their thirties know their hearts and you took mine that first day."

I swooned.

We settled in together, working on our careers, but what we didn't expect was Hollywood to christen us as one of the new 'It Couples'. We had been doing well on our own, but together, our stars rose. We were invited to every movie premiere, every CD launch, every Hollywood celebration. We did photo shoots for Entertainment magazines—together. Bloggers called us for interviews—together. A producer even approached our agents with an idea for a reality show starring the two of us.

Both of us nixed that, but the work kept coming. It was Donovan, though, who kept us focused on keeping our feet planted on solid ground.

"All of this success is good," he'd said. "But what I want to focus on is us. This is all about us getting to the place where we'll get married. I'm not interested in dating. I've been there, done that, and now I wanna have a house filled with little Dobbs who are as handsome as me and as gorgeous as you."

That man kept me in a constant state of swoon-dom.

Back then.

But this was where we were today.

I blinked myself all the way back to the present and focused on the rehearsal across the room. When Donovan put his arms around that Camille girl, my heart turned green and for a moment, I wished that Gwen had put me in *that* role.

"Are you kidding me, Tam," I spoke to myself like I couldn't believe my thoughts. I didn't want to be in this play at all with Donovan, let alone being his major love interest No, being the jilted one was perfect. It allowed me to slap the crap out of Donovan all across America—at least the 'Chitlin' Circuit' part of the country.

And that was exactly what I was going to do.

I couldn't wait.

Chapter 5

Tamara

We rehearsed for three more hours, but I didn't get any more satisfaction. The next scene with Donovan was one of the more lovey-dovey ones. Even though I didn't believe there was a role I couldn't handle, I had my challenges with this one—at least according to Gwen.

"Tamara, you're really gonna have to do something about that scowl on your face," she kept saying.

So, I changed up.

"Tamara, you're really gonna have to do something about that scowl with all of your teeth showing."

Finally Gwen said, "Okay, this is good for the first day. We made progress." She looked at the seven of us who were in the play. "But remember, this is a two-week crash-course. So let's get on our lines."

I was so ready to get out of there and as I grabbed my bag, I wished I was staying in the Renaissance so that I could go straight up to my room, call my agent, then lay my head and all of these burdens down. But since we were going to be in Atlanta for seventeen days (fourteen days of rehearsal and then three shows) I guess they needed the affordability of the Embassy Suites for the cast and crew.

The only good thing was Maury had negotiated my own room, so unlike my other roles where I had to share my nighttime space, I would be able to be alone when rehearsals were over.

Which was exactly what I wanted to do now.

"You sure you don't want to go and grab something to eat," the Clifton-Davis look/sound/act alike gentleman asked me.

"No," I paused, what was his name? I'd been calling him Clifton the whole time in my head. "No, I'm really tired."

"Awww, too bad." Then, he leaned closer and said, "If you need a shoulder to cry on...." He stopped and winked and for at least the twelfth time today, I wanted to puke.

There was bile in my tone when I said, "Thank you, but I don't have anything to cry about. And if I did," I paused so that my next words would stand alone, "I'd be looking for a much younger shoulder."

I didn't bother to look at him as I stomped away. All I could do was wonder had the world gone mad? It had only been eight hours or so and it felt like the earth had tilted off its axis. In just a few hours I'd found out that I'd been tricked into having to earn a check playing the ex of a man who'd made me *his* ex. Then, I'd had some two-bit commercial *actress* come for me. And now, Grandpa was offering me his arthritic shoulder.

I just wanted to get to my hotel room, put my feet up, call room service, order a salad, and hope that the lettuce and spinach would soak up the whole bottle of wine that I planned to buy on my way to the hotel and then finish off before midnight.

But before I could get outside to find my driver, Randy, the band director that we'd all been introduced to this morning, jumped in front of me.

That move startled me a bit or maybe it was what he was wearing that had me off balance. He looked like one of those nerdy guys who tried extra hard to be cool. His Coogi shirt, that had every hue in the rainbow, was about two sizes too big and his silver-rimmed glasses were a size too small.

"Umm, excuse me," he began, shifting from one foot to the other, "I was, umm, I was wondering if we could go over your song real quick?"

"Now?" I asked. "Everyone is leaving for the day." I had to do a kinda bob and weave move to get his eyes to connect with mine.

"Well, I wanted to go over some notes to make sure I had your music just right. You know, like Gwen said, we don't have much time." He paused. "We can do it back at the hotel."

This was so not what I wanted to do right now, but the thing was, I really did want to shine with my song. I didn't sing much, but I was good, in the Southern church girl kind of way. You know, the ones who stood up on a Sunday morning, sang in any one of the twenty-four keys, and rocked the roof off the sanctuary, not stopping until every one of the church Mothers were laid out at the altar. I was that girl, but until now, I hadn't put my focus on singing. But with the acting well running dry, I needed to add singing to my repertoire so that I would be considered a serious triple threat (since I'd convinced the world I could dance in that movie with Angela.)

Having a chance to sing was one of the reasons why I'd taken this role, besides the money. My goal was to turn in a Jennifer Hudson type performance every night that would turn out the audience.

It was because of this that I acquiesced to Randy. "Fine."

He grinned. "You're over at the Embassy Suites with all of us, right?"

I nodded, but I didn't want this dude to think I was going to give him a ride. "I have to make a stop," I said, determined to fulfill my mission to stack my hotel room with dozens of bottles of Zinfandel. "I'll meet you over there."

His whole face was bright, like I'd just told him he'd won one of those Publisher's Clearing House lotteries. "Cool." He nodded and now, he didn't seem to have any problem keeping his eyes on mine. "See you in about thirty minutes."

I exhaled in frustration. People looked at my life and envied the glamour of it all. But what they didn't know was that there was less than fifteen minutes of glamour every day. Besides having to learn dialogue (with all the additions and subtractions) for a whole show in fourteen days, we also had to learn the sets, do blocking and then, there was the nonstop promoting: radio shows, local television programs, magazine, newspaper, and blog interviews. Then add to all of that, my singing. I would be working double-triple-quadruple time.

I needed wine!

As soon as I had that thought, I bumped right into my driver. "You ready?" Greg asked.

I had a personal driver today because in between rehearsing those scenes, I'd had a television interview this morning, and since drivers were hired for the whole day, he would be taking me back to my hotel. But Gwen had made it clear, any time I didn't have other engagements, I'd be rolling with the rest of the crew. When I slipped into the car, I groaned with the thought that this wouldn't be my daily life. I bet Cameron and Jennifer never had to do that rolling-with-the-crew thing.

"So," Greg said when he got into the front seat, "where to? The hotel?"

I shook my head. "I want to first pick up a couple of bottles of wine; then, I'll head...home."

He glanced at me through the rear view mirror, nodded as if he understood and then, eased the car from the curb. I leaned back, closed my eyes, and let thoughts of Donovan and Camille churn through my mind. When we stopped in front of Spencer Wine Merchant, Greg did me a solid and ran in to get two bottles of my favorite Zinfandel. Then within twenty minutes after that, he pulled up to the Embassy Suites.

"Thank you so much, Greg," I said, almost wanting to cry since I wasn't sure when I'd have him to myself again.

"No problem. Let me know if you need anything or need me to drive you anywhere while you're here. I know Gwen said I'd be taking you around some more, but if you need anything else, call." He handed me his card.

As I glanced down at it, I almost wanted to ask him what would his rate be for a daily pickup and return. But then even though I was earning ten thousand a week on this play, I needed to bank every dollar since I wasn't sure when my next gig would be.

So all I said was, "Thanks, Greg," and slipped out of the Town Car.

I was dog-tired, more emotionally than physically when I walked to the elevator. I was glad that most of the cast and crew had gone somewhere to eat and hang out. I didn't want to bump into anyone and I hoped Randy would give me at least a half an hour before he called me.

When the elevator doors parted on the sixth floor, I kicked off my shoes before I even stuck my key card into the door.

Pushing the door open, I dropped the bottles on the table in the front part of the suite, then unzipped my dress as I stepped into the bedroom, turned on the lights and gasped.

"Oh, my...what the hell are you doing?" I screamed.

Randy laid on top of my bed naked as the day he'd popped out of his mama's womb with his hands folded behind his neck as he leaned against the headboard. He laid there, chillin', relaxin', chillaxin' as if I'd given him a personal invitation to get butt naked on my bed.

"Have you lost your damn mind?" I screamed, waving one hand, while holding the front of my dress closed with the other. "What are you doing?"

His eyes narrowed and he tilted his head as if my words confused him. "I...I was waiting on you."

"Waiting for me? To go over my song? Naked in my room? On my bed?" I glanced at his nakedness once again all over my comforter. I ripped it from beneath him. "Get your ass off my bed!"

He jumped and scooted to the end of the bed. "I, umm, you said meet you at the hotel."

"Yeah, I figured you'd call me and we'd meet in the lobby to practice my song, not to have sex."

His head was shaking as he scurried to the chair where he'd left his clothes. "I...just thought, you know, I mean, the way you were looking at me, I thought you wanted me. And you know, I heard you like to, um, you know."

He was back to dodging eye contact, which was fine with me because I didn't want to look at him. "All I know is that you'd better get your nasty behind out of my room!" I shouted as he slid his legs into his underwear. "Wait! How did you get in here anyway?"

He paused for just a moment. "I was gonna wait, but then housekeeping was um, they were cleaning and I just came in." He jumped into his pants.

"Just get out!" I yelled, feeling the strain on my vocal cords.

Randy stumbled with the zipper on his pants. "I...I'm sorry, Tamara. I just thought—"

"That was your first mistake. You need to stop thinking, because it's not working out for you. Just give it up and get the hell out, you nasty mother—"

Before I could finish, he held up his hands and his face stiffened. "Hold up, now," he said, his whole attitude shifting, "don't try to act all holier than thou with me because I know about your history. Everybody knows your history."

"You don't know anything about me!" I said. My glare must have sent a warning that I was on the edge and he needed to back up. Because he dropped his hands and grabbed his shoes.

"This was just a big misunderstanding, okay?" he said backing up toward the front of the suite. "No need to go to Gwen over all of this."

I wasn't thinking about Gwen, I wasn't thinking about anything except getting this pervert out. "Randy," I began, my voice a little softer only because I was sure I was about to burst with fury, "get your perverted ass out of my room."

He kept backing up, but he moved just a little too slow for me and it was anger that made me grab one of the bottles of wine and raise it above my head.

I didn't say a word, just took slow steps toward him. "Whoa!" He took two steps back to my one forward. "Put that bottle down, I'm leaving."

I kept the bottle raised until he backed all the way up and out, then I slammed and locked the door behind him. He didn't have anything to be worried about, I wasn't about to waste a perfect bottle of wine. Instead, I stumbled to the counter, pulled the corkscrew from the bag, popped the cork, then put the whole bottle to my lips. Yeah, there were glasses in the cabinets, but I didn't have time for all of that.

With the bottle in my hand, I staggered into the bedroom, plopped onto the bed, making a note that I'd have to call housekeeping to come and get that nasty comforter. In fact, I wanted a new room.

This was crazy, but unfortunately, it was so ordinary in this business. Something like this had happened to me on every project I'd worked on, though no one had been as crazy to just show up in my room. Not that guys didn't try, though. It was just the way of this entertainment world. Everybody flirted with everybody, then somebody ended up in bed with somebody.

But this guy—in my room. Naked. On my bed.

I shuddered.

I just hoped that he hadn't told anyone that he was getting with me.

I shuddered again. Or maybe, I shivered.

What had I done to deserve this? Donovan, Camille, Randy.

And this was just the first day!

I closed my eyes and inhaled. Then, I prayed. Because if this was the beginning, only God would get me through to the end.

Chapter 6

Camille

It had been hard for me to sleep all night. I hadn't given Randy my telephone number for lots of reasons, but the two most important being that I didn't want any connection between us beyond this play, and the fact that this dude was really creepy. Not only in the way he looked, but with what I knew about him.

But now, as I paced in the conference room waiting for everyone to arrive for rehearsal, I wished that I'd given him something, maybe a throw away phone. Because this waiting, waiting, waiting....

The conference room door opened and I held my breath. An eternity passed before the person walked through the door. And in stepped...Gwen...followed by...Tamara.

"I really think by the time this is all over, you will be so happy with it," Gwen was saying to Tamara as if she were still trying to convince her that this play was the bomb. "I have many more interviews for you to do."

My eyes stayed on Tamara as she stood stiff, arms folded, dressed like she was some socialite wearing one of those designer knit tank tops and matching skinny pants while the rest of us wore jeans.

I squinted, trying to look even closer, trying to get some hint of what had happened to her last night. But if I had to describe her, all I would be able to say was that—she had an attitude.

"Well, I'm here," she said, tossing her hair over her shoulder, "and I'm going to make the best of it," Tamara said to Gwen.

There was nothing! No kind of trauma. She was still in one piece—physically and mentally.

Ugh!

I pushed past the two, though neither made any move like they noticed me and then, I charged to the lobby. What happened? I had to find Randy before we got started. I had to know what had happened.

The Renaissance's lobby was packed with businessmen donned in tailored suits and power ties and women wrapped in designer dresses with matching purses slung over their shoulders. This was the kind of place that I loved to be. Atlanta may have only been a five-hour drive from where I'd been raised, but it was millions and millions of miles away in every other way. Whenever I was away from home, I used the big city as my classroom. I'd sit and watch people, studying what the women wore, how they talked and walked, even imagining what they thought. And I dreamed of the men and wondered what it would be like to be married to someone who worked in a tall office building, making decisions that changed people's lives, rather than being with the guy who worked down at the auto repair shop and came home smelling like car oil with grease on his hands.

But today I was distracted from my normal distraction. I couldn't think of anything else as I paced in front of the hotel's door, not taking the chance of missing Randy. It was a good thing that I didn't have to wait too long because there would have surely been a hole in the carpet with just a few more paces. Randy slithered through the revolving door, not too long after I'd gone in search of him.

We spotted each other at the same time and right when I got to him, I asked, "What happened?" But then, my good sense kicked in. I couldn't talk to Randy about this in plain sight.

I held up my hand, stopping him from saying a word and then whispered, "Give me a minute to go up in the elevator and then you take the next one up. To the third floor, don't go to the second where we are."

After what went down last night—or rather what didn't go down, I wanted to give him clear instructions because clearly, he had messed something up.

He nodded and I felt his glare as I walked away. All kinds of thoughts cranked through my mind. He hadn't hooked up with Tamara. Had he chickened out? Why?

I stepped off the elevator on the third floor, then Randy came up on the next one.

He hadn't taken more than a couple of steps before he said, "Listen, I need to know...."

I put my finger to my lips, letting him know not to speak another word, then motioned for him to follow me to the staircase. We stepped inside the stairwell, but then, the door closed and I faced him. And I realized that being alone in this tight space with this nut wasn't the smartest idea I'd ever had.

"Umm...." was all that came out of me at first.

He said, "I just want to know what kind of game you're playin'."

"I have no idea what you're talking about. What happened?"

His eyes looked smaller than I remembered—small, beady, and dark, too. I took a tiny step away from him.

"You told me Tamara wanted to get with me." His voice was laced with more than annoyance and attitude, there was something else, like a threat in his undertone.

Now, there wasn't much that scared me. I was known for being able to handle myself, especially since I'd grown up with my brother and nothing but male cousins. I didn't fight like a girl and I was hardly afraid of anyone and anything.

But I was also smart enough to know *when* to be afraid and right now, all I wanted to do was knock Randy to the side, then take the stairs two at a time down to safety. But I stayed cool, acted like I was calm and lied with a, "She did want to get with you," that sounded like I was telling the truth.

He shook his head. "Well, she sure didn't act like it. I went to her bedroom and got naked like you said. When she walked in there, she went ballistic."

Until he said it at this very moment, I'd never been sure that he would take my word about Tamara. I'd never thought he'd believe she liked to play games so he couldn't come out and say it, he just had to go to her room. I mean, the story had sounded crazy to me as I told it to him. But I guess everything that I knew about Randy was true—he was nuts.

"So, you got into her room?" I asked.

He nodded, then told me about the housekeeper, how he'd waited, and how Tamara had come in there and threatened him with a wine bottle.

A wine bottle? Really? That was all she had and he hadn't gone through with it?

But staying in my role, I chuckled a little. "Boy, she was just playing hard to get. I told you that's how she likes it."

His eyes narrowed more. "She didn't act like she was playing. She seemed like she meant it to me. She was so mad, I don't even know if I'm gonna still have a job when she tells Gwen."

"She won't tell Gwen," I said, though I wasn't really sure of that. The way this was *supposed* to go down, of course Gwen would find out. But the damage would have already been done to Tamara, and though I knew Gwen would be devastated and it might mess up her play a little, she would recover. Rich people always did. I said, "She doesn't want anyone to know her secret."

"What secret?" There was doubt all etched on his face and inside his tone.

My mind was flipping over with ideas, though, I wasn't sure if Randy could pull this off; but I wasn't going to stop trying.

"Tamara and I go way back. We grew up together in Mississippi."

"Mississippi? She doesn't act like she's from Mississippi."

It was my turn to squint at him. What was he trying to say?

But I forced myself to focus. "*Anyway,* from the time she was younger, she has always liked it rough."

He stepped back. "You really grew up together?"

I nodded, but he shook his head as if he were calling me a liar.

And then, he did call me a liar. "Nah, you didn't grow up with her."

"I did. Why do you think I didn't?"

"'Cause, you're way younger than her."

I released a breath. At any other time, I would have taken that as a compliment. "I am younger, but...." I paused. "She was... friends with...my brother." I didn't even realize that I'd whispered those words until Randy leaned in.

"What? Your brother?"

"Yeah," I said, then swallowed the lump that always formed when I thought of June. "She and my brother...they were the same age and they went to school together until...."

He waited for me to say more, but when I didn't, he asked, "Until when?"

I had to inhale a lot of oxygen for the strength to continue. "Until she went off to college." I had to take this conversation back to where it was supposed to be or else I'd be too emotional. "So, that's how I know her. Yeah, I was little, but she used to talk to me about sex a lot because I didn't have any sisters." That thought took me back to my dark hole. "It was just me and my brother." I took a deep breath. "So, I know she likes it rough."

He nodded, as if he were thinking about my words. "She likes it rough," he repeated. "So what does that mean?"

I blinked back thoughts of my brother and returned to my mission. "I think you know what I mean." He just stood there, so I added, "Like what happened on tour last year. You know, those accusations."

His lips pressed into a tight line. "What...accusations?" He asked the question as if he didn't know that I already had the answer. As if he didn't remember that I'd been there.

Yeah, Gwen had tried to keep it all hush-hush, but the rumors spread at the speed of light. We all knew. And Randy knew that we all knew.

I waited a couple of beats, trying to give him time to change his mind about having me say it aloud. When he just stood there, challenging me with his eyes, I told him, "You know, the rumors that you raped the wardrobe girl."

There was flames in his eyes; I mean seriously, it looked like he was trying to set me on fire with the way he stared at me and I wondered if maybe it hadn't been such a good idea for me to say that to this man, in this small space, with just the two of us. My thought turned into certainty when a second later, he grabbed the top of my blouse and rammed me into the wall.

I screamed.

"Shut up," he demanded.

My heart pounded.

"I'm not trying to hurt you," he growled. "But I will if you say stuff like that."

"Okay, okay. Chill, chill." I held my hands up, trying to show him that I was surrendering and when he finally let me go, I breathed. I really wanted to knock him upside his head and beat him down (like he was the girl and I was a guy) for manhandling me like that. But my mission, my mission. That was where I had to keep my thoughts. And anyway, if this played out the way I wanted it to, not only would Tamara get what was coming to her, but Randy would, too, when Tamara pressed charges. Because it wouldn't go down the way it had last year. Gwen wouldn't be able to pay Tamara off. She'd go to the police, it would be all over the news, and every night, she'd have to relive the violence she suffered at the hands of this maniac.

When my breathing returned to the rate that a doctor would consider normal, I said, "Look, I wasn't saying that you raped her, I said there were rumors. I don't think that you did."

"I didn't," he hissed.

"I don't think that you're like that."

"I'm not and if you know so much you would know that the charges were dropped."

"I know." I shrugged. "Because she was lying."

His face softened with my words. "Yeah," he said his shoulders now relaxing, too. "She was lying," he repeated my lie.

I wondered if this dude really believed that. Was he one of those sociopaths (or was it psychopaths?) who believed their lies were true? He knew Gwen had paid the girl off because she couldn't afford the bad publicity. Her play was up for her second Image Award and she didn't want that kind of exposure; her reputation wasn't yet strong enough to stand what would happen if that news got out.

So, she'd written that two-hundred thousand dollar check for the girl to walk away without talking to the police. She'd given her just about every dollar of the profit she'd made.

But Gwen had made that money work for her because when she told me that Randy was back, I was shocked until she explained, "*I got a great band director for room, board, and minimum wage. It was a good deal.*"

"A good deal? But aren't you afraid that he might do it again?"

She told me she had no fear of that. She believed that Randy had been scared straight, even though she'd found out that there were other incidents in his past.

It wasn't until she told me this a week ago that my plan came together. I was gonna get back at Tamara and do humanity a favor by getting Randy off the streets.

Taking my mind back to Randy, I said, "I bet you I know what really happened with you and that girl."

His eyes narrowed just a little, as if he wasn't sure if I was going to accuse him again. "I bet she wanted a big fine stud like you," I said. I had to pause for a moment because my words had melted him so fast. His lips had spread from that thin line into a wide grin and if he wasn't staring right at me, I would've just shaken my head. And men said women were easy. I continued with my story with, "I bet she did all kinds of things, sent you all kinds of signals. Then, she got up in that room and tried to act all innocent."

"Yeah." He nodded. "She took off all her clothes and let me go down on her, but then, she gon' try to tell me no when I was ready for mines."

I shook my head like I was in utter shock. "See? That's just wrong on so many levels. How a woman gonna let you get to third base and then say can't bring it home?"

"For real!" And then, dude dropped his hand, to the front of his pants...as if I weren't standing there.

Oh, my God! I hoped one day, the police locked this pervert away for good.

I was glad he kept talking 'cause I didn't have anything to say.

He said, "I tried to tell Gwen that!" There was such relief in his voice, as if he was glad that someone finally believed him. "It wasn't my fault."

"I know," I said, stepping right back into my role. "But that's what I'm trying to tell you. That's how Tamara is. She likes to play all innocent, then she just wants a man to take it from her.

His hand was back to where it was supposed to be, though I didn't know how long it would stay there. "Really?"

"Really, I mean, look at it this way. If she thought you did something, she would tell Gwen, right?"

He nodded. "Yeah, that's what I'm afraid of."

"Well, Gwen didn't call you last night after this happened, did she?"

I held my breath; I didn't know the answer, but I was taking a bet based on the way Gwen and Tamara had been in the conference room.

Shaking his head, he said, "No."

"If Tamara didn't want you to do that to her, don't you think she would have told Gwen?"

He began to nod again, slowly, this time. "Yeah, yeah, yeah."

I rolled my eyes, but only on the inside. Men: Easy. Crazy Men: Easier.

Then, he asked me, "So, what should I do?"

I put my finger on my chin. "Let me talk to Tamara for you."

"Okay."

"Now, don't you say a word to her because she's all bougie and everything. She won't want anyone to know about her fetish."

"Fetish?"

"For liking it rough. For wanting you."

This time, he nodded with a grin.

"So, just let me handle this and I'll get back to you, okay?"

"Yeah, yeah. This is good. 'Cause I really like her." Then, his eyes kind of glazed over when he said, "I can't wait."

Okay, that was my signal to get the heck away from him. I told him to take the stairs down and I would catch the elevator, but as I watched him descend, I got this stirring inside, a rumbling in my stomach.

I exhaled, releasing a couple of long breaths when he finally disappeared from my sight. That dude. I didn't realize how scared I'd been until now, and I vowed that I'd never be alone with him again. Any dealings we had from now on were going to have to be in plain sight. I just prayed that he scared Tamara as much as he'd scared me, so much that she had nightmares for the rest of her life.

All I had to do now, was figure out how to set this up again.

Taking a breath, I looked up at the ceiling and imagined that I could see straight through to heaven.

"This is for you, June," I whispered. "This is so you'll be able to rest in peace."

Chapter 7

Tamara

On the meter of pissivity, I was beyond my max!

"Where have you been, Maury?" I asked my agent as I walked from one end of the hotel's driveway to the other. At the first break, I'd cut out of the conference room, rushed outside of the hotel and called Maury the way I'd been calling him for the last three days. And the way I'd started calling him again this morning. "I've been trying to get in touch with you."

"I was asleep, Tam. Have you forgotten you're three hours ahead of me?"

I hadn't forgotten, but that didn't matter. He was my agent, he was supposed to take my calls even if it were four or five in the morning.

"I'm not just talking about today. I've been calling you since Monday."

"And you must've forgotten that I was away. I told you last week that I wouldn't be back in the office until Thursday."

I wanted to ask him what did his being away on a short vacation have to do with returning my calls? Surely, he had his cell phone with him. But instead of focusing on what had passed, I kept my attention on the present. "Well, we have a problem." I didn't even take a breath. "Gwen cast Donovan Dobbs as my love interest in this god-forsaken play."

"Donovan who?"

I frowned. Okay...why was Maury playing brand new? He'd been my agent since before I'd even graduated from Yale. In our final year, all kinds of agents came to the school to sign that next superstar.

You've got the look, kiddo, was what I remembered Maury saying to me. *You look like Muhammad Ali's daughter, you know, the boxer, only not as muscular.*

It had been a strange compliment, but one I'd taken right along with his contract. So Maury had been with me from the day I'd worn that Yale blue cap and gown for the second time. And he'd been there through my love and my loss. Through the tears that I'd shed, through the jeers that I suffered. He'd come to my townhouse too many mornings, rescuing me from drowning in my humiliation. He'd put me back together, then convinced me that the massive success I was about to achieve would leave Donovan the one in his bed crying.

"Hello?" I shouted into my cell. "Are you still asleep or something? I'm talking about Donovan, my ex-dog-of-a-boyfriend."

"Oh! That Donovan. So, he's in the play?"

"As my love interest. And I'm not happy about it so, I've been thinking about it and I want out."

"Now, Tam."

I recognized that tone, the tone a father (or what I imagined a father would sound like if I had remembered mine) who was about to chastise his young.

"Don't 'now Tam' me," I shot back.

"I'm just sayin', you have to play that whole video through. First of all, you have a contract and...."

"There has to be some grounds for breach or something. Remember, I was supposed to approve who was playing opposite me."

He kept on like I hadn't even interrupted his sentence. "Then, you need the money."

I sighed. Well, there *was* that fact. It wasn't like I didn't know that my bank account was dwindling with each bill that came due.

Maury changed up his tone, sounded more understanding when he said, "Plus, Gwen's production company has spent all kinds of money on advertising you as the star. You don't want that kind of a reputation. You don't want it to become known that you're willing to break a contract because of a personal issue."

This was far more of a personal issue, but Maury was right and I knew that, even before I called him. I just needed to vent, I guess and I sighed, a long release of breath that came out in a moan. Sinking onto one of the benches in front of the hotel, I bit my lip, focusing on that pain instead of the ache that throbbed in my heart.

"I know it's gotta be hard," my agent continued, "but you're a professional, one of the best in the business."

Another sigh.

"And you've already almost made it through the first week."

One more elongated sigh.

"And, I have some good news."

I didn't even bother to ask him what he was talking about because nothing he could say would pull me out of this misery.

"Diana Delaney called."

I shot straight up.

"She's considering you for her next movie."

"What?" I lept into the air, not at all concerned about my stilettos. Then, I lowered my voice when I saw a few folks turn to me with that-was-so-ghetto glances. I began pacing again. "Why didn't you tell me? What did she say? What movie? What role?"

It was only when I took a breath that Maury explained how one of the hottest new directors in the business wanted me for her new movie "Girls Night Out."

"She's on fire right now," Maury said when he was finished talking about their discussion of me.

"I know!"

"So, this is good!"

"I know."

"And she really likes you."

"Oh, my God, I can't believe it."

"She thinks you're so strong because of what you went through...and what she had to go through, too."

Yes! I knew all about that. Everyone did.

Diana had lived out her personal drama in the tabloids, too, only hers was worse. Last year, paparazzi had climbed atop the roof of the house across the street from hers and taken zoom-lens photos of her husband and her cleaning lady going at it, not only in their home, but in their bed. After those photos had been published everywhere, it had gone down and had gotten dirty when Diana threw her husband out of their home, filed for divorce and then, her husband began giving interviews.

The interview that everyone remembered appeared in the Daily Intruder with the cover headline: *My Cleaning Lady—The Best Sex I Ever Had.* That headline and story became fodder of late night comedy and I couldn't even imagine Diana's pain. I had cried right along with her when she gave that one interview to Barbara Walters and said that women needed to think about the pain they caused other women.

"*No wife should ever have to go through what I went through,*" she'd said. "*From now on, I know that I will suffer with all wives who have to live through the pain of adultery. And I will always side with the wife against any home wrecker. Even in my movies, even in my scripts, I will not support this kind of thing.*"

"This is her comeback movie," Maury said, though I didn't know what that meant.

Her last five films had all been not only box office smashes in this country, but they'd played and paid well internationally, too, which to this point, had been unheard of for black films.

My agent kept talking. "You know she's good friends with Angela. I think Angela put in a good word for you."

"This is amazing." There was nothing else that I needed to say.

"It is. So, I need you to put your head down and make it happen with this play."

I inhaled.

"We don't need any bad press. Don't need any rumors that you didn't fulfill your contractual obligations."

"Okay." I nodded and since he couldn't see me, that move was more for me. I could do this! I had to do this. This was my hope. This was my future.

"The only thing Diana needs to hear about you is that you're a professional and you killed it on that stage."

"So, being in one of these plays won't hurt me with her?"

"Nah," he said, "everyone understands actors working. Everyone understands actors doing whatever they have to do. She's impressed with that, especially since I told her that you're singing in the play. She said the stage is the best training and that actors never sharpen their skills by sitting around passing up roles."

"Oh, my God. This is huge. Thank you so much, Maury!"

"Just doing my job, kiddo. Always looking out for you. So you think you can make it through this now?"

"Yes, whatever I have to do. I'm gonna work this."

"Okay. Well, I'll keep you posted on how the negotiations are going."

"Whatever you have to do, Maury, make it happen because I want this role, even if I have to take a cut. Whatever!"

"You won't have to do that, but I'll do my part. I always do for you."

"Thank you, Maury. Thank you for this."

When I hung up, I had to repress a squeal. I'd heard about Girls Night Out, but never thought I'd be considered. What was being said among the circle was that the four roles were going to more established, even older stars—like Angela Bassett. Maybe Angela was going to be in the movie, too. Maybe I'd get to work with her again.

Now, I wanted to squeal and jump up and click my heels together, but what I did instead was return to the bench. As cars moved before me, and people scurried around me, I lowered my head. There were a few things I needed to say to God—one of them being an apology.

Here I was complaining, so sad and so unhappy—to be working! How many other actors (African American or not) could say that they'd had the steady work that I had? And if I had to be in one of these plays, wasn't it best to do what Diana Delaney had said and work to sharpen my craft? And wasn't it best to be doing this in a play with Gwen Tanner?

Gwen Tanner.

Diana Delaney.

Life couldn't get any better than this!

I closed my eyes. "Thank you, Lord," I whispered. Then, I opened my eyes, glanced up.

And looked right into the eyes of Donovan Dobbs.

"Are you okay, Tammie-Poo?"

I sighed. My day that had just been made with that news from Maury, crashed with these words from Donovan. "I was okay until you came into my life."

"Why all the hostility?" he asked in a tone that made me think he really didn't know.

Except I knew for sure that he did know. He'd been there. He knew what he'd done. But there was no way I was going to waste my breath on him. Instead, I just stared straight ahead and tried to bring back the thrill of victory that I'd been feeling just moments before.

With unsure motions that made him move like a robot, he finally sat down next to me. I was sure that he expected me to jump up and run away, which was what I'd been doing and what I should have done, but I really wanted to stay in this spot and savor for just a little while longer, the talk with Maury. Because it was that chat that was going to give me the strength I needed to make it through.

My hope was that if I remained silent, Donovan would catch the hint and leave me to my solitude. But as people scooted in and out of cars and strode in and out of the hotel, Donovan sat, though like me, he didn't say a word. For long minutes, we sat together as Atlanta life played out around us.

It was hard for me to return to the place where I was with Maury with Donovan so close to me and smelling like I remembered. Tom Ford's Tuscan Leather—the first gift I'd ever bought him. The fragrance that he promised to wear forever. I guess that was one promise he was able to keep.

I inhaled the scent of leather, jasmine, suede...and remembered.

And then, he interrupted the good parts of my memories. Made me fast-forward through all of that pain I'd had because of him and he brought me back to now when he said, "I wasn't sure if I'd ever have the chance to see you again."

I said nothing.

"That was crazy, though. I should've known that we'd meet up again. We had to. This world is so small and this industry is even smaller."

I kept my eyes on the sights of the cars rolling by and my ears on the music of a workday in downtown Atlanta. I focused my attention on all that didn't matter. I focused on everything that wasn't Donovan.

But even though I wanted to pretend he wasn't there, I still felt him, exactly the way I used to. And I felt when he turned toward me, I felt his heat. "You never took any of my calls?"

He stated that fact as a question. Like a question he wanted answered.

"I really loved you, Tammie."

This time, I had to answer, but I didn't look at him when I said, "I could tell by the way you left me just weeks before our wedding."

"It wasn't because I didn't love you."

I had to swallow my response or else my words would have come out shaky. And then, he would've known that he'd gotten to me.

He said, "I loved you then, and I love you now."

I could not believe he said that. How could he? When he'd left me?

There was no need to sit in this space any longer. The place where I'd been after Maury's call was good and gone and now, I wanted to be gone from Donovan.

I stood and rushed toward the hotel's door.

"Wait!" Donovan called behind me.

I pushed through the revolving glass, but I wasn't fast enough because Donovan went inside through the side door and met me just as I took that last turn. He stood, blocking my way.

"Leave me alone," I said, hating that there were tears in my voice and now, probably in my eyes, too.

"I can't. Because I always wanted to tell you that I was sorry. I always wanted to explain what happened."

"You should've sent me a text."

He shook his head. "No, I wanted to talk to you in person."

I glared at him. "You must have forgotten that you did talk to me. You told me everything that I needed to know. You told me that you got some...chick pregnant!"

I spoke too loudly because faces began to turn and eyes began to pry. It was only because I was whipped up into this frenzy that I let Donovan take my hand and move me to the side. I needed a moment anyway. I didn't want to stumble my way through the lobby.

With a lower voice, he said, "You never gave me a chance to explain it all. It wasn't you, Tammie. It didn't have anything to do with you."

I blinked because I was in a battle with these tears that were trying to seep from my eyes.

"You know how it was with us. It was wonderful," he said. "I wanted you and I couldn't believe God felt I deserved the incredible gift He'd given me in you."

He stood so close that when I lowered my head, my forehead touched his shoulder and I stayed there. Just for a moment, I let my face rest against his chest.

"What the hell is going on?"

The voice startled me, made me look up, made me wonder who was this woman glaring at me and Donovan? But in the next second, I answered my own question. Because once my eyes cleared, I could see her. And I recognized her. From the wedding picture in the tabloids. The woman who I'd always thought was pretty in a plain-Jane type way.

There was fire in her eyes when she hissed, "What the hell is going on," again.

"Latrice, wh. . . what are you doing...back here?" Donovan stammered to his wife.

I took a step back because this was his drama, not mine. Really, I should have taken several steps back and then the fifty or so that would have taken me to the elevator and back up to the conference room. But I stayed because I was curious. I stayed because I wanted to see more and hear more from the woman who'd stolen my heart.

Donovan grabbed her arm and tried to tug her away, but his wife stood like a tree, and would not be moved.

"Answer me!" she demanded of him, though she had turned her glare to me.

I glared right back. Like I said, she was pretty, at least that was what I kind of believed before. It was hard to tell now with the severe chignon she wore and the flowered (yes, flowered) dress that fell right below her knee.

When his wife wouldn't budge, Donovan backed up. Stood next to me. "Nothing's going on, but what are you doing here?"

Now, it was Latrice who was blinking back tears and I wondered if Donovan noticed this sick effect he had on women. And then, I wondered, how in the world had Donovan left me for her? I mean, yes, she was attractive in that what-is-that-librarian-wearing-under-her-ugly-dress kind of way, but I couldn't imagine her laughing with Donovan the way I had, or cheering at football games the way Donovan and I had, or the two of them working out together—in and out of bed.

She finally answered Donovan's question. "I came here to surprise you." She sniffed a couple of times and that made me want to step away for real now. Because though I was sure she was aware that he and I were together when they hooked up (we were all over the media!), I wasn't going to do the same thing to her. No one would ever be able to brand me as that kind of woman.

But just as I began to back away, she said, "What are you doing here with her!" She pointed at me as if she was accusing me of something and I stopped, pivoted, and gave her my woman-you-better-back-up stare.

"What do you mean what am I doing here with Tammie?" he said as if he had no idea what she meant.

"Tammie? You call her Tammie?"

I folded my arms and planted my feet, settling in for the show. It was the first time in the days since we'd been here that I was glad he called me that.

"Look, Latrice, you knew she was in the play weeks ago."

Ding! Ding! Ding! Donovan had just given me proof that Gwen hadn't told me the truth about Jamal, and what I wanted to do was march right up to her and call her a liar. But after my call with Maury, that would have been the only thing that I could do. I couldn't leave this play. And I couldn't do anything about the fact that everyone, including Latrice knew what was going on before I did. Everyone knew, except for me and Maury.

"But you promised that you were only going to be around her on the stage."

That whiney voice brought my focus back to this present-drama.

"And so, what do you think this is? We rehearse in this hotel."

"You didn't look like you were rehearsing anything!"

"We were just down here talking."

Her eyes became slits. "It didn't look like you were just talking."

"I don't care what it looked like; that's all we were doing."

"Then, why is there lipstick on your shirt?"

Donovan glanced down, but from where I stood, I couldn't see what she was talking about. I replayed the moments in my mind and I guessed a bit of my lipstick had brushed against his shirt. But it couldn't have been much. I had only leaned in for a moment.

"How could you do this when you promised?" she cried.

Okay, it was definitely time for me to exit stage right. Her voice had raised and people had slowed as they passed this little trio of a show. I didn't want to be in the middle of any drama that might show up in a video on social media.

"Look, you can't come to my job trippin'," Donovan said. "I'm just working."

I turned, and then, she spat, "I'm tired of skanky heffas like you."

I stopped...again. Pivoted...again. Stared her down...again, to give her a chance to back up. "Excuse. Me?"

She may have looked like a librarian, but she didn't have the brains of one because she took a step forward. "You heard me."

Then the widget had the nerve to get closer and threaten me with, "Stay away from my man or I swear you will regret it."

I'd given her a chance for this not to flip sideways. But she had mistaken my grace for weakness. So I gave her a stare that was designed to melt whatever courage she thought she had. "What you need to do is tell your man to stay away from me. Because I don't want him. At least not anymore." And then my stare, turned into a smile that I knew would piss her off. "I've been there, done that, remember? He was my man first."

This time, when I turned, I was going to keep going. Except behind me, someone grabbed me. Actually tugged and twisted my hair!

"Ahhhh!" I screamed.

I was jerked around and couldn't believe it was Latrice who had me in her grasp. How had she even reached high enough to assault me like this? But I guess jealousy gave way to super-midget strength because before I could get in a single punch, she had me on the ground, straddled me, and began pummeling me in my face.

I screamed, I punched back, and then I grabbed my own handful of hair and yanked so hard that the girl in Asia who originally owned the hair had to feel it.

"Latrice!" Donovan screamed and with a couple of tugs, pulled her off of me.

I was still on the ground when Gwen rushed over to us. "What in the world is going on here?" she asked as she reached down and pulled me up.

Behind her, a crowd had gathered with a few faces I recognized: Camille, Randy.

Ugh! I could not believe this! And I just prayed that this didn't end up trending on Twitter.

"What in the world?" Gwen said again as I straightened out my top and then fluffed my hair with my fingers.

I guess Donovan couldn't speak because he was too busy holding back his wife who was wiggling and waggling like she was still trying to do something.

"I think Donovan's wife caught Donovan and Tamara together," Camille said so matter-of-factly anyone standing there would have thought what she said was true.

I glared at her, but didn't have the chance to say anything because Latrice screamed out and co-signed that lie. "That's right, she was with my husband and I'm gonna teach this heffa a lesson."

"Donovan, get your wife under control!" Gwen barked.

He did as he was told and dragged that crazed woman, still wiggling and waggling, toward the hotel's front door. The air filled with obscenities that were way over the top for what had actually gone down between me and Donovan. It was almost like she had snapped and she was cursing out a year's worth of jump-offs.

But once Latrice and Donovan were gone, the crowd realized the show was over and they dispersed like church-goers at the end of a five-hour service.

Camille, Randy, and a couple of the other cast members lingered until Gwen barked, "Everyone get back upstairs so we can get back to work."

They all moved slowly, though I stayed in place and Gwen did, too. Once we were alone, she asked, "So what happened? She caught you and Donovan?"

"No!" I snapped. "Donovan and I weren't doing anything. I was outside talking to my agent, Donovan came outside, we walked back into the hotel together and the next thing I knew, that maniac attacked me!"

"She must have thought that something was going on."

"I don't care what she thought," I shouted and then rubbed my jaw. I couldn't believe Latrice had gotten all those shots in on me.

"Well, I'm sorry that happened, Tamara. But you're gonna have to stay away from Donovan."

I was pissed on so many levels and for so many reasons. And now, Gwen was going to get the brunt of my anger. "I don't want that man; I don't even want to be in this damn play. But like you and my agent reminded me, I have a contract. And I'm going to fulfill my contract. But if anything else happens to me, I'm walking. And I will tell the world how unsafe it is to be in one of your productions."

Then, I stomped away, sure that behind me Gwen was rolling her eyes and thinking that I was just one of those overly-dramatic actors. But I wasn't playing with this. In the four days I'd been here, I found myself in more drama than Gwen had written into her play. She didn't know about Randy, but she knew about Latrice. And if one more person came after me, I was going to break this contract, sue Gwen, and let the world know Tamara Collins didn't do ghetto-fabulous.

I wasn't worried about the opportunity in front of me. Even Diana Delaney would have to agree with that.

Chapter 8

Camille

I slipped into the ladies room, glanced under each stall to make sure that I was alone, then let out a, "Whoop!" and threw my fist in the air.

It had been almost too easy. Or maybe I was just that good.

What it was in reality though, was that Donovan Dobbs had been a very bad boy. I hadn't been following anything on the blogs about him; he wasn't really on my radar except for when he'd humiliated Tamara and after that, I'd pretty much forgotten about him.

But when a new plan began formulating in my mind after Randy's disaster on Tuesday, I'd found out lots about Mr. Dobbs.

It seemed that in the two years of his marriage, there had been a parade of THOTs and jump offs slithering through his life. I knew having to deal with all of those tricks would have left any woman insecure, and what I also hoped, was that a woman who'd been through all of that could be easily fooled, too.

While I figured out exactly how I was going to use Randy, I wanted to make Tamara as miserable as I could. I might never have this chance again—to be around Tamara every day for an extended time. I had to make every minute of each hour count.

And so I'd figured out a plan. It hadn't taken much time and even less effort, and I was able to execute it right away.

On Tuesday night, as we club-hopped through Atlanta, I'd sat next to Donovan, drinking very little, flirting a lot and after a couple of hours, all I had to do was pretend that my phone was dead.

When I asked if I could borrow his phone to call my mother, Donovan gave it freely (especially when I gave him a little pout and a peek at my boobs) and he didn't even care when I slipped away from the table to make the call. (Though I was sure he wanted me to bring my boobs back.)

Hiding out in the ladies room, I got to work. It didn't take but a couple of moments to spot his wife's number, which was easy enough to find under WIFEY. Then, the texts began:

Get to Atlanta quick.

I wasn't sure if she'd respond right away; not that it mattered. I would have just kept doing it every night until I made contact with her.

But being the wife that she was, probably with her cell at her side waiting for a call or a text from her wayward husband, in two seconds, she hit back with:

Huh? Now you want me to come to ATL?

I smiled.

I'm sorry. This isn't Donovan. I'm a friend of his who's in the play and I don't like what's going down with D and that chick Tamara. She's after your man and I don't play that.

This time, I don't think two seconds passed:

Who is this? What's going on? Where's Donovan? What are you doing with his phone?

My thumbs couldn't type fast enough.

Look, I'm just trying to help. No drama. Just don't like how Tamara is going after him. They're out on the dance floor now and she's all over him. I just wanted to give you this heads up. Get here. Surprise him or something, but get here asap.

So much time passed, that I wasn't sure if she was going to hit back. With what I knew that she'd been through, she might have already been on a plane from Memphis.

But then after about a minute:

Thank you. Thank you so much. I'll be there.

I had wanted to text back and ask when, but I didn't want eagerness to blow my cover or my plan. So, I just deleted the texts that I'd just sent, returned to the table, gave Donovan back his phone (and another peek at my breasts). As I joined back in with the banter and the laughter, I thought about all the things that I could set up so that drama would go down once Mrs. Dobbs got here.

But who knew Donovan and Tamara were going to set that up all by themselves?

Like I said, too easy. The only bad part was that this was my plan and I'd missed it. I wouldn't have seen any of it if Gwen hadn't asked me to walk with her to the front desk to check on a package that she was expecting. By the time we rolled up on Donovan, Tamara, and his wife, wifey had Tamara's back against the floor and she was punching her like she was one of those bags at the gym.

Just thinking about it made me laugh out loud again. I was impressed; Donovan's wife moved her fists so fast, it was just a blur. She wasn't bigger than a minute, but she'd worn Tamara out. That surprised me; I was sure that Tamara could fight—at least, that's what I remembered from back when I was a kid.

The memory of that time snatched my laughter away and I had to brace myself against the sink. Even though I took a couple of deep breaths to steady myself, still when I looked up, there were tears in my eyes. There were always tears whenever I thought of June Bug. His real name was Martin, named after our daddy. Martin, Jr—June Bug was who he would always be to me.

Blinking back tears, I looked up and did what I always did—wished I could see into heaven. If I could have just one more conversation, one more hug, one more moment with him....

But I couldn't. Because for six years now, I'd had to live with an emptiness that was somctimes so overwhelming, I felt like I was drowning in the grief. It didn't have to be this way. Because Tamara used to be part of the family.

February 2, 2001

I tried to hold in my giggles, but it was hard. I was only seven and everything was funny to me. But this was *really* funny. 'Cause June Bug and Tam didn't know that I was hiding from them.

When they came into the living room, I ducked down behind the couch. I knew it! I just knew that they were gonna come in here. And I bet, I would get to see them kissing again. Maybe I would even get to see them doing the nasty the way I saw them the other night when June Bug was laying on top of Tamara. They had their clothes on, but still, I knew that June Bug would get into all kinds of trouble if Mama found out.

I should've told my best friend, Niecy, to come over so that we could watch them again. June Bug and Tam were always kissing and she had never seen them doing the nasty before.

"Don't cry, Tam," my brother whispered right before they sat on the couch and that made me frown. "I don't want you to cry."

My brother's voice was so soft, like he was talking to a baby and I wanted to peek over the top of the couch. But I couldn't take the chance of them seeing me. 'Cause June Bug might get mad and then not give me the fifty cents he'd promised me.

But even though I couldn't see them, I could hear Tamara sniffling. Like really sniffling. Like she had been crying a lot and for a really long time.

Then, she said, "I can't help it. Do you know how long I've wanted to go to Yale."

"I know."

"And now, it's not gonna happen!" Tam sounded so sad, I wanted to cry, too.

I didn't even know where Yale was, but I wanted her to go. Why couldn't she go? Why couldn't June Bug just drive her?

"Let me see the letter," my brother said.

I heard some ruffling, like paper unfolding, and then, there was nothing but quiet. So much quiet, that I almost stood up because I thought they were gone. But I didn't move because even though they weren't talking, I was pretty sure that I heard some breathing going on.

My brother finally made all of that quiet go away. He said, "They are giving you a lot of money, Tam."

"Yeah, but it's nowhere what I need. And I have no idea where I'll get the rest. You know with my mom's disability, she can't help." There were more sniffles. "She tried to save the money from my dad's insurance policy for my college, but it's what we've been living on."

"I know," June Bug said.

I wanted to tell my brother to just drive her over to Yale. Mama would let him drive the car as long as he brought it back before she had to go to the night shift at the hospital.

"Well, what about if you go to Mississippi Valley with me."

"I don't want to go to Mississippi Valley," she cried. "I want to go to Yale. I've wanted to go to Yale my whole life."

"But I'm just sayin', maybe for a year, until we can figure this out. Maybe after a year, this will work itself out and you can transfer."

"Don't you understand?"

My eyes got big when Tam yelled and she jumped up from the couch. I could see the top of her head and it was moving the way Mama's head moved when she was mad at me.

She said, "I don't want to go to Mississippi Valley. I want to go to Yale or I'm not going to college at all. And if I don't go to college, my life will be ruined. I'll never be an actress, I'll never get to leave Mississippi. It will all be over."

The way she shouted and cried made tears come into my own eyes. I wished that Niecy was here with me. Or better, I wished that I was at Niecy's house. Because it didn't seem like there was gonna be any kissing today and I didn't want to sneak around just to hear all of this crying.

"Don't cry, Tam."

Now, my brother stood up, too. And I could see more than the top of his head—I could see his whole face. I could tell that he had put his arms around Tam and he hugged her.

"I'm gonna figure something out. Don't you worry," June Bug said. "I'm gonna make sure you go to Yale. Don't you worry."

He kept saying, 'Don't you worry,' over and over. But even though he said that and even though he hugged her, she still cried and cried and cried. And a few minutes later, I was crying right along with her.

I wiped away my tears now, thinking of that day and thinking about everything that had happened after that. My brother had been such a good guy. He was only eighteen and he'd been willing to give up going to college himself so that he could work and help Tamara pay for school. (I'd figured out that Yale was a college and not just another town in Mississippi.)

June hadn't had to do that since Tamara's mother died right before they graduated and she'd used her mom's insurance money. Still, my brother had been willing. He would have sacrificed everything for her; that's how much he loved her. But she only cared about herself.

Well, the way she had damned my brother, was the way that I was going to damn her. For as many days as I could, I was going to make her life so bad, she'd hope for miserable. I was going to do that until I could figure out this whole thing with Randy. Because Randy was the ultimate to me. Especially with the way he had acted on Tuesday.

Yeah, dude was crazy. And he would take care of Tamara real good, leave her with a permanent pain and I hoped a couple of scars, too.

My tears weren't all the way gone, but at least the thought of Randy being my revenge made me smile inside. That made me smile for the rest of the afternoon.

Chapter 9

Gwen

We'd made it through the first week of rehearsals and all I could say was these pseudo celebrities knew how to dance on a woman's nerves. Couldn't these people see that I was the ally, not the enemy? I was giving these folks a huge opportunity by putting them back in the public eye.

Like Tamara. Yeah, she was a beautiful woman who'd had some success, but recently she'd been in more commercials than anything on the big (or little) screen. Yet she hit my stage every... single...day acting like she was an A list star, especially after that little incident between her and Donovan's wife. That had cost me another ten thousand dollars after Maury threatened me with Tamara leaving the show before our opening.

I was pissed. I didn't believe that she would really leave, but with all that this play meant to me, how could I take that chance? So I wrote another check, though I cursed Tamara and Maury with each zero I had to write.

That was days ago and I was still mad about it. Because it had solved nothing. Tamara was still acting like a prima-donna, though she was acting like one who was taking a walk on the psycho-side.

I rested my elbows on the desk in the makeshift office I was using in the back of the Fox Theatre. Today had been our first rehearsal on the stage, in full costume, and it had gone well... except for Tamara Collins. I swear, she was trying to squeeze the life out of me. Closing my eyes, I remembered what felt like a close call with death.

Ninety minutes earlier...

This was the first time that I'd ever written a dream sequence into a play and I had no idea if it would translate onto the stage the way I saw it in my mind. In rehearsals at the Renaissance, it had worked. But I was eager to see it today with the special effects of the smoke that would surround Tamara and Donovan.

This was huge and I was giddy. If this worked, it would be the talk of the industry. Because I'd written this scene with the drama that had gone down (and clearly was still simmering) between Tamara and Donovan in mind. I knew that once the audience saw it, they would be talking about the wedding that never happened, that finally happened on the stage. And the talk would lead to reviews, and the reviews would lead to...sold out shows!

"Okay, let's do this from the top."

I sat in the front row as the set circled slowly and swiveled to the church. Donovan was in place, the preacher was in place, the extras were in place...and Mendelssohn's Wedding March began to play.

Leaning to the left, I saw Tamara's shadow backstage and I took a breath. I was ready...ready...ready...to see my creativity come to life.

And then...

What the hell?

Tamara sashayed in, exactly the way she was supposed to, holding the bouquet, with a smile on her face as if she were so happy to be walking toward her groom.

Except....

She was wearing black. The heffa was wearing all black. A black catsuit (not even a dress.) Black thigh-high boots (who would wear boots to their own wedding?) And a black fascinator, complete with a black veil that draped her face to her chin.

I jumped up. "What the hell?" I pressed my hand to my chest to stop myself from hyperventilating.

Everyone stopped, though no one looked at me. Every shocked eye in the theatre was on Tamara.

"What are you doing?" I demanded, not quite sure if I was confused or angry.

She turned toward me and stared through her veil. "What?" she asked with the innocence of a seven-year-old.

"What are you wearing? This is the *wedding* sequence. Where is your *wedding* dress?»

She shrugged. "I decided to wear this instead."

I blinked a couple of times. Wasn't this my play? "Tamara...."

"I was thinking," she interrupted me, "this outfit is far better than a regular wedding gown. Because this is how my character would really feel." Her tone was high-brow, as if she suddenly thought this was Shakespeare or something. "My training has taught me to go with the character. After all, that's what I'm doing as an actor, just channeling my character."

"No, what you're doing as an actor is what I tell you to do. And you're supposed to be dreaming." And then I added, "You're dreaming about the wedding that never was," because I was pissed.

She flinched, stomped off the stage, and Donovan ran after her. Right then, I dismissed everyone, knowing I wouldn't be able to get another good moment out of Tamara after that. Plus, I had a huge headache—we'd just have to hit it harder tomorrow with Tamara in a wedding dress.

With my fingertips, I massaged my temples, trying to ease the headache that was still there. I knew what this was—stress, the pressure that came from needing this play to be successful.

What I needed right now was some stress relief.

I glanced at the clock and grabbed my cell phone at the same time. Maybe I could convince Eli that I wanted him, I needed him. He could fly into Atlanta, even if only for one night.

But his phone rang once, went to voicemail, and I tried to convince myself that he must've been somewhere that had a bad signal, rather than thinking that he'd just hit 'IGNORE' so that I'd have to leave a message.

Well, Eli was out. But still, I needed to do something to shake off this drama. From Tamara's many meltdowns, to Donovan and his ghetto wife, who now rang his phone incessantly (after he'd sent her home) and finally to the rumors that Randy had almost gotten himself in trouble again. I'd heard some of the band members whispering about it and I had no idea who his almost-victim was this time. But this was it for me. I couldn't take the chance with this man again no matter how talented or how little I had to pay him. He had a problem that could one day blow up my spot. Yeah, Randy was going to be gone before this production was over, as soon as I had time to focus on that.

I released a long, long, long breath of air and thought about calling Eli again, until, "Ms. Tanner."

I swiveled my chair around.

And looked right into the eyes of that pretty, young specimen—Justin. Like always when I saw him, my mind filled with illicit thoughts. Only this time, what was galloping through my mind was hard to shake away. Or maybe it was that I wasn't really trying.

"Yes?" I said, thinking about what my forty-four-year-old body could do with his twenty-three-year-old one.

"I got all the merchandise accounted for. Everything has arrived." He handed me several pieces of paper. "Here're all the packing slips."

I took the pile from him. "Thank you for your hard work. So, it's all packed away? Ready for opening night?"

"Yes, ma'am."

"Okay, then, thank you so, so much."

He just stood there, and what I wanted to do was just stare back and let the images I had just roll through my mind. But finally, I had to ask, "Is there anything else?"

"I, umm, well, I..."

I let him stutter and do that little side-to-side shuffle just so I could take in that six-foot-one, smooth cocoa-brown, candy bar some more. It took him a little while, before he spoke up,

"I was just wondering if, you know, when I signed on to do merchandising for you, you said that maybe, possibly, there would be a chance, you know, for me to do something else in the show."

I didn't remember saying anything close to that and all I wanted to do was lower my head and bang it against the desk a couple of times. After the day I'd had, this dude wanted to add his desire to be an actor to the list of what-had-gone-wrong-with-my-day? The play hadn't even opened and he was pressing me. Why, oh why did he have to ruin the perfection of his image? Why couldn't he just stand there and be pretty?

It must have been my silence that made him say, "I know it's early, but I got an offer for a job back home in Birmingham. It's not what I want to do, but it's good money and well," he shrugged, "if there's no chance of me ever getting on stage, then I, well, I guess I need to get home. So, I'm not asking for anything right away, but I just wanted to know how realistic you thought it was that I'd ever get a shot?"

I hadn't heard anything after—I need to get home. Go home? My eye candy was thinking about leaving? Absolutely not! Looking at him was the little stress relief that I had.

In those passing seconds, I thought about all of this drama, I thought about Eli, I thought about surviving. "You know what, Justin?" I paused and this time, I let my eyes do a slow stroll up, then back down his body. "Your timing couldn't be more perfect." I reached across the desk and grabbed a script. "One of the guys, Rick, who plays Donovan's best friend, has to leave after Dallas and I wasn't sure what I was going to do," I lied. "I don't have an understudy for him. You would be great for that part."

His eyes widened. "Really?"

"Here, why don't you take this," I handed him the script, "and meet me in my hotel lobby in two hours."

"Tonight?"

"Yeah, tonight. After Atlanta, we hit Dallas and I'd need you ready. So there's no time to mess around on this."

"Cool," he excitedly said. "You're at the Renaissance, right?"

I nodded.

"Okay, I'll get right on this."

"Now, I need this to be between the two of us. When someone from the cast leaves, it kinda makes everyone else nervous, you know? So, I don't want to say anything to anyone until you're ready to step right into the role."

"Gotcha. And thank you so much. You won't be disappointed." He turned and my glance hovered over his firm behind before he dashed out of the office.

I wished I could've just left and hooked up with Justin now. Not that anything was gonna happen...I was too chicken for that. But a girl could look. And who knew, maybe I'd get to touch a little, too.

Turning to the pile of papers, I set my focus on getting this work done: confirming the rest of the media interviews this week, handling tour details, and checking advance ticket sales. I wanted to get as much as I could get done, as fast as I could do it, so that I could go to my hotel and just stare at Justin for hours.

Yeah, I wanted to get to my stress relief.

I walked the two blocks back to the hotel and as soon as I stepped through the revolving doors, I didn't even bother to hide my smile.

"Well, you're certainly on time," I said to Justin who stopped pacing when he spotted me.

"I just wanted to get here and go over the scene you wanted me to learn."

"Okay. Where's your script? We can do a read through and then, if you're good, I'll arrange an actual audition."

He nodded toward his bag. "Right in there, but I don't need the script, I have it memorized."

My mouth opened wide before I said, "You've memorized the lines already?"

With a nod and a grin, he said, "For the most part. It wasn't a whole lot."

"Okay, show me what you got." I moved toward one of the long sofas in the lobby. But as soon as I sat down, I looked at my watch. "You know what? It's late and I'm exhausted. And not only that, I really want to get out of these heels. Why don't you come up to my room and you can read for me there."

"Well...." He did that little side-to-side shuffle again.

I said, "Or, we can just wait until I can fit you into my schedule."

"No, no," he said. "If you don't mind me intruding on your space. . ."

"No intrusion," I said. "I'm in suite 1302. Give me ten minutes, then come on up." I headed toward the elevator.

Exactly nine minutes later, the doorbell to my suite rang. I shook my locs loose, then tightened the belt on the black lounging dress that I'd changed into. Opening the door, I said, "Come on in," with a wave of my hand.

As he passed, the muscles in the very center of me constricted and I wondered how many different ways were there to describe this young buck as some kind of fine.

He stood in the middle of the living room area of the suite as I sat on the sofa. Looking as uncomfortable as he did downstairs, I gave him what I hoped would be a reassuring smile. I wasn't some kind of cougar, waiting to pounce and I wanted him to know that.

After a couple of seconds, his shoulders relaxed and he removed his jacket. "Okay," he said as he hooked his jacket on the back of one of the dining room chairs. "Should I just read the first scene?"

I nodded.

There was another moment of hesitancy before he said, "I've never done this before." He pulled his script from his bag. "Ummm...can you read Valerie's lines for me? That will help."

"Of course," I said, taking the script from him. And then, I leaned back on the sofa.

He took a deep breath and then started what was about eight lines of dialogue, but I felt my eyebrow rise with his first line. I couldn't believe it. This kid was more than good-looking, he was actually pretty good. I didn't really have a role for him, but I began to think that maybe I could write in a character. He would just be another piece of candy, a visual treat for the black women who bought most of the tickets. Now granted, no one knew him, but with his body, in two weeks everyone would know his name.

"Ummm...Mrs. Tanner, it's your line."

His words snapped me from my trance.

"Oh, my bad." Dang! Was it always going to be like that when he was around? I'd have to find a way to concentrate. I scanned the script. "Where are we? Oh, here it is: Why are you doing this to me? You know it's my birthday and..." I stopped and looked up at Justin. "Do you know the second scene, too?"

That side-to-side shuffle was back. "I do." His voice was low.

"Wow, I'm impressed. You really did learn these lines that fast." I flipped the page. "Let's do that scene." I eyed him when he didn't move. "Do you have a problem with that?"

He paused, then said, "No, of course not."

"Okay," I said, now leaning all the way back, as I settled in for what I knew would be quite a show. "The notes call for you to take your shirt off."

The look he gave me said: Do you really want me to take my shirt off?

The look I passed back to him said: I do!

He removed his shirt, strip-tease slow, and at first, I almost passed out from anticipation. And then, I really felt dizzy when half of his body was naked. All I wanted to do was run my tongue over every inch of the terrain that was his chest. "Umm...before we do these lines, can you sing?"

He nodded, though the way he tilted his head I could tell that he was confused since this scene didn't call for any kind of singing. "I do pretty well."

"Let me hear something. Because...you know...I might just write that in."

"Anything special that you want me to sing?"

I had to clear my throat before I said, "Whatever you want." At this point, he could've sang the ABC song and it would've worked for me.

He licked his lips in preparation and then that first note came out:

"Oh, yeah

Got a lady on the line

She screaming, why would she need, oh..."

He'd chosen "Emergency" by Tank, and dude was knocking it out—acapella. Lord, did I want to call 9-1-1. Every word he sang, every note he hit sent my insides into a frenzy. The boy could blow—and how he managed to keep on licking his lips while he sang...I just couldn't imagine. Or maybe the problem was that I could.

"It's an emergency

I'm rushing and I have the mind...."

He came closer, as if he knew he was breaking me down. As if this had been *his* plan all along. He continued, singing something about giving mouth to mouth and I swear, every part of me felt like it was moist. And then when he leaned over me, every part of me became moist.

Oh yeah, he was gonna have a part in my play. Either I was about to write a new role or someone was about to get fired.

"How was it?" he whispered.

I blinked. Had he stopped singing?

I hadn't noticed. But I did notice how he still leaned over me, our faces just inches apart. It seemed that all of his nervousness was gone, replaced by a confidence...or was it cockiness? Either way, this boy had turned me all the way on.

If I were to ever be questioned about my motives, all I would have been able to say was that I couldn't help my next words. They just came out of me without my permission. I whispered, "I'm almost convinced."

The way he raised his eyebrows—oh yeah, he was cocky. "Almost?"

The road I was about to travel wasn't a good one. I knew it, but my body had taken over the driver's seat. "How bad do you want this part?" This time, I was the one to lick my lips.

His response was swift. "I'll do anything to get this part." His cockiness was on full throttle now.

"Anything?" My voice was so deep with lust that I sounded just like him.

"And then some."

That was it—lights out. Literally. I had never cheated on my husband, and never thought that I would. But a woman had needs too, right?

My eyes never left Justin's (or should I say my glance never left that chiseled-carved-to-perfection chest that God had given to him as a blessing) when I leaned back and clicked off the light on the end table. For a moment, I thought about leaving on that light and turning on a few more just so I could see everything he was about to do to me.

But I figured this was the first time, and if it went down the way I thought it was about to, it wouldn't be the last. Next time

I'd get to see more of him. This time, it was going to be all about touch.

My lips went to his first. I just loved being the woman in control. But what I loved even more? A man who was willing to sleep his way to the top.

Chapter 10

Tamara

It was absolutely amazing that I'd made it through these last two weeks and I was still alive. That was my thought as I stepped past security and through the back door of the Fox Theatre. Even though every day brought new drama, I was sticking it out and holding it down. That extra five thousand dollars that Maury had extorted from Gwen for my trouble with Latrice helped. Even after having the agent's fee deducted, I was able to dash over to Lennox Mall and pick up a new designer purse for my pain and suffering. The three thousand dollar price tag didn't concern me at all since this was really a bonus.

Inside the hallway, I paused for a moment for my eyes to adjust to the darkness, then took a couple of steps and wished I could have gone the other way.

There stood Camille, arms folded, eyes glaring, the way it always was with her. She never said a word. Just stared and glared.

Most of the time I turned the other way, but since I had to go past her to head to my dressing room, I marched right up to her and said, "Do you have a problem?"

She responded with, "Only you."

For a second, I paused. She'd spoken only two words, but she'd said them with an accent, a distinct Southern drawl that

I'd heard before. I studied her, then shook my head. "What does that mean?"

Her only answer was a smirk, a turn, and then a strut going the other way. As I watched her, I decided that chick was certifiable. For two weeks, she did nothing but look at me as if I'd stolen something from her Mama. But I was the only one she treated that way. She was always all over Donovan, all the time. Now yes, she was his (other) love interest, the woman he was leaving me for, but she was playing her part like she wasn't acting. Even when she wasn't rehearsing a scene, she was drooling over him with a, "Oh, Donovan," here and a "Oh, Donovan," there. She was playing it like she had really stolen my man.

As if.

And then, I thought about the woman who had stolen my man.

For real.

I shook my head. I could make it through this. We were finally moving from rehearsals to the actual play, which would open tomorrow to a sold-out crowd. Then, I could turn my focus back to the career I was meant to have.

Maury was so close to closing the deal with Diana Delaney. She'd told him that she was glad I was doing the play because I'd come to her movie with momentum. That was a good thing, I guess, but it didn't stop me from feeling like being in this play was me doing penance for some crime my ancestors had committed. Because beyond Camille and her issues, beyond Randy and his issues, beyond Latrice and her issues—there was Donovan and he was my issue.

The hardest thing I'd ever done in my life was share this space with him. He made my head hurt and my heart ache. I hated him!

And that was my issue.

Because I knew the opposite of love wasn't hate—the opposite of love was indifference. And I was a long, long ways from impassivity. Even in my hate, Donovan was able to reach out and touch the deepest parts of me.

Whether he was apologizing for his needed-to-be-committed wife: *I'm so sorry, Tammie. Is there anything that I can do to make it up to you* or whether he was consoling me after Gwen had gone off just because I'd suggested a little costume change in that wedding scene: *She was wrong for talking to you like that, Tammie. Doesn't she get that you're that star*—his presence made me weak, made me want. And I hated him for that.

I shifted my new oversized hobo onto my other shoulder and moved through the corridor of the Fabulous Fox, as those in the industry called this historic theatre.

Turning the corner for the hallway with the dressing rooms, I bumped right into Donovan, standing in front of mine. He stood, like he'd been there for a while, like he'd been waiting for me.

"Excuse me," I said, then I maneuvered to the left, trying to pass him in the confined space.

But he made no moves to move. He just stood there and grinned, blocking my path. "So, you ready for the show tomorrow?" Then, he folded his arms and leaned against the wall, like we were old friends, chatting.

I glared, then snarled, "Look, you low-life liar. If I've told you once, I've told you every day of these miserable two weeks. I'm a professional, so I'm gonna do my job. But outside of that, I don't have anything to say to you, I don't want you to say anything to me, and I don't think your wife would appreciate it—or have you forgotten about her the way you forgot about me?"

He let out a short snort that I guess was supposed to be a chuckle. "I won't ever get over it."

My eyes narrowed. "Get over what?"

"The fire in you when you get mad at me."

It was his cocky smile more than his words that pissed me off even more. "Go work that bull on somebody else because I'm not buying it. I'm not buying anything that you're selling." I tried to step past him once again, but he pushed off the wall and now, he was all in my personal space.

What I should have done was back up, but I figured, why should I be the one to do that? We were standing in front of my dressing room and I wasn't scared of Donovan.

But maybe I should have been. Because with his eyes fixed to mine, he raised his hand...slowly.

I gulped in air, but I didn't move.

The tips of his fingers brushed my skin.

I gasped, but I didn't move.

"That little vein. Right there." He stroked my neck. "It pops up." His voice was low, filled with lust. "It's always been so sexy to me."

I gave in to too many moments of resting in that familiar space. But then, my good sense came over me and I slapped his hand away. "Fool, don't touch me."

He laughed and gave me a reprieve when he took a single step back. "I still get under your skin, I see." He paused, studied my face for a reaction. "That means, you still feel me like I feel you."

I thought about the opposite of love. And I said, "You are a non-muthafu-" Before I could finish cursing him, his mother, his father, and everyone else who shared his DNA, Donovan snatched me, pulled me, pressed against me. I didn't have time to blink or breathe before his lips were on mine. Gentle, at first, until he used his tongue to part my lips, and against every standard and sense in me, I welcomed him in.

Really, I wanted to protest. I wanted to jerk away and give him one of those slaps that I'd had the pleasure of giving him over and over again in the play. But my freaking hormones! And my freakin' heart! My mind was calling Donovan everything but a child of God, but my body, all the parts that made me a woman, was screaming, 'Oh, God!'

I did (kinda) try, though. I did (kinda) try to push away, but when I pushed, he pulled and though it seemed impossible, we were closer, our hearts pressed together like our lips. It was like... we were almost one. The way we used to be.

As my tongue waltzed with his, I became dizzy, but it was from more than just his kiss. I was in a daze, floating between the memories and this reality. Remembering how he'd always kissed me like this, how he'd always left me breathless and spent. Sometimes, even in tears, crying just because I'd been loved so good.

And now, I could feel tears once again as I fell, fell, fell into those memories.

Then...a flash.

Next...a voice.

"Hey!" Gwen's voice.

Donovan and I jumped, leaping what felt like miles away from each other.

Then, another flash. Instinct made me and Donovan turn toward the flash. Toward the man. Toward the camera.

A third, a fourth, a fifth flash.

And I blinked, and blinked, and blinked.

It was happening so fast, but time moved so slow.

"What are you doing?" Gwen called out.

I ducked behind Donovan as Gwen ran toward the photographer, but with a final click, he scurried down the hall.

"Come back here!" Gwen yelled after him, as he shot out of our sight.

Gwen's screams echoed through the hallway as she followed the photographer, but I had no hope.

"Oh, my God!" I shrieked. I pressed my hand against my chest to make sure my heart was still beating.

"What the hell?" Donovan shouted.

He paced in front of me, but I couldn't move. My thoughts kept me stuck in place.

That kiss.

The photographer.

That kiss.

The pictures.

That kiss.

This would be all over the blogs and the magazines and maybe even on TV.

That kiss.

Gwen rushed back into the hallway where Donovan and I stood. "I am so sorry." She huffed and puffed as if she'd ran a mile.

"What the hell?" Donovan repeated, this time straight at Gwen. "What was that? And what was he doing here?"

Gwen trembled as she shook her head. "I have no idea. I have no idea how he even got in. I'm so sorry."

"How did he get backstage?" Donovan snapped.

"I told you, I don't know." She held up her hands in frustration. "And I also told you I'm sorry. I don't know what else you want me to do."

"Well, if you kept your crew under control, they wouldn't have let the damn paparazzi back here!" I growled at her.

I could actually see a little hump in her back rise. "Hold on a minute," Gwen said, her tone and stance filled with attitude. And when she raised her chin, she looked just like an African Queen in that dress and head wrap. "I don't know who you're mad at or why you're directing this all at me. But just remember, I'm not the one who gave that photographer something to capture. I'm not the one who was lip-locked with a man I claim to hate."

I took a step toward her, but Donovan jumped in front of me. "You know what, Gwen?" He held up his hand and motioned for her to back up. "Can you just make sure no more press...or paparazzi gets backstage? That was more than a little messed up."

Gwen stood glaring at me and I gave it right back to her. Who was she to be mad? It was our privacy that had been violated.

After a few seconds of what I guess was supposed to be a New York stare, she hissed, "I'll take care of it. And like I already said to both of you...I'm sorry." Her expression matched her words when she looked at Donovan, but when she turned to me, she stared me down as if I was the culprit in all of this.

Donovan held my hand as if he knew I wanted to go off. Then, he squeezed our fingers together when Gwen finally spun around and turned away.

As she walked from us, Donovan whispered, "Chill, Tammie-Poo."

I snatched my hand away from him. "Don't call me that. And don't try to fight my battles for me. This is all your fault."

"Really?" he said, stepping into my space, getting in my face. "I wasn't the only one in that kiss." Then, he gave me that smile. That smile that I used to love only second to his kisses. "So, now that it's just the two of us again," he leaned in, "can we get back to what we were doing?" His lips were milli-inches from mine when he said, "Because I've missed you so much!"

Then, right before his lips met mine, I leaned back and socked him the way I'd been wanting to for the thirteen days we'd been rehearsing.

He yelped and I grabbed my bag and walked into my dressing room, the place where I'd been headed before I was interrupted. I left Donovan in that hallway still shrieking like a girl.

Chapter 11

Gwen

"Gwen, you sure you don't want to come with us?" Camille asked as I stepped out of the theatre. "Please. You haven't hung out all week."

A bunch of the cast and crew were climbing into what looked like an Uber SUV. I did a quick scan—of course I didn't see Tamara, not that I expected to. The cast had started calling her the Ice Queen since she only mixed with the masses during rehearsals. I had a feeling that her anti-social behavior had more to do with Donovan than anything else; and after the way they'd been caught earlier, I was sure of it.

I waved Camille off. "No, I'm tired and want to be fresh for tomorrow. You guys go on and have a good time, but not too good. Tomorrow is a big night."

Camille wiggled her fingers at me, climbed into the car, then Donovan gave me a thumbs up before he slid his fine self in behind her. His grin showed no signs of trauma from the drama that had gone down earlier.

I watched him until he closed the door and I shook my head. This is one of the perks of my business—working with mad fine black men who took the meaning of hot to a new level of heat.

On the other side of that, though—all of that gorgeousness could make a girl weak. But I never did that business-pleasure-mixing thing. First, because I was married, and then, I was a professional.

Well...that thought made me chuckle. Justin was my exception to the rule that should never be broken. But there was no way my being with him could ever be held against me in a court of law. He wasn't officially in the play, though he needed to be because over the past few nights, dude had nailed every audition. And now the thought of what he'd done to me last night made me sigh with regret.

Earlier, I'd told Justin that we wouldn't see each other tonight, that we would have a major celebration tomorrow. But remembering the last week, now I was tingling all the way down to my toes. Maybe I didn't need a *full* night's rest. Maybe a few hours of those nasty, dirty, amazing things he'd been doing to me would relax me and have me fresh for tomorrow's opening.

Pulling out my phone, I was just about to press Justin's number when a text came in:

Ready to do it?

Now, I smiled for a whole 'nother reason.

Already?

The response:

Yeah, it doesn't take long.

My response:

Where?

The text came back:

Behind the Fox. Is it cool?

I typed:

Yeah, everyone's gone. Can you be there in five.

OMW. I'll be there in two.

Turning around, I walked the half-block back to the theatre, and waited in front until I saw the black Jeep turn into the alley. From the driver's seat, the man's shadow nodded, though I didn't make a move until he was out of sight. Then, I ducked around to the back and walked up to the car. But before I opened the door, I looked to the left and to the right. It was only a precaution; no one would be coming back to the theatre tonight.

Opening the door, I slid inside and grinned. "Great job, Curtis."

The forty-something-year-old white guy who I'd used before for some professional headshots grinned right back at me.

I said, "Or maybe I should wait to compliment you. Maybe I need to wait and see how the pictures turned out."

He opened an manila envelope that rested on his lap, pulled out a couple of eight-by-ten photos, handed me the black and whites, and my smile grew even wider.

"Dang, Donovan and Tamara were really going at it. Tonguing each other down and everything."

"I know, right?"

There were only five photos, but I kept flipping back and forth, from one to the other. "This is absolutely wonderful," I said as dollar signs danced around in my head.

I'd come up with this idea after Donovan's wife had her ghetto moment. She'd been extreme, fighting in the public like she was on some low-brow reality show. But there had to have been something there, something for Latrice to set it off like that.

So, I'd called Curtis, made the deal, had him lurking around, hoping to catch my two stars in a kinda cozy, compromising position. Then, after I'd had whatever he caught them doing published, the public would have to make the decision themselves—are they or aren't they? Are Donomara back together again? The speculation would have been enough for a few more media appearances and a little more interest in the play.

But for the last week, Tamara and Donovan had given Curtis nothing. Then today...these photographs were front-page-tabloid worthy. Donovan Dobbs and Tamara Collins had just gifted me sold-out shows on a platinum platter. And I would be the buzz in this town—Gwen Tanner, the genius who had brought the two of them together. I couldn't imagine the opportunities that would be in front of me if I sold out every show in thirty-six cities. Movie producers would be pushing aside Tyler Perry and David Talbert and would be coming to me to take my next projects to the big screen!

"So, you think these will work?" Curtis asked.

"Don't you?"

He nodded. "I guess."

"Yeah, these will work; they're fabulous." Reaching into my purse, I pulled out the five one hundred dollar bills—the second half to the down payment I'd given him last week. "So, you sure you'll get these out?"

"I already have three places that have their checks waiting."

My legs began to tremble. "How long will it take?"

"Well, one of them is a weekly tabloid so the pictures won't show up there until Friday."

"Dang," I muttered. I wished I'd had this idea sooner because I'd really been hoping to debut these pictures tomorrow—just in time for opening night. "Well, I guess that's still enough time to generate buzz for the Dallas shows."

"Well, the other one is a daily so it'll be front and center tomorrow morning."

"Eeekkk!" I didn't mean to squeal, but the excitement poured out of me.

He added, "And don't forget the blogs. I'll be posting these all over the Internet as soon as I get home."

"Oh, my goodness. I just wish I'd had you stalking them the whole time. You would've gotten some good pictures of Donovan's wife beating Tamara down."

"Get outta here!"

"Yup. I wish I had seen that coming." I paused for a moment, pushed the dollar signs from my mind and thought about something else. "Maybe I can arrange for her to come back."

"Or maybe she'll come back on her own once she sees these pictures."

"True." I nodded. Picking up one of the pictures again, I added, "Yeah, she needs to come back 'cause if that kiss means anything, those two are only a day away from being in bed together."

"You want me to hang around and see if I can catch that?"

I thought about that for a moment, but then made a business decision. "I wish! But that would be too much. Tamara would leave the show for sure and I can't have that." Then, I had another thought. "But when you give them the photos, give them the whole story." I leaned back and told him everything that had happened with Donovan's wife. "So that will heighten the value of these pictures, don't you think?"

"Hell, yeah," he began. "Your play is about to blow up."

"Yes and I so love you for this!" I tucked the photos into my purse. "Now, the papers—they're making the checks out to me, correct?"

His smile faded fast. "Ummm...yeah, about that."

"Don't start none, won't be none." I knew that I was giving away my age a little with that long ago saying, but I said it and then gave him what I called my side-eye-don't-mess-with-me glance. "There is no renegotiating." I twisted so that he could see my whole face and the warning in my expression. "You can try to double-cross me if you want to."

He held up his hands in mock surrender. "Hey, I'm not trying to do that. You just gave me an entryway into a new business."

"You got that right. And, I'm doing a fifty-fifty split," I reminded him.

"Yeah." His hands went down. "But I'm doing all the work."

"True, but you wouldn't have the subjects if it weren't for me."

He nodded, but the way his lips drooped, I knew he wasn't happy. "Just forget that I said anything, okay?"

"Forgotten." I tucked my cross-body bag back in place.

"Do you want me to drop you off somewhere?" he asked.

"Nope." First of all, I didn't want to be seen with Curtis. And now that I had these pictures, my thoughts turned back to Justin. "I'm cool. Just a few blocks from my hotel." I jumped out of the SUV and before I closed the door, I said, "Again, great job. And let me know when we get our checks." I closed the door before he even responded. I'd entertained his gripe long enough. He needed to understand that I was the woman in charge.

That thought took me all the way back to Justin. I waited until I was in front of the theatre, before I pulled out my cell again, ready to text my toy.

But before I could, my cell phone rang, interrupted me again. This time, the number on the screen shocked me.

My heart was punishing my chest by the time I said, "Hello?" If Eli was calling me, someone in my (or maybe his) family had surely died.

"Hey," he said, not sounding at all as if there had been death in either family. "I was just calling to say hello and to check on you, I haven't heard from you in a few days."

"Really? Has it been a few days?" I tried to count the time that had passed in my head, but I couldn't really remember when I'd last talked to Eli.

"Yeah, we haven't connected in about a week."

It had been much longer than that, but I wasn't going to explain that distinction to my husband. Though I had to admit that I was shocked that a week had passed since we'd talked. I guess it was just that I was so busy. My days were packed with all the work I had to do, and my nights were filled with all the work that was being done to me.

"It's been a week? I thought we talked...the other day."

He paused. "No...." He stretched the word out like it had several syllables.

"Oh."

Then the air was filled with silence, the same awkwardness that was always between us. The awkwardness that in the past I tried my best to fill. But tonight, I didn't feel like trying.

"So," he finally said, then paused as if he didn't know what should come after that word.

I said nothing.

Finally, "How's it been going?"

"Great!"

More silence.

"I guess you've been busy."

"I have."

This time, the silence lingered longer and I felt sorry for Eli. It wasn't his fault that he wasn't a good husband. It wasn't like he had a decent role model in his family. His father had been married to the business he started back in the sixties. His mother told me that when she got pregnant with Eli ten years later, she didn't know how it happened.

I swear to you, Gwen, when the doctor told me I was pregnant, I asked him how, Bina Weinstein told to me when I'd gone to her on the first anniversary of my marriage—and Eli had never come home. He wasn't with another woman; I'd found him asleep on the couch in his office.

For the year before, I could count the number of times Aaron had noticed me, let alone touched me. It almost felt like the immaculate conception.

The memory of her words were inside this silence now, and the quiet made me feel sorry for Eli, sorry that he didn't even know how to talk to his wife.

So I said, "I have been really busy, but it's all going well."

"Is it?"

"Yes," I said. "And I promise you, this play is going to make so much money that I'll be able to pay you back every single penny by the final show."

"Gwen...."

"I promise, Eli. That's my primary goal."

He sighed and I frowned.

"What's wrong?" I asked.

"You don't have to worry about paying me back." His voice was softer. "You're my wife."

My frown was so deep now, I was giving myself a headache.

"And that wasn't the reason why I called."

Now that was confusing because money was usually the only thing that Eli ever talked about.

He said, "I was just calling to check on my wife because...."

A lump expanded in my throat. He wanted to check on me? Was he going to tell me that he missed me?

"I hadn't heard from you and...."

Oh, my God! He did miss me!

I had to stop walking; I paused so that I could take in this moment because it had been such a long time since I heard any kind of caring in Eli's voice. And in the seconds that passed, the movie in my mind rewound, then began to play. I remembered how Eli had told me it had been love at first sight for him, though in the beginning, I thought he was just fascinated with my Brooklyn accent, sisterlocs, and the West African prints that I favored.

But I'd been wrong; Eli was in love with me long before I was with him and maybe now, he remembered that. Maybe this was a turning point for our marriage. Maybe when I got home, we could go back to the beginning, go back seven years to how we used to be. My heart swelled with hope.

"And ummm...I called because...."

I closed my eyes. He was going to tell me that he loved me. Oh God—I had cheated on him! And oh God—how was I going to make it up to him? And oh God—I would...I would do whatever I had to!

He said, "Do you know the wi-fi passcode?"

My eyes snapped open. "What?"

"The wi-fi passcode," he repeated.

I blinked and my heart contracted, squeezing the hope out of me.

"I'm having a meeting here in the morning, and I figured you'd be busy so I wanted to call you tonight to make sure that everyone will be able to get on-line."

"The passcode." I didn't know why I repeated it. Maybe it was just that I wanted to give him the chance to take that back, so that he could tell me the real reason for his call—which was that he loved me.

"Yeah. I thought I had written it down, but I can't find it."

There were tears in my eyes when I said, "It's our last name, Eli." I began walking again, almost trotting to the hotel. "The passcode is our last name."

"It is? Weinstein? Wow, that was easy."

The phone was still pressed to my ear when I said, "Is that all you wanted?"

"No, I told you, I wanted to see how you were doing."

"I'm fine and I'm really busy, so...."

"So...."

"Well..."

"Well, I'll see you next weekend."

I said nothing.

He said, "I'm meeting you in Charlotte for your birthday, remember?"

"Okay," I said. "See you then." I hung up, not waiting for him to say goodbye, and absolutely sure that I wouldn't see him at all. Something would certainly come up with his business.

I pushed the hotel's glass door open so hard it banged against the wall. And then, as I marched across the lobby, I punched the keys for my text.

Get here now. I will make it worth you while.

Just a couple of seconds later:

OMW!!!

Three exclamation points. That meant that Justin was as excited as I was. He had no idea what or who would be waiting for him when he got to my room. Tonight, I was gonna turn baby boy out, starting when he walked through the door.

By the time Justin got here, I was going to be butt-naked... that is, if you didn't count the whipped cream that I would have already spread over my body. All he would have to do was lick it off...one inch at a time. And then, I would do the same for him.

Chapter 12

Tamara

The four thousand people were on their feet and the seven of us bowed together. Then, we stepped back and Donovan, Camille and I moved forward. I was in the middle, holding both of their hands and as the audience roared their approval, I gave Camille a hug. I kept my smile the whole time, making sure that none of the people, especially none of the reviewers, saw on my face what was in my mind—how I wished I'd had that knife from my first movie....

The three of us bowed and then stepped back, but then, the audience began chatting, "Donomara...Donomara...Donomara."

I hated that name. Hated it when the world had blended me with my boyfriend as if we were one and I hated it, no, I despised it now. I didn't want to be blended, didn't want to be connected in any kind of way with this dog of a man.

Donovan grinned, reached for my hand, and for a moment, my mind tripped—took me right back to our kiss last night. But then with the deft of a professional, I slid into my actor's persona. And with as coy a smile as I could give him, I took his hand and we stepped forward for a third ovation.

Then a roar that made the theatre's walls rumble began, "Kiss! Kiss! Kiss!"

Even though I wanted to keep my smile, I couldn't. Because the frown was so deep on my face. Why would people be chanting for us to kiss? Donovan glanced at me and together, we bowed. But this time, I couldn't move quickly enough. I wanted to get off that stage.

That was weird, though I figured it was probably something that happened at these kinds of venues. Black audiences always connected with their artists, as if we were family.

So by the time we were backstage, I'd pretty much forgotten about that rude chant and was into the celebration with my cast members. We all cheered and hugged (though Camille passed by me as if I were a ghost). Then, we moved as a group through the halls. We had to go meet the public—a time for autographs and photographs.

After that, "Donomara," chant, along with the, "Kiss! Kiss! Kiss!" I wasn't excited about being among the ticket buyers. What if they started that again? I couldn't guarantee that I wouldn't shout out, "I don't kiss dogs!"

But it was in my contract to meet and greet, mix and mingle. And since I was still on best-behavior-mode (my eye remained on my "Girls Night Out" prize) I was going to go out there and chat and smile for the hour I was supposed to do it.

Right before we got to the exit that led to the lobby, the door busted open and Ted, one of the sound engineers, came in from the outside, stepping in front of us.

"Whoa," Ted said, though it didn't seem like he was talking to anyone because his glance scanned all of us. "I guess none of you know."

"What?" Donovan and a couple of others asked at the same time.

That was when Ted turned his eyes to me as his hands moved to his pocket in the back of his jeans. "I guess no one has seen these." From his pocket, he pulled what looked to be a tabloid magazine. And then, when he unfolded it, I was sure it was a copy of the Daily Intruder. He handed the magazine to Donovan and when I peeked over his shoulder at the cover, I wanted to faint.

"What the hell?" Donovan said.

Camille snatched the magazine from Donovan's hand and gawked at the picture that I'd only glimpsed for two seconds. But I'd seen it long enough. I saw the photo splayed across the cover... me and Donovan...kissing...no, not kissing. That was a tongues-tied, lip lock!

"Oh, my God," Camille squealed. "Secret Lovers Rekindle their Flame on the Set of the Hit Stage Play 'It Should Have Been Me'." She sang the headline, then asked, "Are there any more pictures?" turning the pages as if she were on a treasure hunt.

I wanted to sit down right there and cry.

"This is some bull," Donovan said as he grabbed the magazine back from Camille. "Where did you get this?" He made that demand to Ted.

Ted's eyes were sad as he shrugged and said, "From the convenience store across the street. But they must be everywhere 'cause people are out there lined up waiting for you and Tamara to sign them."

Oh, my God! How had a night that had gone so well have turned into this? As my cast members stood and gawked at the other pictures, I closed my eyes. That photographer had captured everything. Of Donovan and I kissing like we were in love. Or lust. It didn't matter, we were kissing like we meant it and now the world would see it.

Ted touched my elbow as if he knew I needed the support. "Are you all right?" he asked.

I nodded my lie. "I just need...Gwen. Where's Gwen?" I turned to my left, then my right. For the first time, I noticed that she wasn't there. I'd expected her to come out for a bow when we had ours. But she hadn't, and I hadn't noticed because I was caught up in the excitement.

"Excuse me," I said pushing past my cast mates so that I could make my way to Gwen's office. She had to do something about this. At best, she had to get those pictures pulled or at worst, she had to make sure they were limited to just the ones in the Daily Intruder.

Her door was slightly open, but still, I knocked. The pressure pushed the door back just a bit and I saw Gwen on the phone.

"This is way better than what I expected," she said as she swung her chair around. Her eyes lifted, she saw me, and she told the person on her phone, "Let me call you back."

When she clicked off her cell, I stepped all the way inside, "Gwen...." Then, I looked down and saw the tabloid spread on her desk.

I frowned and her eyes followed my glance. She closed the tabloid, turned it over and said, "I was hoping you didn't see this."

My frown deepened. "Did you know about this?"

She shook her head and sighed. "I just found out. While the show was going on and I was so upset...I knew you would be upset and I was seeing what I could do to handle it." She pointed to her cell. "That's what the call was all about."

I remembered her words as I walked in: This is going better than I thought.

As if she read my mind, she said, "I was talking to my publicist. She's trying to track down the origin...."

"We know where the pictures came from," I interrupted her. "That photographer. Who was he?"

She shook her head. "I don't know, Tamara. I am so sorry about this, but I want you to know that we're out there doing damage control."

"What kind of control can you do now? Can you limit it to the Daily Intruder? Because if we can stop them there, then maybe...." I paused when Gwen's cell vibrated again.

She frowned, glanced up at me, then took the call. "Hey, Maury, I'm here with Tamara now. What's up?"

I frowned. Why was my agent calling Gwen?

"Oh, she doesn't have her cell with her; she just got off the stage, but you can talk to her on my phone." She handed me her cell, then whispered, "He wants to speak to you."

My stomach did one of those Simone Biles sky-high triple flips.

There were only two reasons why Maury would be calling me now: one was good, he could be congratulating me. And the other could make this the worst night of my life.

Gwen said, "I'll give you some privacy."

I nodded, took her phone, waited until she stepped out of the office, and then said, "Hey, Maury, what's up?" I was praying that he was calling for the good reason.

"What the hell is going on?"

That wasn't any kind of congratulatory comment.

"Maury...." I sank onto the sofa.

"Tamara, this is not good. This is not the reputation we're working on for you."

"I know; I don't want those photos out there. I don't want to live through this again."

"I get that, but I'm not talking personally. This is a disaster for you professionally." I frowned, but he told me what he meant before I could even ask. "Do you know how hard I've been working to get you that role in Diana's movie?"

His words made my heart stop.

"Well, this might even kill the deal."

"Why?" I asked, though I already knew the reason. Diana and her own drama...with her husband...and the cleaning lady.

My Cleaning Lady—The Best Sex I Ever Had.

Maury interrupted my pain, but he didn't help. He just piled on. "You know how she has publicly stated her disdain for home wreckers."

"But I'm not a...."

"It's not going to matter; I'm telling you, this isn't going to go over well with her."

I moaned.

"Hell, it might even kill the deal."

I groaned.

"I'm sorry to be so rough, but I'm just telling you the truth. What were you thinking?" Again, he gave me no room to respond. "Are you having an affair with him?"

"No! Of course not. I can't believe you asked me that."

"Why not? Have you seen the pictures?"

I closed my eyes, squeezed the bridge of my nose and wished that I could click my heels to travel back, then take back that kiss. "I saw them, Maury," I said, not able to keep the defeat from my tone. "It was just one kiss."

"It must've been one long kiss 'cause they got plenty of pictures."

"I don't want to talk about the pictures anymore. I want to know how we fix this. I want to know how you will still close the deal with Diana."

"I don't know, I don't know how to clean this up."

"Well, maybe it's not gonna be an issue. Gwen is going to try to limit their distribution," I told him, hoping that was what Gwen would do. "So maybe Diana won't see the pictures or maybe she won't care."

He released a long breath. "Do you know how I found out about the pictures?" Again, it was rhetorical because he went right on to the part that broke my heart. "Diana called me."

This time, I moaned and groaned at the same time.

"Yeah, she wanted to know what was going on and if the pictures were legit."

"Oh, God!"

"When I told her I didn't know anything about any pictures, she emailed me a picture of the pictures in the *Daily Intruder.*"

"Oh, God!" That was all I could think of to say because I was afraid to ask the real question. But finally I conjured up nerve that I really didn't have. "What did she say?"

"Nothing. I didn't let her say anything. I just told her I'd get back to her after I found if the photos were real or had been photoshopped."

"Maybe we can...."

"Don't even think about it, Tam. I'm not going to say they're fake if they're not. My reputation is on the line."

"Well, maybe there's something that we can say, some way to explain this."

After he exhaled his frustration, he said, "Well, I'm willing to listen to any explanation you have...."

Then, he went silent and I leaned back against the sofa, silent, too. Because I didn't have an explanation.

"So...." He finally spoke.

Still, I kept quiet.

Maury's voice became softer. "I'm not going to give up, Tam. I'll talk to Diana." Behind his frustration, I heard his disappointment. "I'll talk to her and then, I'll get a PR firm to help us spin this."

"Gwen said that she has someone working on this."

"Yeah, for herself. You need someone working for you." He paused. "I know you don't want to spend the money."

I thought about that designer purse that I'd bought with that little bonus. Wondered if I could dump everything out of it and return it to the store.

"Look, Tam. Go on back to your hotel. I'll handle this and get back to you. I'll let you know how much the publicist is gonna charge you, too."

I nodded because I didn't want to open my mouth and wail into the phone. But Maury was the one who hung up without saying goodbye, and that was when I knew for sure this was trouble. Either he was so distracted or he was so mad—I hadn't experienced either with Maury before.

For awhile, I just sat in Gwen's office. I didn't want to run into anyone, didn't want to deal with the sneers, didn't want anyone to see my tears. And I certainly didn't want to go to the meet and greet with the fans. Fans who would shove those pictures that were death-kisses to my career into my face.

I sat and sat, grateful that Gwen had left me alone. I sat wondering where did this leave me? Was my comeback over before it had started? Would I be limited now to only doing these kinds of acting gigs?

I sat because I was so, so tired. But then, I didn't want to sit anymore. I wanted to lie down, in a bed. I wanted to get to my hotel room and crawl under the sheets. Enough time had passed; the fans should have all been on their way home by now.

Leaving her phone on the desk, I peeked into the hall. There was only a little sound, like a muffled conversation in the stage area and I figured it was Gwen speaking with one of the production people. That meant everyone else was gone, probably out celebrating our opening night and laughing it up about my pictures.

Everyone had probably crowned Donovan as the king and I was labeled a slut because wasn't that the way it always was? A man was a player, a woman was a whore—that was the way of the world.

I was drunk with sorrow and humiliation as I stumbled down the hall and by the time I got to my dressing room, a tsunami of tears blinded me. Right outside my room, I leaned against the wall and slid down until my butt hit the floor. I was just so tired and so afraid that this was the end for me.

How had this happened? Why did I allow it to happen? I didn't even like Donovan. I hated him!

"Tammie?"

It was a whisper and I knew that now, along with everything else, I was losing my mind. Here I was thinking about Donovan and his voice sounded so real in my head.

"Tammie, are you all right?"

Again, it was a whisper, but it wasn't in my head. I looked up, but I had to blink a couple of times to push my tears aside.

"What's wrong?"

I looked up into the face of the man who I had once loved so much. The man who I once thought was my beginning, but who had turned out to be the end for me in so many ways.

Shaking my head, I lowered it again, so that my tears could rain freely. I couldn't see him, but I felt him as he slid down the wall the way I had done just a few minutes before and he sat right next to me.

I sobbed, but Donovan didn't say a word and didn't try to touch me, which pleased me because if he had, I would have hit him. No, not hit, I would have beat him. Right into the ground.

It wasn't until my cries became a whimper, that Donovan spoke. "I know how you feel."

I wasn't even going to answer him because he had no idea how this had ruined me. So instead I said, "I thought everyone was gone. I thought you were gone."

"Everyone else is, but I wanted to wait for you because I knew you wouldn't be all right."

I'd thought my tears were over, but fresh ones were fighting to come through. "I can't believe this has happened."

"Are you seeing anyone?"

I sniffed as I turned to him and cocked my head. Here I was in the middle of this breakdown and that was what he wanted to know? "Why would you ask me that?"

"Because you're really upset. Like I was. Because when Latrice sees these pictures, she's gonna blow a freakin' gasket. So I figured you were upset because...your man would probably do the same."

"Oh." I shook my head. "I'm not seeing anyone."

"What about that guy—the football player on the Jets."

I shrugged. "We saw each other off and on...for a while...but I was really trying to put my focus completely on my career. I figured once that was in place...."

"Oh." There was no kind of smirk in his voice. Good. Because I would've gone right back to thoughts of that beatdown. He said, "I thought that's why you were so upset."

"No. It's something more important."

His glance shifted from the floor to me.

I said, "I'm up for a pretty major role."

"Really? What?"

Most actors didn't talk about things like this, not until the papers were signed, and even then, everyone waited for the official announcements from the production companies and the studios. I wasn't sure if it was because actors were just being professional or if we didn't want to jinx it. For me, it was both.

But I told him about Diana Delaney and "Girls Night Out". I told him how she had come after me for the part and how she was excited and I'd been thrilled. "That role could revive my career." But when I told about the trauma that she'd been through, I couldn't hold my sobs back anymore. "She doesn't like women who did to her what her cleaning lady did." I looked at him when I added, "She doesn't like women who did what Latrice did to me."

"Oh, Tammie," Donovan whispered.

He twisted, rested on his haunches and then with his fingertips, lifted my chin. "I'm so sorry about this. It was my fault."

I swallowed my sobs, nodded, and then said, "What did you tell me yesterday? You weren't the only one in that kiss."

Though his eyes were still sad, he cracked a smile. That smile that I loved only second to his kisses.

His eyes were intense as he leaned so close to me. As if he really wanted me to hear what he had to say. "I don't want you to worry. Because I'm going to pray that Diana Delaney kicks all of this stuff to the curb because she knows how wonderful," he got a little closer, "and special," he came even closer, "and magnificent you are." There wasn't a gap between us. His lips brushed mine as he said, "I'm going to pray that you get everything you want because you deserve that and so much more."

When he pressed his lips against mine, it was so soft, at first. And everything inside of me wanted to protest because this was how we got in all this trouble in the first place.

But I was so tired—of struggling, of almost hitting it big, of all the questions I had between gigs.

And this felt so good.

And I was tired of the drama, the fights, the being alone.

And this felt so good.

That was the only way to explain why when he pushed his tongue against me, my lips parted like yesterday. When he took my hand, I gave it to him. When he led me into his dressing room, I went. Willingly.

I was the one who closed the door to his room behind us. I was the one who pushed his jacket from his shoulders and I was the one who leaned back onto his sofa, so ready for each and every part, each and every inch of him.

Because I was just so, so tired.

And this felt so, so good.

Chapter 13

Camille

I unlocked the door to my hotel room, then kicked off my shoes before I staggered inside. I didn't bother to do anything—not turn on the lights, not take off my clothes—nothing. I just tumbled onto the bed and giggled.

I'd had way too much to drink tonight, especially since I'd never been a Tequila kind of girl. My drinks of choice were always fruity things that were decorated with pineapples and paper umbrellas.

But tonight, I'd hung with the big boys as we partied. Everybody was celebrating the opening of the play and the success of our first night. Everybody except for me. I was celebrating, but it was all about Tamara. She was being destroyed and that brought joy to my life.

Rolling over, I stared at the ceiling hoping that if I focused on one spot, the room might stop doing that tumbling thing. Then, I'd be able to think about how I could push Tamara over, since she was already on the edge.

I wish I'd been the one to think of having a photographer follow Tamara and Donovan around. I was absolutely sure that he'd been hired. First, I'd seen him at the hotel lurking around. I just thought he was some perverted white man who got his kicks from checking out black women. But once I saw him in the theatre yesterday, I knew he'd been paid. I just didn't know who'd paid him, though I suspected it was Gwen.

My girl. That was a boss move. Because like everyone said tonight, all shows would be sold out now. And it would happen at Tamara's expense.

That made me feel wonderful, even though...I was gonna be sick....

I jumped up and dashed into the bathroom, hugged the toilet bowl, released all of the alcohol that was in me, and then sank onto the bathroom floor.

There was no way that I was ever going to drink like this again. Not even when I finally brought Tamara all the way down.

It took a while, but I finally used the sink to push myself up, flushed the toilet, stumbled back to the bed, but this time, I got under the covers, still dressed. But that was all that I could handle for tonight.

I was paying the price, but it was worth it. I wished I could see Tamara right now. Probably crying in her room. I prayed that she was alone, just like I prayed that she would be when this was all over. I wanted her to be by herself. The same way that she had left my brother.

I closed my eyes, wanting to just fall asleep. But when I closed my eyes, all I could do was remember....

September 14, 2008

"What's wrong, June?" I asked my brother. No one called him June Bug anymore. Now that he was grown up.

My brother sniffed. "Nothin'. Just leave me alone, Twiggy."

I stared at my brother, laying on his bed with the cordless phone in his hand.

He said, "Go on, now. Get on out of my room."

Backing up, I pulled the door with me until I was in the hallway and the door was closed. Still standing there, I wished there was something I could do for my big brother since he was always doing things for me.

"AnnaMae," my mother called. She was the only one who called me by my name. "Come on, dinner's ready."

When I got into the kitchen, I sat down at my normal side of the table. Then, I asked, "You want me to get June?"

My mother glanced at my father and then said, "No, baby. He'll get something to eat later."

My father shook his head. "Don't make no kind of sense. The way that girl is treating my boy."

"Hush, Martin," my mother said, giving me a quick glance.

My father raised his eyebrows at my mother. "Why you want me to hush?" Then, he turned to me. "The girl's old enough to know what's going on. Hell, she knows already."

"Martin!" my mother said in the same tone that she used to scold me.

But that's not what had my eyes so wide. My father had just said a curse word! I'd never heard him curse before. I had only heard people curse like five times in my whole life.

"I'm serious, Sarah," my father kept on. "The girl's old enough to know. Aren't you thirteen now?"

"Fourteen," I said.

"See!" He turned back to my mother. "Maybe she'll learn a lesson or two from what Tam did to June."

My mother sighed as she placed my father's plate in front of him, then brought over my plate with hers. When she sat down at the table, my father held both of our hands and we bowed our heads.

It felt funny not to have June holding my left hand since my father held my right one. But for the last couple of days, my brother hadn't eaten dinner with us. He just stayed in his room. He didn't come out for anything except to go to work. But once he got home, he was back in his bedroom.

"Amen," my father said to end his blessing.

It was really quiet for a few minutes, and I kept my head down, just staring at the mashed potatoes and chicken on my plate. Then all of a sudden, Daddy dropped his fork onto his plate.

"This don't make no kinda sense," his voice boomed. "June, get in here and get something to eat."

"Martin!" Mama put her hand over his like she was trying to calm him down.

"Don't Martin me. I need my son to man up. He don't need to be in there crying over no girl."

"But she wasn't just a girl, Martin. You know that."

"I don't care what she was, I know what she is now—a no good, spoiled rotten son of a mother-,"

"Martin!"

"What?"

I sat in my chair and trembled.

My daddy said, "I'm not having no grown son of mine up in my house crying over some two-bit-"

"Martin!"

"Would you stop calling my name? I know what my mother named me."

"And I'm just sayin' give our son some time. This is hard on him. He worked for all of those years so that she could go to school. He put in all of that time for her."

My father threw his hands up the way he did when he was watching football on Sundays whenever a team made a touchdown. "That's what I'm sayin'! He did everything for her and now, where is she?"

My head was kinda bowed, like I didn't want them to really see me, but I was fascinated in a way, too. My daddy was always happy, always laughing or at least smiling. But ever since Tam had moved to California, everybody was upset.

Daddy sat back down at the table and sighed. Mama put her hand over his again.

"This is our son's first heartbreak," Mama said to Daddy. "We have to let him go through it. We have to help him, but let him go through it."

My father shook his head. "No man needs to be cryin' over no woman."

There was a smirk on Mama's face when she said, "How you gonna say that when you cried over me?"

"What you talkin' 'bout? I ain't cried ova you. I ain't neva cried ova no woman." Then, as if he just remembered that I was there, Daddy turned to me and said, "Don't listen to your mama. I ain't cried. And your brother don't need to be cryin'. And what's more," he lifted his fork and pointed it at me, "you don't need to be making no man cry."

"Yes, Daddy."

"I mean it."

"She ain't gonna make nobody cry." My mother smiled when she looked at me. "Are you, baby?"

"No, ma'am."

When my father chuckled, I thought everything was all right again, but then, he sighed. "I just can't believe she won't call that boy."

"I know," Mama said.

"She done gone out there and now she's too good for us."

"I know," Mama said again.

"I should've known she was never gonna come back here. After her mama died, I knew she was gonna go out there and get too big."

"I figured she wouldn't come back, at least not to live anyway." Mama sounded so sad. "But I never thought she'd leave June behind." She sighed. "I figured we'd lose June to that big city life in Los Angeles."

I hated the way Mama and Daddy sounded. I hated the way June was so sad all the time. I wanted everyone to be happy again. That's why I said, "Maybe she didn't call June 'cause they don't have telephones in California. Maybe she's been looking for a phone to call him."

There was nothing but quiet when my mama and daddy looked at me. Of course, I knew that wasn't true, but I was just trying to think of something to say to give them hope.

Daddy just shook his head and Mama broke off the tip of her chicken wing and started chewing.

And I went back to looking down at my plate and hating Tam. I had always loved her so, so much. She was my big sister and did everything with me. She was the first person to take me to get my fingernails and toenails polished, and Mama even let me go to the hairdresser for the first time with Tam. Everything was wonderful when she was around.

But nothing was good now, and it was all her fault. Her fault that my mother was sad and my daddy was cursing. And it was definitely her fault that my brother was crying.

I blinked, but didn't bother to wipe the tears from my eyes 'cause sometimes I felt like I had to cry for June. Tamara had kicked June to the curb like he was a rusted old can of Coke. He stayed sad and that sadness led to a dark depression. Once he got to that deep hole, there was nothing he could do, nothing anybody could do. He got stuck there and couldn't come back.

That's why Tamara had to pay. Because she had driven my brother to that place. My brother, my mother, and my father. And now, I was the only one left.

My head still hurt, but I pushed myself up, then rolled to the edge of the bed. I didn't drink coffee, but I was going to drink a couple of cups tonight. I needed a clear head, not for the play, I'd be fine by stage call. But this I needed so that I could get back to my plans. Tamara was weak now and it was time to break her down. Completely.

Chapter 14

Tamara

I pushed against the back of the sofa to give us more room, then rested my chin in the palm of my hand and stared down at Donovan. I couldn't believe this happened. I couldn't believe that I'd fallen into bed with a married man.

But he was my man first.

Was that a good excuse? I didn't think so. It wasn't how I'd been raised. It wasn't the woman I wanted to be.

But the defense that I would give to any jury was that Donovan had been my sunshine in the middle of this storm today, he was the distraction, the shot of energy I needed to somehow keep fighting.

That made me pause and think about all the other times I'd had those thoughts about the man I loved.

The man I loved.

I resisted taking my fingers and tracing his profile the way I used to—the way I'd done when we were in love. Actually, love wasn't a big enough word to describe the emotions I had for this man. The place that he'd held in my heart was the reason why I still hadn't yet been able to let anyone else in. I wanted a new love, I really did. But because of Donovan, a couple of men had been in and out of my life in the last two years, though no one left a mark. The only love I'd been able to nurture was the love I had for my career.

My career.

Those pictures.

I sighed. I didn't want to think about what would happen now. Just wanted to think about tonight and the way Donovan made me feel. But my thoughts didn't stay with today. Because the more I stared at him, the harder my heart beat. And each beat took me back, back many yesterdays....

January 9, 2014

We never came to Vail to ski. No, on this, our third trip, we came to shop (some of the best shopping in the world was in Vail) and to do this—to hang out in the jacuzzi.

Last year when we'd come to Vail (my first visit ever) two weeks before Christmas, I'd thought it was crazy that the condos had decks with outdoor jacuzzis. Didn't the contractors who designed these units know they were building dwellings where average daily winter temperatures didn't reach double digits?

But it turned out that had been one of the highlights of our four day vacay. Being in the jacuzzi during a winter night when the temperature outside was four, but the water was one-hundred-four aroused my senses. The heat of the jacuzzi against the below freezing air, along with me in Donovan's arms or Donovan in me...yes, being in Vail was the best of times. And here we were again.

I leaned in closer to Donovan, pressing my head against his chest as we both stared into the unpolluted midnight Colorado sky.

I sighed.

"What's wrong?" Donovan asked as he squeezed me even closer. "You cold?"

"No, nothing's wrong. It's just that I really love it here. Those stars," I pointed, "look like diamonds."

"You always say that," Donovan said as he reached up and pretended to swipe the sky. As if he was trying to pull down one of the stars. For me.

I laughed. "And you always do that."

"I'll never stop trying," he said. "I'll never stop trying to get one of those diamond stars for you." Then, he kissed me. One of those Donovan kisses that left no room for me to breathe or to wonder—I knew his love for me was complete. One of those kisses that made me dizzy, made the water in the Jacuzzi feel like it was below zero because of the bumps that rose on my skin.

When he pulled his lips away, I slid beneath the water and he chuckled. "Don't drown." He grabbed my hand and pulled until my head was above water.

"See what you do to me?"

He gave me another kiss, this time on my nose, thank God. Then, he stood.

"Where are you going?" I tugged on his swim shorts

His answer was another kiss, this time on my forehead. "I'll be right back."

As he trotted up the four steps of the jacuzzi, then dashed inside our condo, I leaned back and closed my eyes, basking in the joy that was my life. My heart was so full and it had been that way for two years—every single day. Donovan and I lived together, wasn't that supposed to put a strain on our relationship at some point?

But our experience had been just about love. Every day he told me, and every day he showed me with the flowers he bought, the songs he wrote, and the things that he did—foot rubs and pedicures (he'd taken a class to learn how to do that for me!) to back and scalp massages.

And then, the ultimate foreplay—this man cooked! So well. Almost as well as he made love.

Almost.

My sigh was deep and long. Donovan was just always there, with a hug, a kiss, a prayer—there was nothing like a man who could pray for you.

I had my own prayers, filled with hope that this connection with Donovan would never, ever end. I wanted to carry our love into eternity.

He hadn't said a word, but he didn't need to—we were that connected. My heart felt his heart whenever he was close. So I knew that he'd come back outside.

I opened my eyes, my smile already on my face. But then, the sight in front of me snatched my smile away. And in its place was my confusion.

He stood at the top step of the Jacuzzi, sans swim shorts. Now, we'd skinny-dipped before here in Vail, and in lots of other places, too; that wasn't the shocking part. And though I would have loved to have stared at the man who'd made my heart throb since I was fourteen, the shocker was that he stood there butt naked in the cold that was so far below freezing.

"Donovan, get down in the water. It's too cold for you to be standing there like that."

He shivered, but he didn't move. "I want you to see me like this...."

"Ummm...okay. I love seeing you like this, but...."

"Completely vulnerable. I'm standing before you...nothing but me."

Keeping all but my head beneath the one hundred degree water, I glided to the other side to Donovan. "What are you talking about?"

He raised his hand and for the first time I noticed that, though he was naked, he held something in his right hand. Something that glittered like the stars above in the Colorado sky.

Still, he stood and still, he trembled. Then, he spoke, "Tamara Collins, I love you so much. I have never met a woman like you, never had the chance to be loved by someone as wonderful as you. And now, what I want to do is wake up every morning and love you, take care of you, and call you Mrs. Dobbs. So...." He took a deep breath and raised the ring a little higher. "Will you make me the most honored man in the universe? Will you bless me? Will you marry me?"

He had me at 'Tamara Collins, I love you so much.' And I wasn't talking about when he'd said it just a few seconds ago. I was talking about when he said it the first time, and the sixtieth time, and the one-thousand-twelfth time, and the million other times when he'd made my heart swell with those words.

Tears had already dampened my cheeks when I pushed myself up, and stood in the barely-over-zero cold with my man. I leaned forward, kissing him, letting his lips set my body on fire. We didn't pull away for minutes and when we did, Donovan said, "I hope to God that's a yes!"

I laughed, I cried, I held out my hand for him to slip what looked to me to be at least four carats onto my finger. Once I felt the ring, I knew the weight was at least five carats. Or maybe it wasn't the ring that made me feel heavy. Maybe it was all the love that I had for this man that filled me so completely.

I had to blink a couple of times to make sure that I was here and not back there. Because it felt as if it were happening right now. The way Donovan had taken my hand, led me from that Jacuzzi, and taken me to our bed inside the condo. And then, he had loved me with a gentleness, a loveliness, that I was sure would have filled our lives forever....

When Donovan's eyes fluttered, I left that yesterday behind, came all the way back to now. It took a moment for him to focus, then grin as he stared at me. "Did I fall asleep?"

I nodded. "You did, for awhile now."

"Man, I didn't mean to do that." He reached up and his fingertips trailed my cheek; he'd done to me what I'd wanted to do to him moments before. "Wow."

"Wow?"

"Yeah, wow! I never thought, that I'd have this chance with you again."

I wasn't going to tell him that I felt the same way. "We shouldn't have done this." I shook my head.

"Yes, we should have."

I paused because the words I were about to say, hurt. "You're married." And then, saying those words out loud made me remember I was naked.

As if he heard my thoughts, Donovan's fingertips moved from my cheek to my breast. Made me shiver.

He said, "I shouldn't be married. These two years without you have been a struggle for me. I shouldn't be married unless I'm married to you."

That was my cue to get out of there. Because now, he was reminding me of what could never be. As I moved to slide to the end of the sofa, he grabbed my arm. "I'm serious, Tammie. You never gave me a chance to tell you what happened."

The last few hours had been a fantasy. Why did he have to ruin it with the pain of the truth?

I yanked my arm away, scooted off the couch and snatched my blouse from the floor.

"Why won't you listen to me?"

I slipped my arms into my blouse, not even bothering to put on my bra. "Because it doesn't matter. None of this matters, Donovan. You're married."

"But I want to be married to you."

If he hadn't been hitting my emotions, I would have stopped, I would have laughed. But my heart was starting to cry again; the way it had cried years ago. The way it had never stopped crying.

I had to get out of there. It didn't matter that my blouse was unbuttoned and when I stepped into my pants, I didn't even care if they were zipped. I just grabbed my underwear and stilettos, then stormed from his dressing room. I didn't even look both ways when I ran outside; I just scooted across the hallway to my room.

"Tammie."

His voice was close as I scanned my room, and spotted my purse. I tossed my underwear inside, hoisted the hobo over my shoulder, turned back to the door. And stopped.

Donovan stood there, the way he had that day when he proposed, stood in my doorway, naked.

"Are you freakin' kiddin' me?" I hissed at him. "What are you doing? What if someone sees you?"

Not that I was much better. Yes, I had on clothes, but as disheveled as I was, if a photographer spotted us, he wouldn't have to be a member of Mensa to know what had gone down.

"I'm sure that everyone is gone," he said, right before I pushed past him and rushed into the hallway.

My prayer to God was that Donovan was right, though I was acutely aware that shouldn't have been my first prayer. But I would get to the forgiveness part later. As soon as the Lord got me out of here and away from Donovan.

"Tammie!"

Still holding my shoes, I ran to the back door, tackled it like I was some kind of football player—and nothing happened. I pushed again—same result. "Ugh!" The door is locked? I turned and faced naked Donovan.

As he did what I'd just done, I tried to keep my eyes on his. I really tried as he pushed and pushed. I tried to stay focused on his neck up. I failed!

"Damn," he grunted, then grinned when he saw that I'd lost my focus.

I cleared my throat. "So we have to go out the front?"

Donovan shook his head. "They lock these doors from inside."

"What?"

He nodded.

"That's ridiculous. How can they lock doors from the inside. That's crazy!" I marched past him, this time careful not to touch... him. I had to get out of here, I wasn't about to be locked in this theatre with Donovan all night long.

"Tammie! We're locked in," he shouted behind me.

I kept moving.

"It's two in the morning."

Two in the morning? How had that happened? How had any of this happened?

Still, I kept moving, even as Donovan trotted kinda besides/behind me. But two seconds after we reached the front door, I knew he was right.

"These doors are locked, too," I said as if he didn't know.

Donovan crossed his arms. His smirk was his answer.

"There has to be someone we can call, someone can get us out of here."

He nodded. "There's always an emergency number. We can call that or even call 9-1-1. But, uh, someone is gonna ask what are we doing here...together...in the middle of the night... together." He paused. "'Cause we are...together."

"Would you stop saying that?"

"And if you think those pictures were bad...."

He left his sentence unfinished, though he didn't have to complete it since that's exactly what I'd been thinking.

When he reached for my hand, I should have ignored him. But I didn't because I was starting to have those feelings again—feeling defeated and so tired.

"So, what are we gonna do?" I whined. "Just stay here till morning?"

He nodded. "Security will be here about nine or so, I guess. And then, we can sneak out."

"Together?"

He chuckled. "Nah, I'll let you go out. I'll hang out in my dressing room and they'll just think you were locked in here by yourself—if they see you." He paused when we were back in the hallway, back in front of his dressing room. "That'll be our story." Then, he whispered, "Okay?"

I nodded.

"So," he glanced toward his room, "you wanna come in and talk?"

I didn't. I really wanted to go into my own dressing room. But I calculated the hours and there was no way that I wanted to spend seven hours in this big ole theatre by myself. We couldn't get out, but I wasn't convinced that someone couldn't get in.

So I did what I didn't want to do. This time, I took his hand, and I followed him back inside.

Chapter 15

Gwen

I collapsed, rolled off Justin, then huffed and puffed—Justin had blown my house down! It had been almost two weeks, almost every night and I never got tired of this boy. And what was so great, he never got tired either. I mean, he could go all night in every which a way.

Whew! When God made forty-four-year-old women, he went back into the workshop and created twenty-three-year-old men just for us.

Justin pushed himself up, then looked down at me. "What? You're getting up? I didn't think we were finished."

I laughed. "You're incorrigible."

"I'm just sayin' we can keep going since you finally let me stay the night."

I rolled onto my side so that I could face him, and I marveled at how I still loved just gazing at his face. But then, why would I get tired? No one ever tired of fine art.

"So, you've had enough?" he asked as if his job was to please me.

"I have to get over to the Warner Theatre. And you, sir, need to sneak out of here and get to your room."

"Oh, all right," he said, sounding like a kid about to do something he didn't want to do. When he stood up, I gave him a little slap on his butt and not a piece of skin jiggled. It was like soft stone.

He moved about the bed as if he were looking for something, but I knew his game; he was putting himself on display and I leaned back to enjoy the show that this Trey Songz-looking buck was giving to me. I couldn't believe that I had let Justin stay all night, especially since it was more dangerous here than before. In Atlanta, I had the cast and crew in a different hotel. But here in DC, I'd received such a good deal at the Grand Hyatt that I was able to put everyone in the same place—plus save on transportation since we were so close to the theatre.

Still, I could have stayed in a different hotel, but there was something about taking this risk. Not that I ever wanted anyone to find out about me and Justin. I wasn't about to risk not only my career, but my marriage. It was the thought, though, that we *could* be discovered. It made this affair more illicit, more exciting.

And anyway, I deserved this celebration. Three great shows in Atlanta. Every seat filled, every ticket sold. The sellouts continued—no one could get a ticket for any of these shows here in DC and it was the same for Charlotte and Dallas and Houston ...the list went on.

I sighed when Justin finally stepped into his jeans—without putting on his underwear.

When he saw me grinning, he said, "I'm going to take a shower in my room."

"What are you gonna tell Ted?" I asked, about the sound engineer who was his roommate on the road.

He shrugged. "I'll tell him I was bangin'...."

I frowned.

"Some girl I met at the bar," he finished with a laugh.

I didn't find that funny. I wasn't some girl, we hadn't met at the bar, and he wasn't banging me. But I didn't say anything. Maybe that was just the way young guys talked these days.

"What are you staring at?" he asked.

I blinked from my trance. "Just you."

He held his shirt in his hand as he grinned. "Are you sure you want me to leave?" Then, he tossed his shirt over his shoulder, and took slow steps back to the bed.

Even though my center stirred once again, I shook my head. "I have to get to work."

"Are you sure about that?" With a sudden sweep of his hand, he ripped the comforter away from me, tossing it on the floor. The way he stared at my nakedness, made me shiver and it wasn't from the cool air that brushed my skin.

He didn't say a word, as he leaned over, kissed me and took me to the stars. But then, when he scooted down on the bed and shifted me so that he was between my legs, I knew it would only be a couple of minutes before I shot straight to heaven. And I was right.

I wanted to keep my eyes open to watch his magic. But the things...he...did...to...me. I barely stayed conscious.

He pleased me with his tongue over and over and over. And I shuddered and shuddered and shuddered.

"I...can't...take...any...more," I said, snatching his head up.

I panted as he licked his lips. "Sorry, I got caught up 'cause you...."

I pulled him closer so that I could kiss him. When he pulled back, he asked, "So, did I get the part?"

"What part?" I whispered.

"The part." He stood up straight and took a couple of steps away from me. "The part you had me read with Camille yesterday?"

Oh...yeah...that...part.

I'd done what I said I was going to do. On the flight from Atlanta to DC on Friday, I'd used those two hours to write in a small part, just a few lines for Justin as Camille's brother. And I'd given him a test yesterday, after I told Camille that I'd wanted to add more eye candy to the show.

"Oh, that's a great idea!" she told me. "And thank you for casting him with me! I've been watching pretty boy. Maybe if we have to do some scenes together every night...."

That had almost made me rewrite his part. Put him in the play as a cab driver or something. But then, when he got on stage, I realized that I wasn't gonna have to worry about him spending too much time with Camille because he bombed...and I didn't mean that in any good way. I couldn't believe Justin was the same kid who'd read for me back in Atlanta. On the stage, his voice was loud, his tone was stiff, morticians displayed more emotion.

Even Camille whispered to me afterward, "Uh...dude needs to stick to just looking fine."

I had planned to tell him this right after he came off stage, but he'd met me in the office in the back and started doing stuff to me. Then when I had my second chance to tell him last night, he'd started sucking my toes. I forgot about his stage skills and focused on his bed skills.

"Did you hear me?" he asked. "I could be ready to go tonight, tomorrow at the latest."

"Well, um, yeah, about that." I wasn't sure how I should tell him that there was no way he was going to be in one of my sold-out performances. Everything was going so right—we were all over the media, we were the talk on the blogs, I was even getting calls from promoters who hadn't taken my calls before and now wanted me to bring the show to their city. All of this was happening after just three shows in Atlanta. I wasn't about to take the chance of anything messing up the momentum I had.

I looked up at Justin.

"So, when am I going to hit the stage?" He raised his voice a little and my eyebrows shot up. "I know I hit it yesterday."

I wasn't sure if he was talking about his audition or me. But whatever, he needed to back it up. Just because he could put it down on me—numerous times—didn't mean he could forget who had the power here.

"Look, Justin," I said, grabbing my bathrobe from the back of the chair. I slipped my arms into the sleeves, but I didn't bother to tie the belt. I let it hang open, thinking that I might have to use my body as a part of my negotiation. I might have been forty-four, but I'd had so much sucked and tucked that I looked better than I did when I was a teenager.

Putting my hands on my hips (which actually raised my boobs a bit), I continued, "I was trying to be nice because I didn't want to hurt your feelings. Now, you can certainly sing, but that acting thing...." I shook my head.

His mouth opened. "Excuse me?"

"I'm not trying to be cold," I said, truly meaning that. I wasn't trying to hurt his feelings for a couple of reasons, the most important being that I wanted Justin to stick around 'cause he surely had a future as a maintenance man—and I wasn't talking about anybody who swept the floor. Shoot, I'd put him on the payroll just so he could maintain me. But acting? Uh...that would be a no!

Justin said, "But you said...the other night in Atlanta. In your room, you said that I could act."

"I know." I pouted a little. "I thought you could, but now I realize it was just that I was blinded by all of this." I motioned first toward his chest, and then, I let my eyes go down, down, down and rest right at his part that had made me so happy. "But the reality is, this is not for you, bruh."

He shook his head. "And so what was your plan? To just keep me in your bed?"

Yup, that was the plan, but this didn't feel like the right time to tell him.

"Were you ever gonna let me know?"

I nodded.

"When? You didn't say anything after the audition yesterday."

"I know."

"And what about last night?"

I remembered last night and sighed.

"You didn't say anything then," he said.

"How was I supposed to talk when you were doing that... thing that you do?"

He glared at me and then his bitter chuckle filled my bedroom. He was pissed, and I understood that. But it wasn't like I hadn't given him a chance.

"I'm really sorry," I told him.

"I wanted to be an actor," he said, sounding like the kid who didn't get that toy that he wanted for Christmas. "I know I'm as good as any of those dudes you have on the stage."

I had to focus on something, something that made me sad. Or else I was gonna laugh in this boy's face. Keeping it soft and staying serious, I said, "No, you're not. Justin, you're good for what you're good for." He pouted, but I took a step closer to him. "And truth be told, I don't want what you're good for to end." I took another seductive step toward him and his eyes moved from mine, moved down to my nakedness.

I reached to finger his chest, but he grabbed my hand, stopping me before I could touch him. "So what're you saying? You want me to keep screwing you?"

"Do you want to keep a job?" I felt a little flinch in my heart. This was borderline sexual harassment, but I pushed that bit of guilt away. Men had been doing it for years and I wasn't really threatening him. If he wanted to go, I wasn't going to make him stay.

He raised an eyebrow. "So, now, in addition to handling merchandising, my job is to service you?"

"You don't have to do anything." I shrugged. "You can go back to Salt Lick, Alabama...."

"I'm from Birmingham."

"Wherever. You can go home, go back to work packing groceries at the Piggly Wiggly...."

He glared as if I'd just insulted him. "I've never worked there."

"Or you can keep doing the fabulous jobs you do, which by the way, you do both so well that you deserve a raise. I'm thinking about maybe doubling," I paused and with my eyes drank in more of him, "no, not doubling, tripling your salary."

"Triple?" At first, his eyes widened, but then the room filled with that bitter chuckle again. "Just wow. Now I'm a male prostitute?"

I was getting tired of this negotiation. Glancing at the clock on the nightstand, I said, "I really have to get going." My eyes turned back to him. "You can make this sound whatever way you want; I've made you an offer. And now, it's up to you."

He let a couple of seconds go by, then shrugged. He grabbed his shirt from the floor where he'd tossed it. "It is what it is." He didn't bother to button his shirt; he just grabbed his wallet from the table, then moved toward the front of my suite. "Guess I need to get back to my other job."

I stopped him before he reached the door. "So, will I see you back here tonight?"

His glare gave me my answer, then, he opened the door and I sighed as I watched the love of my body's life walk away from me. I almost wanted to cry.

But then, before the door closed, he turned back and said, "See you tonight. Same time, this is the place."

My joy came back!

But then, he said, "And Gwen, I know I'm still young, but I do know that you can't keep screwing people without sooner or later, somebody screwing you back." He shut my door, pulling it hard so that it would slam a little.

His words lingered in the air, and made goosebumps rise on my skin. But then I shook my head and that feeling of foreboding off of me. What could he do? He was twenty-three and I was Gwen Tanner.

But maybe it was time for me to make one of those smart head-chick-in-charge decisions. Maybe it was time for me to end this thing with Justin. Especially since Eli would be here in just six days for my birthday, though that was still conjecture since my husband's promises were filled with as many holes as a homeless man's shoes.

Still, if Eli did meet me in Charlotte, that would show some kind of effort on his part, right? And then, I could make an effort, too. Now that I'd had this itch scratched, maybe I could find a way to make my marriage work.

As I turned toward the bathroom that was my thought. I was going to end this with Justin—right after tonight.

Chapter 16

Tamara

It took her all of this time?" I wanted to shout, but these dressing room walls were really thin, much thinner than they'd been in Atlanta, and DC. Even though the Belk Theatre was one of the newer venues where we would be performing, new construction couldn't compare to buildings from the '50s and '60s.

"Tam, the mere fact that I was able to stretch this out over two weeks is a sign of not only how hard I was fighting, but how much Diana was still considering you."

I massaged the bridge of my nose.

"If it's any consolation, she said it's not because of the pictures...."

"Yeah, right."

"...she just decided to go in a different direction."

Maury could spin this any way he wanted, but the fact was I'd blown the one promising lead I had because Diana hated home wreckers. I plopped onto the sofa, that seemed the best place to cry.

"What am I going to do, Maury?"

"You're gonna hang in there, kiddo. You're gonna hang in there and know that I'm working for you. And what is it that I hear people say? What God has for you, is for you."

If he'd been standing in front of me, I would've punched him in the eye. Why did people say that when it was so untrue? If that were the case, why did we strive for anything? Why didn't people just sit back and wait for God to give us what He had for us?

But I wasn't about to lecture Maury on the falseness of that statement and the truth of scripture. I had my own issues after what I'd done, my own issues with God that needed to be worked out before I could set anyone else straight.

"Okay," I whispered.

He said, "Look, you still have that gig with Gwen and with all the publicity you're getting, I'm wondering if maybe you and Donovan should set up some more shots."

"First of all, I already told you there isn't anything going on with me and Donovan." I crossed my fingers like a ten-year-old. "And even if there were, why would we do that? The publicity hasn't been good."

"Not true. It may not have worked with Diana and maybe it didn't because of her personal situation. But I'm getting other calls."

"From who?"

"No one I'm ready to talk about. Let's just say that your name is out there now and I have a feeling that you're gonna get something better."

His pep talk was such a lie. Something better than working with the hottest director, next to the hottest actor, on the hottest movie?

"I'm gonna keep working for you and you do your part—you keep acting on that stage and getting those great reviews where even the reviewers are wondering if something is going on between you and Donovan."

If only he knew.

"Any way, I gotta go. Keep your chin up, kiddo."

Before I even clicked off the phone, I knew what I was going to do.

I was gonna get out.

If Diana Delaney had said no, then there was no reason for me to continue doing what I hated. No, hate wasn't even a strong enough verb for what I was feeling about this play. It was because of this play and those photos that my name was being thrashed around the country as Donovan's mistress. Every interview we had (and since those photos appeared, a lot more radio and magazine and even TV entertainment shows wanted to talk to us) was about me and Donovan.

"Come on, you can tell us," the DJ of the most popular morning show in whichever city we were in would say. "Y'all are kicking it, right?"

And Donovan and I would laugh. (Although my chortle always sounded like a growl to me.)

It was Donovan who spoke for both of us, "Nah, I can't believe y'all let Gwen set you up like that. She staged those photos."

And everyone said, "Yeah, right."

If the media was tough, the audience was tougher.

Every autograph we signed was about me and Donovan.

"I'm so glad Donomara is back together!"

"No, we're not," I said fighting to keep my smile every time. "We're just friends. Remember, he's married."

"That ain't stopped y'all from kissing! Will you sign this magazine for me?"

It went on and on like that. Our denials, and their winks and, 'yeah rights.'

It was hell for me and what I needed was for Stephen, John, Spike, Tyler, somebody, anybody to call me so that I could do some real acting and make some real money and have some real peace. Because I would never have peace as long as I was in this play and...as long as I was sleeping with Donovan every single night.

God help me, but every DJ, every blogger, every magazine interviewer...and every fan was right. The night we'd been locked in the theatre in Atlanta was only our beginning. Even though, that night, we really had gone back to his room just to talk. We really talked. About what happened between us. Talked about how we should have really been together....

Thirteen days before....

I followed Donovan back into his dressing room, my heart pounded with each step I took. When he closed the door behind us, I said, "You can keep that open."

He shook his head. "No; you don't want anyone to see us.... by accident."

That was when I realized that I was still holding his hand. I let it go, folded my arms and smirked, "There won't be anything for anyone to see."

He gave my smirk right back to me. "I know. Whatever will be happening in here will be completely innocent, but someone might peek in, see us…talking, maybe…sleeping and get the wrong idea."

I knew he was right, though I didn't want to tell him that. So instead, I stomped to the sofa, slumped down, crossed my arms once again, then said, "Talk."

He chuckled a bit, shook his head, then shrugged. But before he opened his mouth, I held up my hand. "Wait!"

He frowned. "What?"

"We're not talking…until you put some clothes on."

It took him a moment, he looked down, then when his eyes came back to mine, he grinned. "We used to always talk like this."

"We're not who we used to be." His grin faded a bit, and then I took it completely away when I added, "And you have a wife."

He sighed, grabbed the jeans he'd had on before, slipped them on, then sat down next to me. At first, I was gonna protest. Ask him where was his shirt. Tell him he was only fifty-percent dressed. But I kinda liked the fact that he was fifty-percent naked, especially since this would be the last time we'd be like this.

He took my hand, I took it back. He sighed, I waited.

He said, "I am so sorry that I hurt you, Tammie. So sorry, and you've got to know that's never what I meant to do."

From the moment Donovan had come home two years, three months, seven days…and if I looked at my watch, I would even be able to add in the minutes, and told me that we couldn't get married because of another woman, that was all that I wanted to hear. I didn't need the details, didn't want the details, was too afraid the details would crack open the half of the heart that I had left after he'd said, "I'm sorry…but I can't marry you."

I didn't want to hear it then, I didn't want to hear it now. "All that matters is that you left me."

There was such sadness in the way he shook his head. "I didn't want to."

That made no sense to me. Because grown people did what they wanted to do. But his—*I didn't want to*—made me curious. Made me not tell him to shut up. So, I shifted, opened up, and without saying a word, told him to continue.

He said, "This wasn't an affair...."

I raised an eyebrow.

"....at least not in the way you think."

I smirked.

"I knew her before I knew you."

That made me squint and frown and tilt my head. For these two years, I'd assumed that Latrice was someone Donovan had met on the road. Some groupie, jump-off who'd had sex with my man and for a reason that I wouldn't understand got promoted to wifey. That was where the story began and ended. I never asked myself why she was chosen and I wasn't. There was no way I was going to drive myself bitter with that question.

He went on, "Remember when I didn't go right back to LA after our movie, after we met?"

I nodded. I remembered that well. We were both so excited about returning to Los Angeles, so that we could be together away from the set, anxious to see if our chemistry would extend beyond the fantasy. I headed straight to Los Angeles, but Donovan didn't come home right away. I never asked why, didn't ask where; always assumed it was a previous engagement and he would be home to me soon.

Donovan said, "I didn't tell you something about that trip, about where I went."

I swallowed.

"I went," he took a breath, "back home to Memphis."

And then, he told me the story.

"I had a girlfriend, back home. Latrice."

That made me raise an eyebrow.

"I'd been seeing her off and on since high school, if you could believe it."

His words made me think of my own home, my own high school, my own boyfriend. I could believe it.

"I knew we weren't going to make it. It wasn't Latrice's fault, we were fourteen when she became my girlfriend and two years later, I was on the road and everyone was calling me a star. Then, I lived a little bit of that life...."

I knew what he was talking about. It felt like he'd lived what happened to me.

"My life became so different from hers...."

I understood.

"God help me, I just didn't think that she would fit in...."

The air I sucked in expanded my chest, made me shift a little with uncomfortable memories.

"But Latrice didn't believe it, no matter what I told her, no matter what she read about what I was doing on the road, she believed I'd want to settle down one day and we'd be married. So...whenever I went home, we kicked it together. I was always honest with her, but she just kept holding on. Every time I went back to Memphis I expected her to tell me she'd met someone, but she kept asking if I'd ever heard of Magic Johnson? And how his high school girlfriend waited for him, and how they'd been married for decades now. So she would wait for me...until I got it all out of my system."

I closed my eyes and remembered—not the same words, but the same sentiment.

"But she kept waiting for me. And since I never met anyone." He looked up and into my eyes. "Not until I met you."

When he took my hands into his, there was no way I could pull back from him now.

"When I met you, I went home to Memphis, told Latrice that I'd met the woman I was going to marry and I wanted her to know it. I told her that I was going to marry you before I even told you. I told her that I was going to marry you and we'd known each other just that month on the set."

I felt the heat of tears building in my eyes.

"I wasn't trying to hurt her, but I'd always been honest with Latrice. And that day when I walked away from her, I walked away from all the others, too. For me, there was only you."

I wanted to pull Donovan into my arms, tell him that I understood. But there was still the question of... "So what happened? How did you decide...."

He took a deep breath, then another. And another. "After that, I didn't see her the entire time we were together and then, just a few weeks before I asked you to marry me, her dad died. I went back for the funeral, remember that?" He didn't wait for me to respond. "I told you I was going home for the funeral of my high school coach. Her dad had been so good to me, I had to be there. Then, I had to comfort her. And the night of the funeral, we were talking, she broke down, we were in her apartment and she was crying because she said that she felt so alone. She still wasn't seeing anyone, still said she loved me, was so afraid now that her father was gone...." He sighed. "I shouldn't have had sex with her. But she was kissing me, she was so sad, and we ended up in bed."

I cupped his face with the palm of my hand. "You could have told me. I would have been upset at first, but I would have understood."

He nodded. "I told Latrice I was sorry, it never should have happened, but I was going to marry you."

"So...." I shook my head in confusion.

"She got pregnant."

It took a couple of seconds for me to say, "What?"

He nodded, letting me know that I'd heard him correctly. "She got pregnant that night. When she called me, she was four months pregnant, told me she'd had an ultrasound and that we were going to have a son."

I blinked. "You...you have a son?"

In the way he blew out a breath, I had to sit back, put a little space between us.

"But how? How?"

He gave me a sideways glance.

"I mean, not how. I know how. But, you have a son? I didn't know."

"We did a great job of keeping my life out of the news. My agent hired R. Kelly's publicist because no one even knew R. Kelly had a wife until she divorced him. That's what I wanted. I didn't want anyone to know. I guess because I was ashamed."

"Of what? Not your son?"

"No, not him. I love that little boy." The way he smiled, warmed my heart. Almost made me smile. He kept on, "But there were so many other things. Latrice didn't mind us keeping Don out of the news, but when I tried to keep my wife out, too, she refused."

It was like I didn't hear what he'd said about his wife. All I heard was the name that we'd talked about—if we'd had a son. "Don."

He nodded. "My son." Both of us let time pass before, he said, "So, I married her. Because she was pregnant—with my son. It was hard, but I thought I was doing the right thing." He looked at me. "But Tamara, I shouldn't have done that. Because I never loved Latrice. That's why I've never been a good husband to her. I've had such a hard time...being faithful." He paused after that confession. "Because I never stopped loving you."

It wasn't those words that got to me. It was Donovan's story. His story that was my story...well, all except the baby. But everything was almost the same and he didn't even know it.

It was because of his story that I reached out, wrapped my arms around him, pulled him close and gave him the gentlest of kisses.

Leaning back on my sofa, I could feel that kiss even now. And the thousands of kisses that had followed. That was where it all began. With that kiss. Or maybe it was with his story. I wasn't really sure.

But even though it wasn't real, and even though I knew it couldn't last, I was living in the best of times, right inside the worst of times. It was the best knowing that Donovan loved me, the best knowing that he'd always loved me.

But it was the worst because no matter what, Donovan and Latrice had a son. And I would never do anything to come between that.

So I had to find a way to get out. Get out of this play and get away from the man I would probably always love. I didn't know what I would do, but I would find something!

Chapter 17

Camille

I'd wanted to watch Tamara suffer as she worked with Donovan every day. I'd wanted to catch her crying in between her scenes, tears pouring out so much that she couldn't even speak.

I'd imagined going back to my hotel room every night filled with hope and happiness as I watched her breaking down. And then, when she was at her very lowest, I'd send Randy in to finish it all.

But Tamara wasn't suffering, she wasn't miserable, she wasn't breaking, and she hadn't shed one tear. She was having a grand ole time because she and Donovan had hooked up. Yeah, they told everyone that nothing was going on, but a chemist couldn't create what was happening between those two. They were sleeping together, I was sure of that. Tamara had been doing too much smiling, no, she was grinning and she was giddy. She was happy and I wasn't.

It was time to hand her over to Randy.

The thought of that made me shiver, though it didn't make me smile as I walked into the lobby bar. It was full, just about every seat taken, which was a good thing. I needed to do this in plain sight. I'd decided to meet Randy right here, like talking to him here was no big deal—we were just colleagues chatting for a moment, the way everyone in the cast always did. No one would think anything of it and it was much safer than being alone with him in a stairwell.

I tugged my purse closer to me as I made my way to the end of the bar. Just as I expected, the guys from the band were all hunched together at the other end, their eyes on the basketball game on the screens above. I motioned to the bartender and he raised a finger. Then, I turned my attention to Randy and I got that stirring inside, the upset stomach feeling that I got every time I saw him.

He sickened me, not only because of what he'd done to me in the staircase, but he was truly a pervert. Always staring at women, then always doing things with his hands....I shuddered. After he took care of Tamara, I prayed that she'd report him so that he could spend the next ten decades of his life in prison.

But before that happened, I needed him; so I stared at him, one of those looks that made men with egos always turn around to see who was looking at them. It didn't take even a minute before Randy glanced at me.

I nodded, smiled, nodded again. He frowned, at first, so I gave him another nod, another smile. That was when he got it. That was when he nodded back. I watched him as he did one of those country-boy struts toward me and that wasn't an insult. I recognized that walk—my brother used to do it all the time, trying to impress Tamara.

"What's up, Camille?" Randy said as he slithered up next to me.

I cleared my throat. "Nothing. Just you." I took two steps to my left, wanting to make sure there was enough space between us and others so that our conversation wouldn't be easily overheard. Not that I was too worried. The cheers from the game drowned us out.

He rested his beer onto the very end of the bar. "So, you wanted to talk to me?" Then, he leaned in a little to add, "Or we could find a place more private than this."

I rolled my eyes, and he laughed.

"So this ain't about you and me?" he asked. "Let me guess. It's your favorite subject. Tamara."

"You and Tamara," I whispered back to him.

"I dunno why you still tryin' to make it seem like she wants to get wit' me." He shook his head. "She all up with that nigga, Donovan now."

"Could you not use the n word around me?"

"What?" His face was scrunched like he was really confused. "You don't want me to say ‚now'?"

It was a good thing he busted out laughing right away or else I would've just walked away. ‚Cause if he was that stupid, he wouldn't be able to pull this off with Tamara.

"I know what you mean, girl."

I gave him my ‚really' look.

"Okay, I won't say it anymore. So," he looked over to the bartender, held up his glass and the bartender gave him a nod. Then, he asked me, "You want somethin'?"

"No, I'm good," I said, remembering what I'd done opening night in Atlanta. Clearly, drinking wasn't my gift.

As Randy waited for another beer, I rolled over the script in my head and worked hard to press down my nerves. I had no idea why I was so nervous. It was all planned out with just two unanswered questions—the first being what I would say if Randy told anyone that we'd spoken. He was crazy, everyone knew that. That would be my defense—I had no idea what that nut was talking about.

When he turned back to me, I said, "So, what I wanted to talk to you about...."

He nodded. "I know. Me and Tamara. Why are you so interested in this?"

"I already told you. You would make a cute couple and then, she's the one who got me all involved. Carrying all of these messages to you."

"I just don't get it. She's a grown woman. Why can't she tell me herself? And why she always acting like she can't stand the sight of me?"

"And I already told you that part, too. She wants to keep up impressions. You know, she went to Yale and everything."

His eyes narrowed and I could almost see the flames of anger beneath his skin. "She doesn't think I'm good enough for her?"

"No, she just wants to make sure the chemistry is right between you two first before she makes any kind of public announcement."

"Chemistry?"

"You know, sexual chemistry."

"Oh, yeah." He grinned and he dropped one hand to his crotch.

Right away, I yanked my eyes back to his. Once again, I got that stirring inside, making me wonder if I should just walk away. But I couldn't. I had to remember my family. I had to remember how Tamara had never called back, never came back. And so, my brother decided that life in heaven was better than life on earth—without Tamara.

He didn't leave a note, but I was sure that was the reason why when I came home from my job at Betty Bea's I found him in bed, only this time, surrounded by all this red. That was the first time I understood why people sometimes said it was a pool of blood. Because there was so much blood and it looked like my brother was swimming...with his gun right beside him.

That alone was too much to take, but Tamara's betrayal didn't stop there. Next, came my mother. Who couldn't imagine life on earth without her son. That was why her heart had attacked her a little over a year after June died, leaving just me and my dad. My dad with all of those bottles of Crown and Irish Turkey to numb his grief. And I had my revenge.

"Hey, hey."

I blinked.

"You okay?" Randy asked as he tapped my hand with his fingertips.

I looked down to where he'd touched me and remembered where his hand had been a few moments ago. As I jerked away from him, I wondered what I could use to sterilize my skin.

"You good?" he asked.

I nodded, blinked some more, reached into my purse, and then with a quick glance around, I slid the white envelope onto the bar.

He didn't touch it at first. Just looked down, then back up at me. "What's that?"

"Something for you." I lowered my voice even more. "But be discrete." And then, I prayed that he knew the definition of that word.

He didn't pick up the envelope, which was a good sign. He lifted up the flap and the way his eyes got wide, I was afraid, he would pick up the envelope and show it around.

"There's money in there."

This guy was a genius!

"What's this for?" he asked.

"For you."

"Why you giving me money?"

"For Tamara."

His frown was so deep, I was afraid someone might notice and think we were arguing or something. "If Tamara really wants to get wit' me, why you givin' me money?"

Okay, he wasn't as dumb as I thought, but I was ready.

I shrugged, as if I hadn't been prepared for this question. "I don't know. This isn't my money. She gave it to me to give to you. She said it was a promise." I shook my head as if I were confused. "I have no idea what that means, but she said you would understand."

At first, he frowned, but then, he grinned. "Oh, yeah." He nodded. "I can get wit' that. She wants to take care of me. Okay."

Then, I blinked and the envelope was gone. That fast. I couldn't believe it and my first thought was that if this creep hadn't been into assaulting women, he might have had another career as one of those two-bit thieves on the street.

"So, how much is in there?" he asked, tapping the inside of his suit jacket where (I guess) he'd stuffed the envelope. "How much does she think I'm worth?"

Now that wasn't a question I was prepared to answer, but I didn't want to pretend that I didn't know. I couldn't have him pulling the envelope out, and counting the money in front of everyone.

I said, "She didn't tell me, but I think it's a couple of thousand."

He nodded. He grinned. He was pleased.

"So, what's the plan?" he asked.

"She wants to see you tomorrow night, after the show." His hand dropped to the front of his pants again, and this time, I kept my eyes right on his. "But she wants to role play. She doesn't want you to walk right in."

"What do you mean?"

"When you knock on her door, don't say, 'It's Randy.' Be creative...say you're with room service, or something like that."

He shook his head, then shrugged. "If that's how she wants to do it, but she sure wants to go through a lot when I have so much to offer. She needs to just be waiting for me in the bed."

"Who says she won't be?"

He licked his lips like a hungry wolf and I felt that stirring again. "Okay, then. It's done. Tomorrow night, right?"

I nodded. "And she said she's going to be in full role mold." I shrugged. "I don't get it, but she's an actress and I guess that means she always has to be acting."

"I get it now. Thanks, Camille. You sure are a good friend."

I didn't say anything since I was ready for him to get back with the guys and away from me. But as he did that country-strut again, I thought about his words: a good friend.

That, I was. I was a good friend to my brother. And my brother was finally going to have his revenge so that he could rest in peace. I prayed that Tamara would be left as heartbroken and despondent as she had left June.

I stood at the bar, not wanting it to seem like my purpose for being there was only to see Randy. As I sipped my wine, I smiled as others motioned for me to come their tables. I nodded as if I would join them, but there was only one thing I wanted to do tonight. I had to get back to my room, so that I could answer the second unanswered question: How was I going to separate Tamara and Donovan tomorrow night?

Even now, they were the only two missing—as if we wouldn't know that they were together. It was like that every night; it couldn't be like that tomorrow.

I'd figure it out, I was sure of that. But first, I held up my glass, asked the bartender for another glass—just a coke, this time. But then, I changed my mind and asked for another glass of wine. My second. This would be my last one, but right now, I needed something to calm all of this rumbling going on inside.

Chapter 18

Gwen

"Yes!" I whispered and pumped my fist in the air as I walked down the hall toward my office in the back of the theatre.

We had added another city, Memphis, and I couldn't wait. I couldn't imagine the publicity we would get when we got there—Donomara...and his wife?

What a threesome! Oh, yeah. This was going to be epic.

Just as I had that thought, I felt a tug on my arm, and then a push and a shove into what looked like a storage room.

"What the…?" I screamed.

My heart was pumping, my fists were clenched until I turned around. And then my heart pumped some more, though now, it wasn't from fear.

"Oh," I said, relaxing my hands. I smiled as I wrapped my arms around Justin's neck. "This is different. We've never done it rough and we've never done it in public."

This *was* different...and reckless in so many ways. Not only were we about to have a quickie in the theatre, but really, we shouldn't have been having this quickie. The promise I'd made to myself to give Justin up hadn't come to fruition at all. This boy was like crack, or at least what I imagined crack to be since I'd never done any kinds of drugs—I hadn't even smoked weed when I was an undergrad at Brooklyn College.

But I couldn't get enough of Justin. And I justified it by saying it was going to make me better for Eli. If I were in a good mood when he arrived tomorrow (if he arrived tomorrow), it would be better for my marriage.

I leaned in for a kiss...and Justin pushed me away.

That made me smile. "What's wrong? You scared?"

His face was set with the hard lines of a statue. "We need to talk."

"Okay." I dropped my arms. "But I don't think this is the place to do it. We'll talk tonight," I told him.

He shook his head. "No, we'll talk. Right here, right now."

There were lots of reasons why I wasn't going to stand here and talk to Justin—the first being he needed to learn that he couldn't tell me what to do. I gave him one of my best sister-girl stares before I said, "Didn't I just say...."

"And I just said, we're gonna talk here. I was trying to respect your privacy. That's why I pulled you in here. But you know what," he stepped back as if he was making room for me to move to the door, "we can certainly go into your office and have this talk. And then, we can wait to see who will walk in and overhear us."

My eyes narrowed. "What do you want to talk about?"

"That's better." He took a breath, then, hunched his shoulders twice like he was preparing for a fight. "Now...." He paused.

Did he really just pop his collar?

"I needed to talk to you about money. I don't think I'm earning enough for the job that I'm doing."

This was why he was putting on this show? For a few extra dollars? "Really? I'm already paying you triple minimum wage."

He nodded. "Okay, well then. I want a bonus. Ten thousand dollars."

I didn't know which opened wider, my eyes or my mouth. But that lasted for only a moment before I laughed. I leaned forward so that I could laugh right in his face, sure that would rattle him a little bit. But he wasn't moved.

He didn't blink, he didn't snicker, he just stood stiff and waited until I finished. Then, as if my laugh didn't matter, he said, "When can I expect the cash? And let me repeat that because I want it in cash."

I raised my eyebrows.

He made a grand show of raising his arm, looking at his watch. "I want to get to the bank before five."

This dude was serious. Like, really serious. I had too much work to do to be playing around with him like this.

"I'm not giving you any money." I tried to push by him, but Justin blocked my way. Looking up, I kept my voice calm and steady, but I added an edge to let him know that I was already tired of this little game. "Little boy, I don't know who you think you're messing with."

That made him laugh. Now, I was the one who had to wait until he got it together. "I wasn't a little boy when you were riding me and calling me Big Daddy."

My quip came hard and fast. "I've ridden better and the Big Daddy was just so I wouldn't hurt your *little* feelings."

Now, that was a lie, but it hit its mark.

Justin stiffened, from his forehead to the way his shoulders tightened...my words had done what I planned. And if he hadn't demanded money from me, this would have been the perfect time for some great make up sex.

"Well, whatever you want to call me, call me Mr. Bucks 'cause I'm about to get some money."

"I'm not giving you a dime!" And then, I took a breath, to bring down my voice and my temper. It was bad enough that I was having this conversation; I didn't need to be overheard and caught in this storage room.

His tone was cool and casual when he said, "I beg to differ. In fact, the price just went up for my effort here. Fifteen thousand. And, since you're being such a bitch, you're gonna give me a role in your show like you promised."

I didn't even laugh this time because now, it wasn't funny. "I wish I would."

"I wish you wouldn't. Because my next stop will insure that I get even more money. Maybe not the part in the play, but I'll be talking about getting ten times what I just asked you for."

I glared at him, but didn't say a word. I wasn't going to ask him, knowing that he'd show his hand, he'd tell me his plans.

And, he did. "First, I'll go to your husband. He's going to be here tomorrow, right?"

I inhaled, and Justin caught that because he smiled.

He said, "I'm sure he'd love to know what his wife is doing out here on the road."

Now, I ground my teeth.

"And then, after I talk to Mr. Tanner...."

I didn't bother to correct him.

"...I'll set up a meeting with an attorney to file sexual harassment charges."

My fingers curled into fists.

"Finally, you might not put me in the play, but I will get my fifteen minutes of fame when I get a starring role at a major press conference. Can you imagine me telling everyone how I was just an innocent struggling college student who was trying to break into the business before you took advantage of me?" He turned his face from the left to the right. "Which is my best side? Which way should I look at the camera?"

It was when he faced me again, with that smirk, like he was the one in control, that I lost it. I lifted my hand and with all the power in me, I slapped him. Actually, I was surprised that he was still standing there because I'd hit him so hard, I was sure that I'd knocked him straight to next Tuesday.

His palm went straight to his cheek, and he rubbed it for a moment before he laughed. "This is perfect. We can add assault to the list. Sweetheart, that just cost you another five grand," Justin said. "Have my twenty thousand and my script for my role." He turned toward the door, but then, over his shoulder said, "Oh, and I'm taking the night of...from your play and from your bed." Then, he strutted out of the room like he was already twenty thousand dollars richer.

I stood there for a moment, stunned and silent. I was being blackmailed...by a kid...from Birmingham.

And the biggest problem—Eli would be here tomorrow. Would Justin really go to my husband? Standing there, I tried to imagine what that would be like…what Justin would say, what Eli would believe.

No! I couldn't let that happen. I wasn't sure what I was going to do, but I had just about twenty-four hours to figure it out. Maybe I could call Eli. Make up some excuse for why he couldn't come to Charlotte.

I'd tell him I was sick, on my period, something, anything to make him change his plans. That wouldn't be too hard; Eli would be happy to have an excuse not to spend the time with me.

Nodding my head, I took a deep breath. That was what I would do. I lifted my chin, rolled my shoulders back, straightened up and walked out of that storage closet like the woman in charge that I was.

Once I kept my husband away, I'd find a way to deal with Justin. That little blackmailer was going to regret the day his tiny brain had come up with this little scheme. By the time I finished, he'd be paying me twenty thousand dollars. I was going to make sure of that.

Chapter 19

Gwen

Unfortunately, my twenty-four hours were up!

My time ended when I stomped from that storage closet and went a few feet down the hall to my makeshift office.

When I entered, I was about to hurl my tablet across the room—except it would have hit my husband right in his chest.

"Eli," I said, with surprise all in my voice. "Wh-what are you doing here?" I felt like I'd just walked into a sauna, the way perspiration covered my body in an instant and my heart raced.

"I could ask you the same question." His glance roamed the room and I saw the disdain in his eyes. "This is an...interesting place to work."

"It's not a real office," I said moving past him. "It's just a space that every theatre has for the director."

He kinda shuddered...like a girl. "I don't know how you do it." He turned to face me.

"Not all of us need to sit behind an ebony desk to work." I strode toward the table that had been set up for me, a cheap piece of furniture that had probably been purchased at Wal-Mart.

"You're right." He gave me a smile that wasn't filled with any kind of heart, and that made my heart sink to my feet. I sat there, waiting for him to kiss me, hug me, something, since we hadn't seen each other in a month.

Of course, he made no moves like that. Of course, he said nothing kind. Of course, he sniffed as he gave my office another swift one-hundred-eighty-degree glance. "But still, this place is repugnant."

I glared at him. "I'm sorry this doesn't meet your standards, but I have no control over the scent of the theater."

"I know that. It's just that I can't figure out how you can work like this." Then, he had the nerve to shudder (like a girl) again. "You know, I've been thinking. I know you love doing this, but maybe it's time for you to give this up."

I had to shake my head a couple of times to clear whatever pebbles had somehow found their way to my ears. "What?"

"I'm just saying, this...you don't have to do this. You can come home."

"And do what at home? This...what I'm doing is my passion. It's taken me years to get here."

"I know, but it's a passion that I fund."

"What difference does that make?" I snapped. "It's still my passion, you wanted to fund me, you offered to do it." I felt like I always had to remind him of that. "I'm good at what I do; I've won awards...."

He yawned!

And I tried not to let that hurt my heart.

"....and now, I'll have the money to pay you back. All of it. At the end of this run."

He raised his eyebrows.

I waited for him to say something because I knew he didn't believe me. Actually, I was lying, but not by much. I'd cleared all the money for Atlanta and DC and with advance ticket sales in upcoming cities, along with the merchandising, I had close to one hundred thousand dollars—after expenses. By the time this tour was over, I expected to net at least one mil.

But Eli didn't need to know that, not yet. I'd write him a check for 250K at the end—just in case anything came up.

Like this situation with Justin. Especially with Eli here now, I just might have to write a check to that boy.

He said, "Well, let's not talk about money right now. I came for your birthday."

I knew I should have said thank you, but what came out was, "I thought you were coming tomorrow."

"That had been the plan, but I thought I would come early and surprise you. I thought you'd be happy since you're always complaining about how I miss you birthday and our anniversaries and everything else in between. I was trying to make all of that up to you."

All of that? With a weekend visit to Charlotte, North Carolina? I nodded a little. I needed to be understanding. I needed to appreciate his effort.

He said, "I stepped away from a big project to come down here, Gwen."

The way he said that, like I should get down on my knees in gratitude, made me take back the little bit of appreciation I had.

But I didn't have any time for a reproach because of the quick knock on my open door. And then, Justin stepped in.

"Mrs. Tanner?" Justin peeked his head inside, his grin so wide on his innocent-looking face. "I just wanted to let you know the merchandising is loaded and ready to go for tonight."

My slow, steady breaths belied the flip flops going on in my stomach. "Thank you, Justin, but umm, I thought you were taking the day off."

"At the last minute I decided I was feeling okay." He turned to Eli and extended his hand. "Hello, I'm Justin."

Eli hesitated, then shook his hand. "Eli Weinstein, I'm Gwen's husband."

"Oh," he looked from me to Eli, then back to me. "Your husband? Gwen Tanner?"

I hadn't slept with Justin because of his IQ. "My full name is Gwen Tanner Weinstein."

"Yes," Eli said, "I couldn't get my wife to drop her name and take just mine."

"It was a professional decision," I told Justin, then paused. What the hell were we doing? Having this discussion in front of my blackmailer?

"Oh," Justin said. "Well, it's a pleasure to meet you finally. Mrs. Tanner has told me so much...so many great things about you."

Eli's head bounced back a little. "Really?" He smiled. "Well, what do you do around here?"

"Oh, merchandising, and really just providing other services... as needed." He licked his lips, my insides begin to throb and I cursed the parts that made me a woman, then I cursed Justin.

"And, Mrs. Tanner has also been gracious enough to give me a small role in the play for the rest of the run. I go up in the next city." He grinned and if we'd been alone, I would've slapped him again.

"Glad you're feeling better, Justin," I said, stopping him before he said anything else. I needed to break this little buddy-fest up. "But now that you're going to be here tonight, I'm sure you have a lot of work to do."

Justin looked at me, then turned to Eli. "Actually, Mr. Weinstein, how long are you in town?"

"For the weekend; I'm here for my wife's birthday."

"Well, I know you're a busy man, but I'm interested in accounting."

"Really?"

He nodded. "And I understand you own one of the largest accounting firms in the country."

Air filled Eli's chest making him look like he gained ten pounds of muscle. But my focus was on Justin. He knew about Eli being an accountant? What had he done? Researched him on the Internet? I would have been impressed if my feelings for him weren't now bordering on hate.

"Yes, I own a firm—actually it's accounting and financial planning," Eli said.

"Wow, I'm impressed. I had to take a year off from school for financial reasons, but I've come into a little money and I'm confident I'll be able to go back to school in the fall."

"Well, that is awesome news, ummm. . . Justin, isn't it?"

"Yes, sir. And I understand education is key so I am determined to go back to school."

If I'd had a spoon, I would have stuck it down my throat. No, I would have stuck it down Justin's throat.

"Anyway," Justin continued, "I'd love to talk to you. Maybe tomorrow, I could treat you to a cup of coffee while I tell you a little about myself," he glanced at me, "and what I've been up to."

That made me jump from my chair. "Justin, tomorrow is my birthday and my husband and I will be spending time together."

"Oh, I'm sorry," Justin said.

"Well, we will spend the day together, but not every moment," Eli said. "I'd love to take a little time out to talk to you." He slapped Justin on the back. "I always love giving advice to young people who are working hard for their future."

"That would be great," Justin said, and if I didn't know hat he was a liar and a blackmailer, I would have thought his enthusiasm was real. "Mrs. Tanner has my number, so you just call me when you're ready."

"I'll do that, son."

Justin smirked at me before he darted out of the room, not giving me a chance at all to wrap my fingers around his throat.

"He seems like a nice young man," Eli told me.

Yeah, if you like punk-ass-criminals. It took everything in my power to force a smile before I sat back down in the chair. "So, I have some work to do before the show tonight. Do you want to wait for me or just meet me in the room?"

"Uhhhh...."

My eyes narrowed.

"Well, I'm not going to the room right now."

"Fine, you can wait for me."

"Uhhhh....no," he looked down at his watch, "I have a meeting."

"A meeting? Here in Charlotte?"

He nodded. "There's a potential client down here, a prestigious firm that would be a coupe if I could snag it. I have a meeting with them today and then dinner with them tonight."

I shook my head. "So, you won't be coming to the play." That wasn't a question.

"Uhhhh....no. Not tonight."

"Unbelievable."

"You weren't expecting me today anyway, remember? And tomorrow is your birthday."

"Would you have even come down here if you couldn't make it a business trip, too?"

"What difference does it make?" He shrugged. "I'm here now, right?"

"Whatever." I waved my hand.

He sighed. "I made this effort."

There was nothing left for me to say. I looked down at my tablet, opened my emails and began reading. But the moment Eli stepped out of the room and closed the door, I placed the tablet back on the table.

I didn't know why I was fighting it, why I was trying to make Eli into a man he could never be? Maybe I should just let Justin tell Eli because then one of two things would happen—either he'd get jealous and he'd step up. Or he'd get jealous and toss me out. But was I ready to give up my lifestyle? I mean, it wasn't like he was cheating on me.

I sighed. I wasn't sure what to do. But the more I sat there, the more I began to wonder...maybe both Eli and Justin needed to be taught a lesson. Maybe I should just let what was going to happen, happen.

The only thing was, I wasn't sure if I was ready to live with the consequences.

Chapter 20

Tamara

With the tip of the towel, I wiped the shower steam that had fogged the bathroom mirror, then stared at my reflection. I stayed there for a moment, wanting to be sure that I could still look myself in the eye, even though it had been ten days—no, not days. The days didn't count because we worked during the day. It had been ten nights. Ten glorious nights since Donovan and I had been back together.

Though it didn't feel like only ten nights. It felt like ten weeks, ten years, ten forevers. It felt like the way it was supposed to be.

That was the thought that made me look down, turn away, and grab my robe from the hook on the bathroom door. My skin was still a bit damp and so the satin clung to me as I tied the belt around my waist. But the whole time, I kept my eyes away from my reflection. Away from the reflection of the other woman.

This wasn't who I was, wasn't who I wanted to be and if that last part of my thought was true, then the ten nights had to come to an end. I couldn't be with Donovan anymore.

This was not a new revelation. Every night since the first night, I'd said the same thing—the first night and the third night and the eighth night and last night. I was sure I would've been telling myself the same thing tonight if Donovan hadn't had a meeting with one of our cast mates. Something about someone wanting advice for her brother. I hadn't even asked Donovan who he was meeting, because that didn't matter. What mattered was that this was divine intervention—God giving me a way out. A chance to break this trance I was under. Being away from Donovan tonight could be what I needed to make last night the last night—for real.

A bit of steam wafted from the bathroom when I opened the door and stepped into the bedroom. I pressed the mute button on the TV remote, then tossed it onto the nightstand. It was much too early to sleep, at least for me—it was just a little before eleven; the show had only ended about two hours ago and tonight, we didn't have a meet and greet. Gwen's husband was visiting for her birthday, so all of us were where we wanted to be at least an hour earlier than usual.

I was used to getting in bed around midnight and since I hadn't been going to bed alone, sleep didn't come until many hours after. So tonight, adrenaline was still pumping through my veins, even as I crawled onto the bed. I didn't disturb the duvet, just leaned back, closed my eyes and thought about how I would never be with Donovan again.

That truth hurt my heart, though, so much of this didn't make sense. When I met Donovan, I'd been sure that God had sculptured us just for each other. From the beginning, we were every way soul mates: from how we were both fanatics who cheered for the best in all sports: the Lakers, the Cowboys and the Yankees. How we both ate too much chicken (was there such a thing, we used to ask), dark meat only. How our televisions only seemed to receive signals from two TV stations: ESPN and CNN. And then, there was our reading. Both of us were voracious readers, carrying a book with us at all times, though our favorites differed—he loved Richard Wright and Donald Goines, while I favored the Russian playwrights like Tolstoy and Chekhov.

But the most important thing that we shared was that we were each other's first loves. Or at least that's what he'd told me and that's what I told him. I'd hidden my past from him, though I hid it in plain sight. He knew I was from Itta Bena, but he knew that I hadn't returned to Mississippi once I completed undergrad. There was no reason for me to go back, no family, no one that I really called a friend. Nothing and no one...except for Martin.

The thought of June made me open my eyes, made me shift, made me remember. Who would have ever thought that who you loved at sixteen wouldn't be who you loved at thirty-two? Back in 1990, when we met in Sunday School, I was so in love. I may have only been six, but I told that little boy that he was gonna be my husband.

I smiled, remembering that, then laughed as I recalled the way June Bug said that was fine with him. And that was it—we were together from that moment. The prince and princess, who grew up to be the king and queen of Itta Bena, destined to be together.

We had the kind of love that not only grew, but often made me cry—I cried as we danced at our Senior prom, and I cried when June vowed to get me through Yale. Then, the way he held me when my mom died, for days, as long as I needed.

That was love.

At least that was love then.

It was a heart love, but not a soul love.

Sighing...I opened my eyes. I hadn't thought about June this much in years, and it was strange thinking about him as I thought about Donovan. Not for the first time, I wondered what June was doing. I had no doubt that he was married by now, a girl from Itta Bena, of course. Maybe even my best friend, Maxine because though she never told me, I knew that she loved June in high school, even as I loved him, too.

I really prayed that he was happy and that his happiness made him forget all about the hard breakup that we'd had. I hoped his happiness made him forget the plans we'd made to leave Mississippi together and move to Hollywood so that I could be an actor and he could be...well, we'd never thought that far ahead.

And that had been our problem. Because maybe if we'd thought ahead, maybe we would have been able to see what was clear to me my first day in Los Angeles. There was nothing heavenly about the City of Angels. It was a hard life, a struggle, even for a person with an undergrad and grad degree from Yale. So what would it have been like for a guy from Mississippi with only one semester of college because he just didn't like school?

Even now, all of these years later, that question in my mind made me shake my head. I couldn't imagine how out of place June would have been in Los Angeles because it had always been such a nightmare for him when he came to New Haven. From that first time, when he visited me at Yale, the first time for homecoming.

I'd only been away from home for two months, but when his parents said that they would chip in money so that June could make the trip to New Haven, we had both been giddy with excitement and anticipation. I wanted June to see everything that had amazed me when I first arrived in this big city.

But when he got there, though his eyes were big with wonder like mine had been, it wasn't for the same reasons. He wasn't interested in all the plans I had for us: he didn't want to take the walking tour across campus to marvel at the buildings that had been around since the seventeen and eighteen hundreds. He didn't want to see the ten million books in the Yale library nor hang out with the black students at the African American Cultural Center.

"This is too big, Tam," he complained. "Too many people."

June had come back again, but it hadn't been any better when we went out to Gino's Pizza with my roommate, Corrine and her boyfriend, Lloyd (of the New York Vanderbilts, he told everyone).

"Twiggy was drownding and she wasn't even in the deep end of the pool." June laughed as he tried to tell us a story about his sister. "I kept yelling to her to stand up."

But while I giggled with him, Corinne and Lloyd frowned. "Uh?" Corinne began. "Drownding? What's that?"

Before I could say anything, Lloyd chimed in, "That must be Mississippi speak for drowning."

Then Corinne and Lloyd busted out laughing.

My face heated with embarrassment, but not for me. It was the look on June's face that made me squeeze his hand, kiss his cheek, then lead him away from that pizzeria as Corinne and Lloyd's laughter drifted behind us.

Those were just horrible days that never got better and made June's visits dwindle to nothing. But then, I didn't know that my years in New Haven were the beginning of our end. I didn't know that until I left Connecticut for California. The moment the wheels of my plane hit the tarmac of Los Angeles International Airport, I knew Martin Wilson would never be able to make that place his home.

August 4, 2008

"It's still gonna take me a couple of weeks to save the whole four hundred dollars," June drawled.

I'd never noticed it before—the way June spoke so slow yet all his words still ran together.

I closed my eyes and did that pinching thing on my nose that sometimes took away the pressure. But it wasn't working this time. "You may need more than four hundred dollars."

"Why? Did the cost of the airplane ticket go up?" There was so much innocence in his voice; he just didn't know.

Even though he couldn't see me, I shook my head. "No, it's just that I haven't found any work yet...."

The way he laughed made me sit up straight, made me frown.

He said, "You've only been out there for two months, boo. You have to give it some time."

I don't have time! That's what I wanted to scream. But I kept it calm and said, "Well, I said that because I'm still sleeping on somebody's couch...."

"Somebody? I thought you knew the girl."

See...this was one of the problems. He didn't get it and I had to explain everything.

"Of course I know her. I mean, I know her through Maury. He's her agent, too. But what I'm saying, June, is that when you come, where are you going to stay?"

He didn't say a word, but even though we were almost two thousand miles away from each other, I knew his expression, I knew his body language. He was probably sitting on the edge of his bed, frowning, like he was trying to make sense of my words.

"Well...." He dragged out the word making it sound like it had a dozen syllables. "Are you saying that you don't want me to come?"

"No, that's not it at all," I said as quickly as I could. "It's just that when you get here, I can't ask Alexa to let you sleep on the couch."

"I don't mind sleeping on the floor."

Inside, I sighed, though I wanted to scream again right in his ear. He didn't understand that this wasn't the South. There wasn't hospitality of any kind in this place, at least not where I lived. Alexa Matthews had also graduated from Yale Drama, two years ago. That, along with us sharing the same agent, was the reason why she'd opened her one bedroom condo to me.

In the beginning, she'd invited me in with a huge smile, but as the weeks passed and turned into eight, her smile was gone, replaced by a you're-still-here scowl every time she looked at me. So I couldn't imagine asking her if my boyfriend could invade her space, too.

"You want me to speak to your roommate?" June asked after I was silent for too long, I guess. "You know how charming I can be. I can convince her."

He chuckled and I tried to swallow what felt like a boulder growing in my throat. Why couldn't he understand what I was saying? How was he supposed to visit when we had no place to be together? And even once I got a gig and a place, how was June supposed to live in LA when he couldn't even take New Haven?

"I'm coming anyway, Tam," June said. "We'll figure it out. Your roommate won't have a problem, once she meets me."

I shook my head, but said, "Okay," anyway, because I didn't know how to explain it anymore. I didn't know how to explain anything anymore.

My words were slow, and there were already tears in my eyes when I said, "I'll talk to you tomorrow, June."

Clicking off my cell phone, I sat on the sofa for a few minutes, swiping away my tears, before I grabbed my purse and headed straight to AT&T. On the whole walk over, I tried to figure this out in my head. June and I loved each other. We'd be together. One day. Just not this day. Once I was able, once I was settled, I'd call him back and explain what I was doing, why I'd done it this way. I knew June—he would understand, he always understood.

When I got to AT&T, I went to the salesman and said, "I want to change my number."

He nodded, but gave me a kinda side-eye glance that let me know he wasn't sure he should help me. It was probably because of the tears that gushed from my eyes and then the sobs that seeped through my lips, even as I tried to push them back inside with my fingers....

I'd changed my number (and email, too), that day. But the next day, I'd written June a letter. Told him that I would always love him, but that this was best. At least for this moment. I told him my plan, asked him to just give me time to get situated and then I would call him. But for now, I needed to focus.

There was a part of me that hoped June would still get on that plane, track me down, and do what he always did when we were in Mississippi—take over and fix it.

But I never heard from him and he never heard from me.

The memories made more tears stream from my eyes. Eight years ago, I'd given up my heart love and now, I had to give up my soul love. Was one person supposed to lose so much love in one lifetime?

These memories, these thoughts made me weary with sadness. So I did the only thing that I could do.

I closed my eyes...for just one moment.

Chapter 21

Tamara

I was dreaming...I knew that. One of those dreams where I kinda knew that I wasn't awake, but I wanted to stay in this fantasy place. Because I was dreaming of Donovan.

And our wedding.

It was finally happening.

My eyes were down as I looked at my bouquet, and tried to steady my hands. I didn't need to be nervous. This was our time. Finally. Our meant-to-be. Finally.

So, I raised my eyes.

And screamed.

I screamed into the blackness.

Why was the world all black?

The chords of Mendelssohn's Wedding March began to play, the doors opened and there stood our hundreds of guests. All looking at me, all grinning.

All dressed in black.

I screamed even louder.

It was the veil. My veil made me see the world in black. I dropped the flowers and raised my hands, trying to rip the veil from my head. But it was affixed to my scalp. Like the blackness was something that would never go away.

"Donovan! Help me!"

"Tamara!"

"Donovan!"

I tried to scream myself awake, but my eyes were squeezed shut. Then, I heard a bold knock and I bolted up.

Donovan!

Jumping from the bed, I ran to the door, swung it open...then, blinked, blinked, frowned.

"What do you want?" It was only because I was groggy that I even asked the question instead of just slamming the door on Randy who stood in front of me with his buck-toothed grin.

"Come on, I know you want to play, but...."

Playing was not what I wanted to do; I raised my hand to make a dramatic move and slam the door in his face. But, Randy moved faster. His foot was in the door, stopping me from closing it. Then before I could react, he pushed the door, causing me to stumble backward.

I caught myself right before I hit the floor, then struggled to stand upright. "Have you lost your damn mind?" I yelled, wide awake now. "Get out of my room!"

"Look," he motioned with his hands, "calm down." Then, he closed the door. "I can never tell with you. I can never tell if this is part of the game or not."

I hardly heard his words because every part of me was focused on his hand. His hand that had moved to the door...then twisted the lock, bolting us inside.

I stepped to move past him. If I got to that door, I was going to get out and scream until the roof on this building blew off. But he blocked my path, making me back up and away from the door since I didn't want to be that close to him.

He said, "I'm not going anywhere until we figure this out." Before, all I'd heard was his craziness. But now, there was a desperate edge in his tone that made me more afraid.

"Randy." My voice was calm, a lesson I'd learned from one of Oprah's shows. Try to speak sense to people who were speaking nonsense. "We don't need to figure anything out. There's nothing we need to talk about. I'm tired and I just want you to leave."

He took a step toward me and I took two steps back.

"If you don't leave my room right now, I'm going to call the police."

Him: another step forward. Me: another three steps back.

He said, "Why you gotta bring the cops in this?" The edge was still in his tone, but now, it had moved to his eyes. At least that was the reason why I thought his eyes widened, looked glassy.

"Randy." I wasn't sure how I was doing it, but I kept my calm. "Randy...you need to leave."

"Nah." Then, he shoved me and I stumbled back again, this time, falling hard onto the bed. "I know your type." It was his voice that was rising now. "You act all high and mighty, playing games with people. Why you got to keep playing games with me?"

I had no idea what this fool was talking about. I hardly saw him and when I did, the only words we exchanged were professional, always about my song.

"You keep saying you want me, and then you say you don't."

I didn't say a word because my fear barometer had crashed off the charts. There wasn't a word for what I felt now, and so, I scooted up on the bed, trying to get away from him.

But for some reason, that made him smile. No, smile wasn't the right word—he sneered.

"Yeah, that's what I thought," he said. Then, his eyes lowered away from mine. When he looked down, I grabbed the hem of my robe. I'd forgotten what I had on. Just the robe that barely covered my butt.

His eyes were on my thighs and he licked his lips. "Look at all of that sweetness."

I wanted to scream, but I was afraid that I wouldn't get a word out before he grabbed me. "Randy," I made a point to say his name again. "I don't know what you think, but I don't want... this." That was the word I chose, not wanting to say directly that I didn't want him.

But I wasn't sure he heard me. Because he unfastened the buckle on his belt, swiped it from his waist, then unzipped his pants. I moved again, but I was already leaning on the headboard.

"I promise, once we're done, you're gonna wish you didn't wait this long and played all these games...."

"What are you talking about?"

"You're gonna wish that we got together sooner, instead of sending your girl to set us up."

My girl? Set us up?

He was insane, but his words were distracting because I didn't see him reach for me. But even if I had, I was sure that I would have done the same thing. Because it was a torque reaction—he touched my left leg and my right leg swung out. With all the force within me, I kicked, my heel aimed for his groin.

I kicked. I screamed.

He wailed.

As he bent over to save himself, I jumped from the bed and scrambled toward the door. "Someone help me!" I shouted.

"You slut!"

I wasn't even halfway to the door before he grabbed my hair, jerking me backward. When he swung me around, I used my fist and socked him as hard as I could.

But it wasn't enough. Because this time, he was the one with the torque reaction and as my right fist *tried* to do damage, his right hand did—he slapped me so hard, I wilted to the floor.

Before I could blink or breathe, he straddled me, pinning my hands to the floor. "You were the one who wanted to play this game and I was willing to go along. But no one gets away with attacking me like that."

I struggled under his grasp.

"You wanna play games?"

I wiggled, but between his legs and his hands, I couldn't move. So, I was going to have to use all that I had left. I was going to scream to the heavens.

But just as I opened my mouth, he moved one of his hands. I tried to push myself up, but then, I saw the silver flicker of a Swiss Army knife. Just like the one I'd used in my first movie. When he pressed it to my neck, I gasped, knowing the damage that it could do. I wanted to cry, really, I did. But the sharp, pointy steel kept me silent.

"That's better," he said. He released me from the grasp of his other hand, but how was I supposed to move with the knife still against my throat?

When he pulled his penis through the opening of his pants, I whimpered, "Randy, please...."

He pressed the knife deeper into my skin. "Shut the hell up," he said and I did what I was told. "You're the one who wanted to play it like this."

The way my eyes widened, I was able to take in all of him. I took in his deranged stare, the way he massaged himself, the way his lips curved when he said, "Oh, yeah, this is about to be good."

He moved the knife up to the bridge of my nose. "And if you try to scream, or do anything stupid again, I won't hesitate to kill you."

I squeezed my eyes shut. "Randy." His name came out in a whimper this time.

"I said, shut up!" When he pressed the knife into my cheek, I felt my skin tear. "You said this is how you wanted it. So just shut up and take it."

He was bat-shit-crazy, but what was I supposed to do? I couldn't scream, couldn't fight. Because I knew he'd do what he'd said—he would kill me and get pleasure from it. So, I relaxed my body, though I cried. He couldn't stop me from crying.

God, why was this happening?

That was my thought as he climbed on top of me. That was my thought as he pushed my legs apart. That was my thought as he pushed inside of me.

I cried.

"Oooh....this feels so good."

I cried.

"I knew it would be like this, baby."

I cried.

I cried until he finally grunted, finally exploded.

And a piece of me died.

There was silence in the room, except for Randy's huffing. There was no sound from me; I'd stopped breathing a long time ago.

Finally, "Oooooh, dang, girl. That was so freakin' good." He pushed himself up, though, he kept that knife near my nose. "Tell the truth, you were getting into it." When I said nothing, he shouted, "Answer me!"

The shock of his scream made me jump, made me say, "Yes," because I wanted to live.

He smiled. "Good." His voice was softer now. "You know what?" He lowered his head to mine. "I got a little left in me. What about you? You ready to go again?"

Oh, my God! No!

"Answer me!"

I trembled with fear but said, "Yes," with a strength that I didn't know I had within me.

"That's better," he told me.

That was when he made a decision—he pulled the knife away from me.

That was when I made a decision—I forced myself to smile.

I thought of this as a role when I said, "Yeah, I'm ready to go again."

If he'd known anything about me, he would have heard the tightness inside my calm. He would have become suspicious and he should have been afraid. But my calm was meant to distract and relax.

And that's just what he did. His grin widened as he laid the knife on the floor.

He said, "I guess it was kind of good, that role-playing that you like to do. What role do you wanna play this time?"

From the corner of my eye, I saw the knife. Right next to me. I measured the distance.

My hands were shaking as I lifted them to the front of my robe that had somehow stayed closed during his attack. I parted my robe, revealing all of my nakedness.

He gasped. "Damn." His eyes stared at the fullness of my breasts, then, he did what I knew he would do. He leaned over—without the knife. Took my left breast into his mouth—without the knife. "I like this role," he said as he slurped.

I pushed him away, just a little. He looked into my eyes and frowned. I looked into his eyes and smiled.

"This time, I want to be the one on top," I said, my voice still tight.

"Oh really?" He laughed, like he was the man.

I nodded and rolled over, careful to keep us in the same position on the floor. Straddling him, I leaned over and my hair spilled onto his face.

He moaned.

I shifted, so that my breast filled his mouth.

He moaned.

And as his tongue flicked my nipple, my fingers wiggled against the carpet until I felt the edge of the knife.

I pushed myself deeper into his mouth. I curled my fingers around the handle.

He groaned and looked up at me. His eyes were glassy as he asked, "How does that feel?"

I took a breath. I said, "It feels just like this," as then with a move that happened before a second passed, I plunged the blade into his stomach, praying that everything I'd learned from my first acting role was true.

He screamed, but hardly moved and I pulled out the knife and stabbed him again. I did it over and over, never planning to stop.

And I didn't stop, until I heard that knock on the door.

Chapter 22

Camille

Donovan glanced down at his watch once again.

And every time he did that, I took another gulp of my wine. Which is why, after about an hour and a half, I was sipping/swallowing my fourth glass of the hotel's house wine.

"So...." Donovan kinda sang that word like it was a whole note, but then, like he didn't have any words or notes to follow that one.

I nodded, trying to think of something else, anything else to keep Donovan down in this bar. It had just barely hit midnight and I wasn't sure if that was enough time for Randy.

The thought of that made me turn up this fourth glass and with one last swallow, I finished it off. Not looking at Donovan, I raised my glass to the waiter who'd been serving our booth and when I turned back, I saw the frown on Donovan's face.

"Are you all right?" he asked me.

No!

It was a good thing he couldn't hear the way my heart screamed that word out to him—or maybe my heart was yelling at me. I wasn't all right because I wasn't sure if what I'd done was right.

Why was I doubting myself? I couldn't figure it out. My brother was dead and Tamara needed to pay. At least she was going to still have her life.

But I thought about Randy...and Tamara being locked up in that room with him.

I'd paid him to rape her!

Rape. Her.

The ultimate crime that took power away from a woman. It was a hate crime! I hated men who committed rape!

But wasn't that what I wanted? To take away Tamara's power like she'd taken mine? And June's and my mama's and daddy's?

But Randy?

But rape?

I shuddered and waved at the waiter, wondering where was my next glass of wine?

"I've never seen you drink this much," Donovan said. "You sure you're okay?"

I nodded. "I'm just gonna have one more glass. It's not like I have to drive."

When the waiter placed the fresh wine in front of me, Donovan glanced once again at his watch. Before I could raise my glass to my lips, he said, "Let me walk you to your room. Make sure you get there."

"Why?" I blinked, trying to focus on the fuzzy edges of his two faces. "You're ready to leave? It's still early."

"Well...I think I answered everything you asked for your brother."

I nodded. "Yeah, my brother." I tried not to cry.

Resting his arms on the table. "Camille, it seems like there's something....are you sure you're okay?"

"I told you," I snapped, teetering on the corner where sadness and anger intersected. "I'm fine."

He leaned back and held up his hands. "Oh...kay." Another glance at his watch. "Well, listen, it was good talking to you. I hoped I helped."

As he slid across the booth, I asked, "Where are you going?"

When he stood at his full height, he looked down at me with one of those 'nun-yur' looks. But he was too polite to tell me to mind my business, so he just said, "I hope you'll be ready for work tomorrow."

I swallowed the stones in my throat, nodded, and prayed that he wasn't heading to Tamara's room. Because if Randy was still there....

"And listen, tell your brother to call me if he has any questions. You have my number, right?"

I nodded again, even though I didn't. How would I have his number? He knew he'd never given it to me. But I nodded because what else was I supposed to do?

"What's your brother's name again?"

I looked up and the question that was in my eyes made him repeat his question. Then, I said, "June?" I whispered. "My brother's name is June."

He nodded. "That's cool. Like the month."

"Like June Bug. Like Junior. Like he was Martin Wilson, Junior."

Donovan frowned. "Was?"

I had to blink a couple of times until there was only one face in front of me.

"Hey, y'all."

Donovan and I turned to the voice.

"What's up, Justin?"

I watched as the two gave each other the brother-brother handshake/hug/slap on the back. Then, Justin turned to me, "What's up, Camille?" Before I could say anything, he added, "Y'all been over here a long time. Private meeting?" He looked from me to Donovan and then settled his eyes back on me.

Donovan said, "Yeah, we were just talking business." He glanced at his watch again. Made me take another swallow of wine. He added, "But we're done now. And I'm headed," he paused for a moment, "upstairs."

Justin slid into the booth, holding a glass of beer. "Good deal. Then, I'll keep this beautiful lady company."

Donovan nodded. "Yeah, do that. Make sure she gets to her room."

"Will do," Justin said, glancing at me.

Donovan gave us both a nod and then, trotted out of the room. He literally trotted, like he couldn't get to where he wanted to be fast enough. I raised my glass again.

"So, what's up with you?"

Justin's question made me shift my eyes back. I blinked some more to focus and when his face became clear, this dude was licking his lips. I sighed and for a moment, forgot what was happening on the sixth floor.

There was no doubt that Justin was too fine, and I'd really been sad to find out that his looks was all he had going for him because dude couldn't act. I'd had such hope when I'd done that audition with him, even thinking that he and I could have one of these little road flings. I'd done that on the last two plays—no biggie. Everyone did it. Everyone was sleeping with somebody.

Sleeping with somebody.

That thought brought my mind back to where I'd been and why this was my fifth glass of wine. Before tonight, I hadn't had five glasses of wine all year.

That had to be the reason why I asked Justin, "How old are you?"

He leaned, then stretched across the booth and it was only because the booth was so wide that his lips didn't touch mine. "Old enough."

That sent a shiver that was different than the others that had filled me all evening. But even though there would have been nothing better than dragging this boy up to my room, I had to stay focused. Exactly the way I'd been focused for the last two weeks.

He was still leaning across the booth and so, I did the same thing, though I didn't have to move as much since he was so close to me. My lips were within inches of his when I said, "I'm not interested."

He leaned back and laughed, then shrugged. "So then, let's change the subject; why're you down here by yourself drinking yourself into a stupor?"

His question made a scene flash in my mind: Tamara.

"I wasn't by myself. You saw Donovan...and...now...I'm waiting on someone."

"Oh. You just have men coming and going, huh?"

"How do you know it's a guy?"

He shrugged. "Because first, you're not interested in me and there has to be a reason for that." He paused, like he was waiting for me to do something, say something. I didn't move. He continued, "And you don't strike me as the type of woman who has a lot of female friends. I mean, you and Tamara don't even seem that close even though you work together every day."

Another flash: Tamara and Randy.

Why did he have to say her name? "Oh, God," I whispered and squeezed my eyes shut.

"What's wrong?"

I shook my head. "I'm not sure anymore. I'm not sure if I should have done it?"

"What?"

Tears were already blinding me and when I raised my eyes, two tears rolled down my cheeks.

There seemed to be so much concern on his face and I was sure of it once he slid out of the booth and slipped onto my side. "Camille." His voice was filled with care. "What's wrong?"

"My brother died!" I sobbed.

"I didn't know that. I'm so sorry. What happened?"

"Tamara killed him."

His frown was deep, his lips were twisted when he grunted, "Huh?"

It was hard for me to look into his face because my tears blocked my vision. But I had to make him understand. I had to make them all understand what happened. That was why I started talking: I told him about Randy and his issues. I told him about Tamara and what she'd done to my family.

"That's why I had to do it. I had to make her pay. Because of what she did to my brother."

"So, what did you do?"

The way he said this, I could tell that he was really concerned about me. "I paid Randy...to rough...Tamara up a bit." That was all I could say, I couldn't speak the word—rape. "I wanted her to hurt the way my brother hurt."

When he put his arm around me, I laid my head on his shoulder and just cried. And I would have stayed there for the rest of the night if Ted hadn't come rushing into the bar.

He stopped right at the entrance. "Has anyone seen Gwen?" he shouted.

I sat up just as Justin jumped up.

"Yo, Ted, what's up?" Justin asked his roommate.

As the rest of the patrons in the bar looked on, Ted rushed over to us. "Have you seen Gwen?" He huffed, so out of breath.

"Nah? What's up?"

He shook his head. "It's bad, man." He rubbed his hand over the scalp of his bald head. "It's bad. Something happened to Randy."

"Randy?" I pushed myself up, and out of the booth. That was and when I saw police officers rushing through the lobby.

As patrons stood and pushed toward the commotion, I staggered past as many people as I could.

"This way!" a bellhop shouted to the two paramedics barreling past. The young man led them to the elevators. "The sixth floor."

My heart was already pounding at a level that I knew it could not sustain, but when I saw the medics, my heart stopped. Had he hurt her that bad?

Oh, God.

The young men led the medics to the elevators and I followed. But the police pushed me away.

"I'm just trying...to get to my room," I said.

"You'll have to take the next elevator," the policeman told me.

I waited behind what seemed to be an army of people, then turned toward the stairwell. But before I could push open the door, someone else did. I looked over my shoulder.

Justin.

I said nothing, and I rushed up the steps. I couldn't speak because of all the thoughts that swirled through my head. Randy must have hurt Tamara pretty bad—exactly the way I wanted, right?

So why, was I crying? Why did my heart hurt?

But when we got to the sixth floor, I stopped. The police were there which meant that Tamara had probably called them. They were going to arrest Randy, he was probably already in handcuffs. But what if he saw me? Would he point me out? Right now, if he'd said anything, it probably sounded like the ramblings of a crazy man.

But if he saw me....

"What's wrong?" Justin said.

I looked up and into his eyes. I was about to tell him that I was afraid, but then, my lips snapped shut and my head cleared as if all the wine had been sucked out of me. I had already told him too much!

"Come on," he urged in a voice so soothing, I followed him. I had the feeling that no matter what happened, Justin would protect me.

He opened the door and we stepped into the mass of chaos. The hall was filled with people and a security guard stopped us as we moved toward the room where so many stood outside. "You need to stay back."

"My room," I pointed in the direction of what I knew to be Tamara's open door. And then I saw them.

Donovan, with his arms around Tamara, leading her into the hallway as she wailed.

"That's my friend," I lied and pushed by the guard who had little control. It took a lot of effort, but I was able to push out the two words, "What happened?" I spoke to Donovan and Tamara at the same time as I searched Tamara's face for signs of a struggle. But except for a tiny cut in her cheek, there was no signs of trauma, just that her eyes were puffy and crimson red.

Her head was resting on Donovan's shoulder until she looked up. "Camille," she breathed my name like we were good friends. "Oh my, God," she cried. "I killed him. I really killed him!"

I stood there stunned, as she rested her head back in the crook of Donovan's shoulder. *What had she said?*

Before I could have another thought or ask a single question, Donovan said, "Here," and then he passed Tamara off to me. "Can you stay with her for a moment? I want to talk to the police and...." He left it there as if I would know what he had to do.

I expected Tamara to say something like, 'Don't leave me with her.' I didn't expect Tamara to turn from Donovan and wrap her arms around me, sobbing now, into my shoulder.

"Oh, my God," Tamara sobbed over and over into my shoulder, repeating what she'd said before—I killed him.

Randy? Dead?

And then, I asked the question that was in the center of my heart—because of me?

At first, I felt like a statue, standing stiffly, saying nothing. And then instinct made me wrap my arms around Tamara, but not so much for her comfort; it was for me. So that I could find a way to keep standing, to survive through this moment.

Then a stretcher was being pulled-pushed from the hotel room and though the body was covered from the top to the toes, I knew it was Randy beneath that white sheet.

"Oh, my God!" I cried as the stretcher rolled past us. Even though Tamara and I were holding each other, I fell against the wall and slid until my butt hit the floor. I didn't know how—but Tamara ended up sitting next to me.

"Oh, my God!" I cried again. And because now, I just had to know, I leaned away from Tamara. "What happened?" my question came out in a whisper.

Her voice was as soft as mine. "He raped me. And I...killed him. I took his knife and killed him over and over and over and over...."

I put my hand on her shoulder, stopping her. Because if she had said that one more time, I would have died, too.

She lowered her head again and this time, I pulled her to me. And as we sat there, sobbing together, a pair of black Timms stopped in front of me.

"Donovan," I whispered. But when I looked up, I looked into the eyes of Justin.

Though it wasn't his eyes that set my heart racing at a sonic-speed. It was his lips and the way they curved into a smile, no a grin. A grin, that would fit the face of a character in a horror movie. A character who knew your secret and a character who looked like he was ready to bring you down.

He grinned, then brought his index finger to his lips, as if he were telling me to be quiet. Or maybe that was his signal that he would be the one who wouldn't say anything; I wasn't sure.

Then with his finger still in place, he backed away, though his eyes stayed on me. He stared and stared until he turned and disappeared through the stairwell door.

That was when I began to shiver. Or maybe it was that I had never stopped. Maybe I'd been shivering since I put this plan into motion.

Whatever it was, I shivered, feeling like I would never stop.

Chapter 23

Gwen

My favorite food was Italian, while Eli preferred French—which was why, even though it was my birthday, we'd had dinner at Lumiere French Kitchen.

"You heard from him already?" Eli spoke into his cell phone.

I looked out of the back window of the Town Car as we sped down I-85.

"Well, I knew our meeting went well, just not this well. I planned on having coffee with Mr. Anderson tomorrow before I flew back, but...."

My eyes had glassed over hours ago, from Eli's conversation (or lack of) and the bottle of Dom Perignon that I'd finished off pretty much by myself, the benefit of dining at a French restaurant if you were willing to drink your dinner.

But now I wished that the champagne had done something to my ears, too, and blocked Eli's conversation with his father. No matter what, no matter where, no matter when, business still took precedent over me and my birthday.

Well, maybe not my birthday. I glanced at my watch, it was well after midnight. I could no longer claim any kind of special place in Eli's life now. That thought made my heart hurt and took my eyes back to the darkness of the city as the car carried us toward the hotel.

Why had it all changed? Where was the Eli Weinstein that I'd met on that weekend in August back in 2008, the man who'd been enamored with me from first sight.

August 8, 2008

I'd registered for all four of Eli Weinstein's classes because he was the reason why I'd even signed up for this workshop. This for me, was the cherry on top of my educational cake. The process had taken quite long, though. Years of planning, then mixing it up and finally, the baking. All of it slow, all of it a struggle.

First, I'd worked four years after high school so that I could go to college debt-free, since my education was completely on me. After working double shifts at two restaurants for four years, I enrolled in Brooklyn College, majoring in psychology because even though I wasn't quite sure of what I wanted to do, I knew I'd need to understand humans and their behavior to be successful.

It was in my Senior year, when Tyler Perry came to speak that I discovered the passion within me. His story of poverty was my story, his story of dreaming was mine, too. But I was determined to give myself advantages that he didn't have so after graduating from BC, I went to work, three solid years of regular and overtime hours at two more jobs. And then, I was accepted into the prestigious Tisch School of the Arts. My chest had been poked out big time three years later when I received my MFA from NYU.

But since then, I'd been working and saving, studying and saving, networking and saving, struggling and saving, and now, I was sitting at the feet of one of the partners from Weinstein and Ernst (the most prestigious accounting and financial planning firm on the East coast). My hope was to soak up as much as I could from these Master Classes in Money Management so that I could come out of the box with the success of a million dollar project.

I sat, I listened, I took notes, I asked questions. Eli was friendly and patient, giving me all of the information I needed and at the end of the last workshop, I stepped to the front of the room, ready to thank him for dropping so much knowledge.

But before I could tell him that, he said, "I'd love to give you my number."

I guess it was my raised eyebrows that made him speak faster.

"So that we can stay in touch and I can answer any questions you have. I can feel your passion and I'd love to help if I can."

That surprised me and thrilled me. And I have to admit, it amused me, too. It was the way Eli Weinstein, stood there in his three-piece suit (even in the dog-day August heat of New York) shifting from one foot to the other.

"I'd like that," I said, getting one of his business cards and writing my number on the back.

I took his number, thinking that maybe if we stayed connected, his firm might consider me for some kind of diversity project and my play could be even more successful.

Then true to what he'd told me, Eli called. Just two days later.

"I'd love to take you out to dinner this week, if your schedule permits."

I accepted his invitation, told him I'd be available tomorrow and then, I gave him a dare, though I didn't quite put it that way.

"Let's have dinner at Caribbean Breeze."

"Where's that?"

"Right here in Brooklyn," I said, leaving out the part that it was on Nostrand Avenue in the heart of Bed Sty.

"That's great. I'll find it. See you tomorrow."

For all the hours between that call and me standing in front of the restaurant where the smells of curry and coconut, jerk spices and garlic wafted outside, I'd wondered if Eli Weinstein would really show up.

But he did, at seven o'clock exactly, still in his three-piece suit with spit-shined shoes. And he sat down like he didn't notice he was the only pale-face in the place.

I was impressed.

It was a great connection for me. The weeks that followed were filled with Eli always on my calendar. Almost daily talks on the phone (always about me), dinners a couple of times a week (always about my plays) lots of in-office (his office) meetings (always about my business plan). And then, came the time when he wanted me to go with him to meet his parents.

"Really? Dinner? With your parents? Why?"

"Because they want to meet you."

"Why?" I repeated, truly not understanding why the Weinsteins would have any kind of interest in their son's African-American friend.

"They're as intrigued as I am and they can't wait to meet a young playwright." Then, he lowered his voice. "And secretly, I think my dad has always wanted to be a writer."

"Okay," I said, thinking that when I showed up to that Fifth Avenue penthouse, this would be the end to my friendship with Eli. He was a grown man—in his early forties—but still, when his parents saw me....

I showed up, wrapped in one of my West African print ankle-length skirts, with a matching headdress (though my locs still flowed from underneath) and a big billowy yellow blouse. Oh, and of course, my dozen wooden bangles that I never left home without.

But either his parents didn't notice or Eli always brought home African-American women who looked more African than American. The conversation all night was about me and how they wished me massive success.

From there, our friendship kept on and on, until we had a seismic shift. It was one of those nights when Eli insisted on driving me home rather than me taking my preferred mode of New York City get-around...the subway. We were sitting in his Jaguar, in front of the brownstone where I lived in the third floor apartment. From one of the first floor windows, I could see the curtains moving and I knew it was my landlord/kinda friend, Sheila monitoring my date. She wasn't a big Eli fan—Have you noticed that he's white?—she asked me more than once. But I ignored her every time, just like I ignored her now as Eli and I talked about how it was time for me to finally move forward. But then, Eli was the one to move. Forward. All the way forward until his lips were against mine.

"Whoa!"

At first, that was all I said as I sat there in a couple of frozen seconds of shock. But then, I didn't know what it was—maybe it was because he cared so much and no one had ever cared about me—I charged him and pushed my lips into his, not caring one bit if Sheila was watching.

That had been our first kiss, and now, as I looked out into the darkness, I realized that I remembered my first kiss with Eli eight years ago, but couldn't recall the last time that our lips had connected.

"What time does his plane leave?"

That made me turn my head back to Eli just as he turned up his watch. Just as the driver rounded the driveway of the hotel.

When the car stopped, Eli glanced at me, "Uh, Dad...hold on a second." He paused, but I didn't wait for him to give me whatever excuse he had for deserting me again. I pushed open my door before the driver could get to me.

"Gwen...."

I slammed the door on his words.

If I'd been in private, I would have burst into tears, but I was far from being alone. My steps slowed as I took in the ambulance and more than a couple of police cruisers that lined the hotel's driveway.

"What's going on?" I asked, though I wasn't speaking to anyone in particular in the crowd of dozens that had gathered outside of the hotel's revolving doors.

And then, a stretcher rolled outside, carrying a body, I could see that from the outline below the white sheet. But I couldn't tell if it was a man or a woman since every bit of the form was covered.

"Oh, my God," I whispered, pressing my fingers to my lips. My mind began cranking, I couldn't stop it. And I imagined the scenarios that had brought this person to this end: a heart attack. No, she was having dinner with her husband and she choked on the tip of a hot wing.

"Gwen!"

It was Ted's voice that saved me from myself. Before I could say a word, he said, "It's Randy. I've been looking all over for you."

I blinked and frowned and tried to make sense of the first two words Ted had just spoken. "What's Randy?"

As if he had no more words, he pointed to the stretcher that was halfway inside the ambulance. My eyes stretched wide. "That's Randy?" I gasped. "Oh, my God. What happened? Is he...."

Ted nodded without me even saying the word and I cried out. "What happened?"

He grabbed my hand and pulled me inside, which was a good thing since I wasn't sure if I'd ever be able to walk on my own again. Inside, the lobby was filled with just as many people, more really, even though the midnight hour had long passed.

As we moved through the crowd toward the steps, Ted talked. "I don't know everything, but it seems Tamara killed him."

I stopped moving again and it took a tug from Ted for me to put one foot in front of the other again.

He led me to the stairwell as he explained that the elevators weren't opening on the sixth floor. "But they haven't blocked the staircase," he said.

I followed as he continued, "Randy was in her room and somehow he ended up dead. I don't know if she invited there or what."

It was hard for me to keep breathing because I knew from what Ted said that he didn't know. I knew that Randy had not been invited in by Tamara. This was just like the last time.

Oh God! Why had I hired Randy back?

I was still asking myself that question when we reached the sixth floor. At any other time, I would have been huffing and puffing, but it was either adrenaline or fear that had given me what I needed to make it to the top floor of this hotel, like climbing six flights of stairs was my regular exercise.

When we opened the stairwell door, there were even more people, packing the space and I wasn't able to move. I stood on my toes and through the heads and shoulders, I saw Tamara on the floor, sitting next to Camille, and Donovan just feet away from them talking to a sandy-haired white guy in a sports jacket and jeans.

I tried to press through, but even when I got past the three or four who blocked my path, a security officer stopped me from going further.

For a moment, I wanted to explain to the officer who I was, but then, I backed up. I needed to find out all that I could first because there was a chance I could be implicated in this situation somehow, since he was my band director and she was my star.

Oh, my God!

Backing up, I bumped into someone. "Excuse me," I said out of my instinct to always be polite.

"No problem."

His voice made me whip around and my eyes narrowed. Still, I backed away from as many people as I could because I didn't know what would come out of this boy's mouth.

We were steps away from everyone when Justin said, "So how did you do it?"

"What? You think I did this?"

"No." He chuckled like he'd heard a joke and like he wasn't standing feet away from a crime scene. "I'm talking about your husband. How did you keep him away from me today? I wanted to have coffee with him, but he never called."

I couldn't believe that this was what he wanted to talk about. "I don't know what happened," I lied. Of course, I'd made sure that Eli wasn't going to get anywhere near Justin. My plan had been to make love to my husband. But that hadn't happened. Instead, when he'd gone into the shower and his cell phone rang, I took his phone to him. When I saw it was his father calling, I knew they would talk until at least noon.

And that's just about what he did. So when he asked about Justin, I told Eli that it was too late—that Justin was working with the merchandising and there would be no chance for the two to meet.

"Well, I hope I get the chance to hook up with him. Where is he?" He looked around the crowded hallway as if he expected to see my husband as one of the gawkers.

"He's not here."

"Well then," Justin stepped closer, all into my personal space and with both hands, I pushed him away.

"Have you lost your mind?" I hissed. Then, I stomped toward the staircase. Not that I wanted to be alone or anywhere near this guy, I didn't even want him in my zip code. But I couldn't take the chance of anyone overhearing his nonsense.

He followed me into the stairwell, and closed the door behind us. "This is better," he said, leaning into me and I shoved him away from my space once again.

"What's with you?" he asked, holding up both hands. "I just figured you were probably a little stressed from all of this and I wanted to help you out."

"I'm fine. You need to stay away from me."

He shrugged. "All right. Fine with me." This his smile dropped and the concern in his tone did, too. "You got my money?"

I shook my head. With all that was going on now? "Look-"

"Ah, ah, ah." He wiggled his finger in my face. "You know, it's not too late for me to find Mr. Weinstein."

"He left already," I said, not even sure if I was telling the truth. For all I knew, whatever Eli had to do had been planned and his bag was already in the back of the Town Car. Or maybe he didn't have his bag and he'd just ask me to ship it back to him. I didn't know anything about my husband, but what I knew was that this fool wasn't going to be anywhere near him.

"Awww, too bad," Justin said like he was really disappointed. "I really wanted to get to know him. I figured he and I could compare notes on how you are in bed."

I raised my hand but he caught my wrist before my fist made contact with his face. "The price just went up."

"You bastard."

"Do you want to keep going? Because if I can't get to your husband, I won't have any problems getting to the media. All the tabloids have been hanging around, reaching out to us, trying to get more dirt on the cast. They all know there are more stories there."

My eyes narrowed, but I was as upset with myself as I was with Justin. I was the one who had opened the door, letting the tabloids in. Just like I'd let this devil in.

He said, "My story will replace all the news about Tamara and Donovan, especially by the time I finish telling it. By the time I finish, the world will believe that you had me as some kind of unwilling sex slave."

"No one will believe that."

He shrugged. "Let me tell it and we'll see."

I inhaled, then exhaled all of the air.

"That's better," he said, letting me go. "Now, I want twenty-thousand."

I tried my best not to move any muscles in my body. Didn't want this blockhead to redo the math. He'd said the price had gone up, but I guess it hadn't.

He said, "And, I want you to give me Donovan's spot in the play."

I was pissed, but that was funny. So I couldn't help my laugh. "Really?"

He didn't bat an eye.

"You think you can handle that part?" I didn't wait for him to answer. "First of all, nobody knows who the hell you are so why do think you'd get the starring role in my play? Secondly, you suck. And thirdly, do you see what's going on right now? I don't even know if this play is going to continue."

He nodded. "You have a point and I'm not unreasonable." He paused. "If there is a show, I want Donovan's role."

I glared at this boy who had clearly been born without a mother. He thought he was in control, but I'd shut the show down before I let him blackmail me into giving him the lead. Hell, with his talent or lack thereof, the show would close the second night he was on stage anyway.

"But either way," he interrupted my thoughts, "I want twenty-five grand tomorrow."

I blinked. "What? You just said-"

"I know. I just wanted to see if you were going to be honest and remind me of the price." He laughed as he brushed away lint that wasn't on his jacket. "I guess you should've paid me when you had the chance."

"Go to hell," I spat.

He chuckled. "Only if you come with me. We can have a good ole time down there, 'cause for an old lady, you sure know how to...." He leaned forward, his lips aimed for mine and this time, I didn't move. Because when he got close enough, I was going to bite his lips right off of him.

But he didn't touch me, at least not in that way. He only squeezed my chin, then trotted down the stairs. I stood there until I didn't hear his footsteps anymore.

And then, I breathed, thankful to God that He'd made Justin leave when he did. Because with all the police here, it would have been really easy to find me after I choked him to death.

Because right about now, not only did murder feel like a good idea, if felt like my only option.

Chapter 24

Tamara

There were two kinds of movies that I said I would never do—erotica and horror. And, I'd been right about both. Because tonight had been a nightmare that had me more afraid than I'd ever been.

Three hours before....

It wasn't until I heard the knock on the door that I realized I was screaming.

"Tamara!" I heard someone shouting my name.

At first, I thought it was Randy. Even though his lips weren't moving, who else would be calling me? So, I kept stabbing him so that I could be sure that he didn't get up. Because if he got up....

"Tamara!"

That made me pause, though I kept the knife right over Randy.

"Donovan?" I whispered.

"Tamara! What's going on?"

It sounded like my door was about to be busted open and that was when I pushed myself up...then looked down. "Oh, my God!" I screamed.

His eyes terrified me. His eyes that were open, but I could tell that he saw nothing. Stumbling to the door, I swung it back, then fell into Donovan's arms.

"Oh, my God," he whispered when he saw me. Then, he repeated those words when he saw Randy sprawled on the floor.

He didn't even ask me what happened, at first. It was like he knew. All he did was walk me to the other side of the room, sat me in the chair, then closed my robe and tied it before he grabbed the blanket from the foot of the bed. He wrapped it around my shoulders, then held me for a moment.

He began to move away, but it was too soon for me to be alone. "No!"

"I'm going right over there," he whispered.

"No!" I shook my head. "Don't leave me."

"I won't." His voice was so soft. "I'm just going over there." He pointed toward the bed. "I'm going to use the phone."

It took me a moment, but I nodded, though I kept my eyes on him. I didn't want to see the filth that was on the floor. Then, when Donovan finished with whomever he was speaking to, he took my hand and made me stand. But he didn't make me walk—he carried me from the room.

He waited until we were over the threshold, before he sat me down on my feet and asked, "What happened?"

It was hard to see Donovan because of the tears that blurred my eyes. "Is he dead?"

He nodded. "I think so." He paused. "What did he do to you?" I lowered my head and sobbed. He held me and whispered, "Did he attack you?"

I nodded into his shoulder.

He asked, "Did he rape you?"

I nodded again, and he squeezed me tighter.

But that only lasted for what felt like a moment, because the hallway filled with people. It was hard for me to comprehend it all, but it seemed like first, every security guard in the hotel filled the space, and then, the next elevator load brought police and EMTs, though a couple of officers came from the other end of the hall and I assumed they'd taken the stairs.

"What happened?" everyone wanted to know.

Donovan didn't say a word, not until Camille came up and he handed me off to her. She sat with me on the floor, protecting me on one end, while Donovan handled the questions on the other end.

I just sat there and cried; Camille just sat there and held me, never saying a word. It had felt like that was going to go on forever until Donovan came back (with a white guy behind him), knelt down, took my hands and told me that I had to go to the hospital.

"Okay, I just want to put on my clothes," I sniffed.

But the man who stood above us shook his head. "We have to take you the way you are," the man, who I assumed was an officer, said. "We don't want to destroy any evidence." Then, as if he were doing me a favor, he added, "You can keep the blanket," and I was so grateful to Donovan for covering me with that or else I would've been walking out of the hotel half naked.

That had been hours ago, though it had been the longest hours. I was so grateful that the officers let Camille and Donovan accompany me, though neither had been allowed to come into the examination room, which was probably why I was trembling now. This was the first time I'd been alone since Randy....I closed my eyes and just said the words inside—since I killed Randy.

I had actually killed a man! Taken a life away from this earth! How would I ever be able to live with that?

"Ms. Collins." I turned to face the black woman, dressed in a white lab jacket and khaki-colored pants. My first thought was that she looked like Halle Berry, and then my second thought: wouldn't that have been a great solution. This wasn't real—this was a movie.

She smiled and held out her hand. "I'm Doctor Williams, I'm a sexual assault forensic examiner and I'll be doing what we call a rape kit with you."

I'd heard of a rape kit, of course. Unfortunately, I'd known too many women who'd been raped. But an assault forensic examiner? That was different and just the way that title sounded made me tighten the blanket around my shoulders.

The doctor said, "I'm going to do a number of different things and this is going to take a while, okay?"

Again, I nodded at her professional, but compassionate tone.

She said, "If at any time you feel uncomfortable, let me know." She paused. "And I'm going to explain everything as we go through each step."

"Okay." I couldn't stop myself from nodding. "How long will this take?"

"About three to four hours."

My eyes got so wide. "What? That long?"

This time, she was the one to nod. "We're going to do a number of different things, but I'll try to get you out of here as soon as I can, okay?"

She took my silence as permission to proceed. I guess it was, it was just that I didn't have the words within me to tell her to do it.

"First," she said, "can you get completely undressed behind that curtain, making sure that you stand on the paper?"

I looked down to where she'd pointed.

The doctor explained, "This will catch any hair or fiber evidence."

I sighed. It wasn't like I had much on, just my robe and the blanket. But still, I did as I was told and once I undressed, I paused. What was I supposed to do now?

The doctor answered my silent question right away. "When you're ready, you can come from behind the privacy screen and I'll be taking photos of you."

"Pictures?"

"Yes, we want to preserve any evidence of bruising or any trauma."

Pictures? Of my naked body? Not that I was ashamed of how I looked, but pictures? Nude pictures of actors were always leaked. No matter what. I didn't care that these were being taken because...of what happened to me. Really, that reason would make the pictures more valuable.

It was a shame that this had to be my calculation right now. A shame that I had to think about this. A shame that I had to make this decision. "Do I have to do this?"

From the other side of the screen, she said, "No. There is nothing that you have to do, but I want to encourage you to let me gather as much as I can."

I thought about it for another moment. There would be enough evidence. "I don't want to do the pictures. I'll do everything else, but not the pictures."

"Okay," she said. After a few moments, she handed me a paper robe and I stepped back into the open space.

From there, she took me through so many procedures: a pubic hair comb, she took swabs of the outside and inside my vagina, and then, a speculum exam which wasn't any different from my regular pap smear—I hated that then, I despised it now. She scraped under my fingernails, and even combed through my hair.

Finally, she asked, "Would you mind if I took one picture?"

I said nothing.

She said, "There's a cut...on your cheek. I want to take a picture of that side of your face."

Her words made me raise my hand, made me feel the scar. I'd forgotten that he'd cut me. I nodded, giving her permission.

That was the end of the couple of hours that made me feel like I'd been the one to do something wrong. When she said, "I'm finished," and I had never been more grateful to hear two words.

It wasn't until I sat up from the examination table that I realized that all I had was this paper robe, since they were keeping my robe and the blanket. What was I supposed to wear back to the hotel?

As if she'd read my mind, as if she'd done so many of these that she knew the next question, she said, "Here, you can put on these."

She handed me a pair of navy sweat pants and a white T-shirt. It must have been the look on my face that made her explain, "These are donated for the rape center here at the hospital. You can wear that home and then...you can do whatever you want. You can even bring them back and we'll wash and use again. It's up to you."

"Thank you," I whispered, and then, with another nod and a smile, she left me alone. I was only half-dressed when a knock came on the door.

"Tamara?"

"Come on in," I told Camille and when she walked inside, I gave her my first smile of the night.

"I just wanted to make sure you were okay," she said in such a small voice. "The doctor said it was all right to come in."

I slipped the T-shirt over my head and nodded. "I'm fine. I'm just ready to go."

She nodded as if she understood and not for the first time tonight, I marveled at how this woman, who'd never spoken more than a dozen words to me away from the stage (and none of those words had ever been kind), had become the one I depended on through this. I was so grateful for not only her familiar face, but her soft, soothing voice, a Southern drawl that I'd come to love. She kept me calm, never leaving one side as Donovan never left the other.

She said, "I know this was horrible. What happened to you?"

"It was awful." I closed my eyes for a moment. "This whole night...." I wondered if there would ever be a day in my life when I didn't think about the fact that I'd taken a man's life.

Even though I hadn't answered her question, she said, "I'm so sorry."

Her apology for something that she didn't do made me smile again. Camille was just being a woman, always taking responsibility for an affront (or a crime) that didn't belong to us.

Then she said, "I just want to let you know," with her slow drawl once again, "the police are outside."

"For me?"

She held up her hand. "Don't worry. I think they're just gonna ask you a few questions. And Donovan already got an attorney for you. He's here."

An attorney? I needed an attorney?

The questions in my head must have shown on my face because Camille assured me, "You don't have to worry. The police officer told us that this is all just procedural."

I wasn't sure what made me do it, what made me rush to her and wrap my arms around her again. She stood stiffly, shocked again, I was sure of that. But, I would never be able to thank her enough. She'd stepped up as a friend, something I hadn't experienced too many times in my life.

When I moved back, my plan had been to just look into Camille's eyes and give her my sincerest gratitude. But when I looked at her, there was something—something so familiar, though something that I couldn't place.

Her eyes widened a bit and I watched as she took a couple of swallows. I couldn't be sure, but it seemed almost like...she was afraid.

She whipped her head away from me, and then her words rushed out, "If you're ready, let's go so that we can all get back to the hotel."

"Okay." I nodded because I did want to get back, not only for me, but for Camille and Donovan who'd had their nights turned upside down because of me.

The moment I stepped out of the room, Donovan wrapped his arms around me like he planned to be my forever protection. And I stayed in his arms as he led me to a man who was standing just a few feet away.

"Tammie, baby, this is Lewis Angleton. My agent recommended him and he's going to help you."

The first question I wanted to ask Lewis as I reached to shake his hand was, why did I need a lawyer? And my second—was he Matthew McConaughey's older brother?

Lewis said, "I'm sorry about what happened to you and I'm gonna make sure that you don't have to go through anything else."

"Thank you."

"The police do want to talk to you."

"What for?" My voice trembled, which is why I was sure Donovan tightened his arm around me. "I didn't do anything. I was protecting myself."

"I know. And the police know that, too, from what Donovan told them. But they have to hear it from you." He took a step closer. "If you're not ready, I can postpone this, but I recommend that we get your statement taken so that you can move on. My plan is to only give them one shot at you."

I glanced at Donovan and he nodded.

Lewis said, "Okay, let's go. I arranged to talk to Detective," he paused and looked at a notepad in his hand, "Liu. Detective Liu. He's waiting for us in a conference room down the hall."

We moved in that direction, but then, I stopped when I realized that Camille wasn't where she'd been the entire night; she wasn't by my side. Looking over my shoulder, I saw her standing in the spot where we'd just walked away. Her arms were bunched across her chest, not like she was mad, but as if she were cold.

"Come on," I said. "I want you with me, too."

She stayed steadfast and shook her head. "No, you go on. Donovan will take care of you now," she said. And then after a pause, she urged, "Let him." She sounded like there were tears in her voice.

I reached out my hand to her, but again, she shook her head. "I'm going back to the hotel." A beat. "I'll be waiting for you there."

I stretched out my arm even more, hoping she would change her mind. But when she didn't, Donovan tugged my shoulder a bit and I began to move once more with him.

Still looking back at her, I mouthed, "Thank you," and Camille nodded. I faced forward, but then seconds later, right when we rounded the corner, I looked back...and she was gone.

Inside the conference room, a tall (almost six feet) Asian man waited alone and I nodded my greeting to him as soon as we stepped inside. I was surprised that he was by himself—didn't all police travel in gangs of at least two?

But like Lewis promised, my time with the detective was short, it wasn't painful. In just over five minutes, I told the Detective how Randy had come to my room, and raped me. I told him about the knife, showed him where he'd cut me, then told how I'd tricked Randy when I thought he was going to rape me again.

"My plan had been to just hurt him so that I could get away because I knew that if he got up, he would kill me."

I covered my face with my hands and trembled.

The detective asked, "Did he say anything to you?"

I shook my head, though my mind took me back to those incoherent moments. When Randy rambled about my girl...a set up...wanting to play games. Was any of that important? Finally, I told the detective, "No, he didn't say anything...nothing that made sense," because I knew what Randy had said were just the scrambled thoughts of a psycho.

"I think that's enough," Lewis interjected. "You have everything you need, correct?"

The detective nodded. "For now."

"Well, you have my number and I'll make sure that you're able to speak to Ms. Collins if you need to. But I'm sure her statement will line up with the evidence."

Lewis shook hands with the detective, then we all walked out of the room. The detective left us alone to ride the elevator to the lobby, and I was a bit surprised that it was still dark as we piled into Lewis's SUV. This night was just going on and on and on. Donovan sat in the back of the truck with me, still holding me as if he never planned to let me go.

The truth was, though, he would have to let me go. And it was going to have to do that very soon. I knew this was the end, for a lot of things—for the play and for me and Donovan.

But for these last moments, I kept my head on his chest, rolling the thoughts in my mind. Wondering about all of the things that could have changed this night. What if Donovan hadn't been called away? What if I had peeped through the door before I opened it? What if I had only stabbed Randy once and then ran?

"Ugh! I didn't think of this."

I lifted my head as Lewis drove slowly by the front of the hotel where a gaggle of photographers loitered. There was even a news truck set up. Lewis kept the car moving.

"I can go in and set it up with security for you to go in through one of the other doors," Lewis said.

"Yeah, let's do that," Donovan replied for the both of us, though I knew it was going to be impossible to dodge the media forever. But if I could get an hour or two, just a little time to let this all set in, then I'd be able to handle this.

Lewis eased the SUV to the curb three blocks away from the hotel, then he jumped out and I watched as he trotted from the truck, back behind us. When he was out of sight, I sighed.

With his fingertips, Donovan turned my chin so that I faced him. And instantly tears swam in my eyes.

"I'm so sorry," he said.

Like Camille, he was apologizing for a fault that wasn't his.

I nodded and lowered my head once again onto his chest. "I'm sorry, too. I'm so sorry, Donovan."

"Why are you apologizing?" He kissed the top of my head.

"Because you should have never been involved in this...and you should have never been involved with me."

Even without looking up, I felt him shake his head. "No, I'm so glad Gwen set this up, set it up for us to do this gig together. Because this just proves what I've always known. That we were meant to be."

Now, I sat up. Now, I looked at him. "We weren't. You have a son."

"I can work all of that out."

I shook my head. "You can't. Because you don't want to leave your son. You don't want him to grow up the way you did," I said, repeating words that he'd told me years ago.

He held out his arms for me again, and I did what he wanted...I rested again on his chest. This time, I closed my eyes and for a moment, I feared that I would see Randy's face in the darkness. But whatever vision that waited for me behind my closed lids was faded out by the rhythm of Donovan's heart.

And so I squeezed my eyes tighter, and focused on his heart. I wanted to remember this moment and the heart that I knew still beat for me.

His question came long after we'd been silent. Like he'd been trying to think of the right words to say. He asked, "So, what are you saying? That we can't...."

The SUV door opened and Lewis jumped back in. "Okay, we have a plan. There is paparazzi at all the exits, but security is back there now telling everyone that you're about to come in and will make a statement." He turned around in the seat. "Donovan, if you're up to it, we'll use you as the decoy."

"That's fine with me."

Then, turning back to me, Lewis added, "And while Donovan and I are rolling up to the hotel, Tamara, you can dash around to the side."

I breathed. "Thank you, Lewis."

He nodded. "Also, here's a key—when Donovan first called me, I got in touch with the hotel. Had them move your clothes and everything to a different room."

I hadn't thought of that, hadn't thought about the fact that I would have never been able to walk back into that room. It was probably still a crime scene anyway. "Thank you so much."

Another nod. "Okay, so we'll go back toward the hotel and a block away, you'll get out, then, I'll drive up real slow to the front of the hotel to give you room to escape."

This time, I squeezed his shoulder to show my gratitude.

He smiled and that did it—I knew for sure he was related to Matthew in some way. He said, "So, y'all ready for this?"

Donovan and I nodded together. As Lewis started the car, I leaned back again, once again savoring what would truly be our final moments. Seconds later, Lewis eased the car to a stop. "Okay, you have my card, right?"

"I do."

"I'll give you a call in a couple of hours; I'm gonna head to the police station, just to get a feel for what's going on, to make sure this is done."

"Okay." And then, I turned to Donovan. I smiled.

His eyes searched mine as if he were trying to figure out my thoughts. "What room are you in? I'm coming there as soon as I get inside."

I shook my head. "No, let me get settled first."

He hesitated before he nodded. "Okay, but as soon as you do, call me and I'll come there. Or you can come to my room because I don't want you to be alone." He lowered his voice when he added, "And, we need to talk because I'm not letting you go."

Leaning forward, I kissed him gently, another moment to memorize. I didn't want to pull away, but when I did, his face was covered with a frown.

"All right, Tammie? Call me?"

I was sure his words were meant to be statements, but he sounded so unsure, they were questions. All I did was say, "Goodbye," then jumped from the car.

As the car rolled away, I pressed back my tears. Then, dashed around to the back door of the hotel. Using my key, I scurried inside, then dashed down the hall to the first floor room.

Once inside, I bolted the door behind me, then leaned against it, my eyes searching the room. It looked the same as the one I'd had on the sixth floor and my eyes lowered to the space that was the same as where Randy had attacked me, where Randy had died.

I waited for something to come, some kind of hysteria. But nothing rose inside of me, except for overwhelming sadness that came with so many degrees of death. There was so much loss between last night and this moment.

I opened my two bags, one that had been left on a luggage stand and the other was on one of the Queen-sized beds. I scrimmaged through, checking to see if the staff had collected all of my clothes, but it was hard to concentrate on this task. Because right now, clothes didn't matter to me. I really didn't care what I left behind.

Heading to the shower, I peeled off the T-shirt and then before I was in the bathroom, the sweatpants were off, too. My plan was to get out of this hotel, out of this city, out of this nightmare as soon as I could. But first, I had to scrub the feculence of this night completely off of me, though I wasn't sure that would ever be possible.

But inside that shower, I would try.

Chapter 25

Camille

I slid the washcloth from my forehead and tossed it across the bed. The cloth hadn't held the heat from the hot water for more than sixty seconds, so my head still ached.

Rolling over from my back to my side made my head throb more, so as slowly as I could, I pushed myself up and eased my legs over the side of the bed.

Sitting on the edge, I had to use my hands to hold myself up as I stared out the window at the blackness, though it was much closer to morning than it was to night. In just a little over an hour, I would have been awake for twenty-four hours straight, though the last five hours had felt like five days.

Even with the trauma of last night, at least I was awake. Randy would never be awake again.

"Oh, God," I groaned at that thought.

How had a plan that had felt so right have ended so wrong? That was the question I'd been asking for the last two hours or so, since I'd left Tamara and Donovan at the hospital. And it had gone wrong on so many levels—first, I was the one consoling Tamara...and then now, I had to grieve Randy.

Randy. Was. Dead.

And it was my fault.

Oh, God!

That thought made me pop up from the bed, even though the sudden movement messed my head up even more. But I couldn't sit down, so I began to pace, though it was really more like a slow stumble across the room.

"This wasn't my fault," I said aloud to the thought that dogged me. And then, I started a conversation with myself when I added, "But Randy wouldn't have done it if I hadn't put him up to it." Then, my mind swiveled back to all the issues Randy had. I had nothing to do with all of that. He was either born that way or something traumatic happened in his childhood or he hated his mother. Maybe his mother hated him.

Whatever, Randy was who he was and he would've done what he did even without me, even without the money.

The money.

I felt like I was never going to stop groaning.

Supposed this turned into a full-fledged investigation. Would they find the money I'd given Randy? If they did, would they think that cash was suspicious? And if they thought it was suspicious, would they dust the bills for prints and find mine?

Easing myself back onto the bed, I tried to calm my thoughts. This wasn't "Law & Order." This was a real life sexual attack and what happened was that the woman attacked protected herself. That was all there was to this—this case was shut before it was even opened. That was all I had to remember—that the blame belonged to Randy.

But even if I were able to convince myself of that, how was I going to handle thinking about what happened to Tamara? What I *caused* to happen to Tamara?

I closed my eyes, trying to bring back the memories, wanting to recall the reasons why I'd done this. But I couldn't remember the hate that had fueled my revenge. I tried to find it, but all that was inside of me now was the fact that Randy was dead, too. Randy was gone, just like my brother, just like my mother. And he was gone because of me.

Tamara and I were the same.

That made me want to just lie here and cry forever, but then, the knock on my door shocked me. Made me freeze, at first. Then, it came again and I sat up. Who in the world would be knocking on my door before the sun even rose?

Tamara! She was probably back from the hospital.

I stumbled to the door, but right before I opened it, I peeked through the peephole. When I didn't see anyone, I asked, "Who is it?"

Then, the image came into view. "Justin," he said.

Justin!

I had forgotten about him. But I hadn't forgotten about what I told him.

My heart started pressing hard against my chest, but still I opened the door. I hadn't thought about him since I'd gone to the hospital with Tamara, but it was good that he was here; I needed to talk to him, needed to find out what he thought he knew.

"Hey. I was just checking on you," he said when I gave him room to step inside. "Wanted to see how everything had gone."

As I closed the door behind him, I studied him. His words said he was concerned, but his tone didn't sound that way. I didn't have time to play around, this was too serious. "Everything's fine, but let's just cut to the chase," I told him.

He frowned as he lowered himself onto my bed as if I'd given him an invitation. "I don't know what you're talking about.

I crossed my arms in front of me. "Why are you really here? What do you think you know?"

He leaned back on one arm, crossed his legs, and shrugged. "I don't know anything."

I exhaled.

But then, he took my breath away when he added, "Except for what you told me," with a smirk. He put a finger to his head like he was thinking. "Something about you paying Randy to rough up Tamara."

I glared at him. "I was drunk when I said that."

He nodded slowly. "True, but haven't you heard that the truest things are said when you're drunk?"

"I've never heard that."

He shrugged as if that was my problem. "It's true. Even the cops know that."

I waited a moment; if my head didn't hurt so much, maybe I could find a way to outsmart him. But I didn't have the brainpower, I didn't have the energy. "So, what do you plan to do with that information?" I finally said.

He put a hand over his heart and feigned shock. "I'm hurt. What makes you think I plan to do anything?"

Oh, my God. I'd worked myself up for nothing. It wasn't until that moment that I noticed my shoulders had been hunched up to my ears. I relaxed. "I just thought... you know, everyone in this business is out for something."

He sat up and slowly slid his tongue over his bottom lip. "Well, I'm just a lowly merchandising guy, so technically, I'm not in the business."

For the first time in all the hours that passed since I'd started drinking in the bar last night, I smiled, feeling even more relief set in.

Then, he added, "But, I'm learning how far knowledge, of say, inappropriate behavior, can actually get a person."

That smile I had didn't last long. "What does that mean?"

"It means," he paused letting the room stay quiet for too long, "what is my silence worth to you?"

I took a deep breath, then released it slowly. I should've known, remembering now, how he'd left me last night.

He leaned back on the bed once again, this time resting on both of his elbows and he spread his legs.

Men were such pigs!

Fine! I stepped toward the bed, and didn't say a word as I reached for his hand and led him right to my sweet spot.

"Ummm," he said as he massaged me through my skirt, "you feel good."

I had screwed for less in my life so this was actually a very small price to pay for what I'd done. I sat down on the bed and put my hand between his legs. "You feel good, too." I couldn't even get my voice to sound like I meant it. Yeah, Justin was a sexy man, but something about blackmail messed with my libido.

I pushed his hand away for a moment, then stood and lifted my skirt, ready to kick off my panties. But he held my hand, stopping me. "But even though you feel good, you know what would make me feel so much better?"

My frown was really deep. What did this freak want me to do? "What?" I asked, already imagining some crazy sexual fetish. I was a country girl, raised with good-girl Mississippi Christian values. There weren't too many things I was going to do—even in a blackmail situation.

"Twenty grand."

"Twenty grand what?"

He laughed as if I'd told a joke, though I was sure I'd never spoken more serious words.

"You're funny," Justin said with a grin. "I never knew you were a comedian." Then, that smirk on his face went away and he became as serious as I was. "Dollars. I'd feel so much better with twenty thousand dollars."

I gasped. Now, of course, somewhere inside I knew he was talking about money, but I had been giving Justin a chance to take back that craziness. "Are you kidding me?" I asked, dropping my skirt down.

"No, I'm not."

"And where am I supposed to get twenty thousand dollars? I don't have that kind of money."

He shook his head a bit. "Well, you need to find a way to get it."

I crossed my arms.

"Or I go to Tamara, and the cops."

I let my arms fall to my sides.

"And not only will your career be ruined, but you could possibly go to jail."

"Are you freaking kidding me?" Now, my hands balled into fists. "You're really blackmailing me?"

He sat up straight and looked at me as if I'd just called him and his whole family some kind of bastards. "What? Blackmail? That's not what this is." He shook his head. "I prefer to call it a transaction. I'm giving you something and you're giving me something. My silence for your cash. That makes sense, right?"

I backed away, afraid that I was about to wail on him the way my brother had taught me to do if I was ever attacked. And then, Randy might not be the only one who would need to have a funeral planned. So, I kept backing away and all I said was, "Wow."

He grabbed the remote and flipped the TV on as if we were about to just chill. "I'm not an unreasonable man." He pressed the channel button over and over. He wasn't even looking at me when he added, "I'll give you till tomorrow morning to get it."

I pressed my feet into the floor or else I was going to rush over to him and start swinging. "From where? Where am I supposed to get that kind of money?"

He shrugged. "Ask your new BFF. I'm sure she'll help you out with the way you rushed to her side."

I glared at him.

"Or go prostitute yourself."

Now, I wondered what happened to the knife that Tamara had used.

"I don't care what you do. Just do it 'cause I don't know what's gonna happen with this play." He clicked off the TV and shook his head. Looking at me, he said, "You know it's a mess. Who knows if Gwen will be able to keep this open."

Then, he pushed himself from my bed, strolled to me, and said, "Eight o'clock. Tomorrow morning." He leaned toward me and I backed away. That made him chuckle as he strode toward the door.

My teeth were grinding as I followed him with my stare. When he put his hand on the doorknob, he paused, looked at me, said, "Eight o'clock. Tomorrow. Or I'm gonna have some story to tell."

"How am I supposed to get that kind of money on a Sunday?"

He paused, as if he hadn't thought of it, then turned and his eyes rolled over my body as if he might be considering that other offer. I prayed that he was. He said, "You're right. Today is Sunday. The day that the Lord hath made."

Then he chuckled, and I took a step back. Just in case God was about to do me a solid and strike this heathen down.

But no lightning came and Justin said, "Well since this is the Sabbath, and since I'm a reasonable man, I'll give you a little more time."

That didn't make me feel any better. He was still blackmailing me for twenty grand.

"I'll give you till tomorrow night. Eight PM, just in case you have to rob a bank or something." Then, he had the nerve to laugh as he stepped into the hallway and closed the door behind him.

But I rushed to the door and opened it, just so I could slam it. The moment I did that, I wished that I hadn't because his laughter was louder now.

Ugh!

I pressed my hand against my chest, trying to calm my breathing. I was hyperventilating and needed to get myself under control. I didn't want to die just because of that dude.

But if he went to the police, I might as well be dead. Twenty grand? I released a long breath because the thing was, I did have the money. I still had about fifty thousand left from my mom's insurance policy, but how could I give Justin almost half of that? I'd been living on that money since the acting gigs weren't coming fast nor were they coming often.

You won't need any money if you're in prison.

Lord, Jesus, I had no idea how I was in the middle of this nightmare, but what was clear was that I was going to have to pay Justin. The thought of that brought tears to my eyes, but I had no one to blame except myself. Now, I understood what my grandmama used to say: He who seeks vengeance must dig two graves. One for his enemy and one for himself.

She ain't never lied because even though I was going to give Justin this money, who was to say that hc would never come back for more? And who was to say that the police wouldn't find out about what I'd done anyway? No matter what, now I'd spend the rest of my life fearing Justin and fearing the unknown. I'd be living in prison anyway.

I glanced at the clock and the red digital numbers blinked 5:57. Twenty-seven hours before I could even get the money. So I did the only thing that I could do—I laid down, but this time, I didn't lay down because my head hurt. This time, I laid down and did all that I had left—this time, I laid down and cried.

Chapter 26

Gwen

Daylight was beginning to peek into my bedroom, but I hadn't closed my eyes since I climbed into my bed a little after one. My insomnia had started with the text that had come about ten minutes after I laid my head down.

What is going on? You know Tamara is gonna want out and I won't be able to stop her. Call me.

I'd read Maury's text and just laid back down. He wasn't telling me anything that I didn't already know. How would I even ask Tamara to go on stage after what happened? Even if I postponed the show for a few weeks, that was going to cost me a lot of money.

It was those thoughts that had kept me awake, those thoughts, along with the feeling that at any moment, police would come banging on my door. They had to be unfolding Randy's history and as they did, they'd discover that I knew all about his past. So their question would be, why had I hired him?

I had my story ready, though. Randy had been accused, but never convicted. Hell, he'd never even been arrested! So I was just one of those good people who believed in giving bad people a second chance.

That made me sigh. Because no matter how I spun the story, the star of my play had killed my band director. It would be in all the trade papers, all the tabloids, on all the blogs, and would probably make mainstream media, too.

Rolling over and facing the door reminded me that Eli hadn't even come back to the room. I wasn't even sure if my husband was still in Charlotte. Not that I wanted to complain too much about this. I couldn't even imagine what it would have been like if Eli had walked into the hotel with me last night. And I didn't want to imagine what he was going to say about this now. Especially if what I believed came true—if I had to cancel the play now, I wouldn't be able to pay Eli back his money. And if I couldn't pay him back, would he ever be willing to fund me again?

It was amazing that I had to ask that question when Eli was the one who had made pursuing my dream part of the deal. He'd woven that all into his marriage proposal....

April 4, 2009

"I know you may not feel about me the way I feel about you, but I want to take care of you, Gwen."

I shook my head, but I wasn't doing that just because of his words. It was the ring that he held in front of me that had me shaking my head to make sure that my brain and my senses were still in place.

"Uh," I began, not looking at him; how could I when there was all this bling shining in front of me, "I don't want anyone to take care of me."

"Well, maybe I'm not saying it the right way," Eli said. "Maybe what I want to do is help you achieve your dreams. You inspire me, and this is what I want to do."

I couldn't believe this was happening to me. Not that I didn't enjoy being with Eli, these past seven, eight months (I wasn't sure, I'd kinda lost track) had been so much fun. But I think it was more about how much he liked to talk about me: always asking me questions about how I'd grown up (I always thought people from Brooklyn were the coolest), why I wore my hair the way I did (So what's the difference between braids and Sister Locs?), and his fascination with my clothes (You don't go to Africa to buy them, do you?)

Even though some of his questions made me ask—are white people really that out of touch—I knew that Eli questioned me with the best intentions. He was just a curious white man who'd never had to walk inside a black world.

That was all there was to it because whenever he stayed away from my race, our conversations made me feel wonderful: You're as talented as any of those playwrights on Broadway; that's where I want to see you one day—on Broadway.

But even with all the time we spent together, it wasn't like I'd ever imagined us as a couple. I mean, I guess we had been dating if you called going to the movies and dinners, and kissing and making out afterward, dating. But we hadn't even slept together.

And now, he wanted to get married? How could I say yes? First he was older (by ten years), then he was richer (by at least ten zeros) and finally, he...was...white! I couldn't marry a white guy—I was the one who had thought about changing my name to Adaeze, my favorite West African name.

I hesitated, but that didn't indicate a denial to Eli. He talked me into taking the ring.

"Just hold onto it, for a day or two. And then, we'll talk about it some more."

There didn't seem to be any crime in that.

I couldn't wait to get home and tell Sheila. I expected her to be excited, but when I told her about Eli's proposal, she looked at me (and the ring) in horror.

"Gal, tell me that you are not going to marry that man," she said, her West Indian accent thicker with her appall.

Her attitude made my own enthusiasm dip. "I don't know. I haven't decided. But why would you say it like that?"

She tsked, then said, "Because that man doesn't want to marry you."

"Uh...." I held the ring up in front of her face.

She slapped the box away. "He doesn't want to marry you." My frown made her continue. "Think about it. Look at that man. Why would he, with all of his money, want to marry you?"

"Gee, thanks," I said, plopping down on her couch.

"I'm just keeping it, how do you say, real...I'm just keeping it real. I think he's just fascinated by you. He gets to take a trip to Africa without getting on a plane. You're exotic and he's black-curious, you're his forbidden fruit."

"Black-curious?" I was both insulted and fascinated by that expression that I'd never heard. "If that was all I am to him, then he wouldn't have to marry me."

She nodded. "Oh yes, he would. He doesn't see you as a whore, he sees you as a Madonna."

"Huh?"

"Look it up on the Internet, but I'm telling you, he will marry you, but when the newness of it all wears off, when he finds out that you are just a black woman, and even worse, just a woman...."

She sure knew how to mess up a good marriage proposal. "Why does it have to be all of that?" I folded my arms. "Why can't it be that he just loves me?"

She mimicked my stance. "Did he say that he loved you?"

"Yeah," I said, though that was a lie. I couldn't remember. I scrolled through the words that I knew he said...that I was special, that he'd never met anyone like me, that he wanted to take care of me and help me achieve my dream.

"And let me ask you this?" Sheila stepped all over my thoughts. "Do you love him?"

I pressed my lips together, saying nothing. If she had asked me this question first, before she'd gone off on me, I might have told her my truth. That I didn't really love, Eli— yet—but I really did like him. But what I did love was the thought that I wouldn't have to struggle anymore. I had been struggling for so long, since I was four really. When my mother had me shipped from Haiti because the wife of the man who was my father, threatened to have me taken away from her.

It didn't seem to occur to my mother that she lost me anyway, since in my three decades on this earth, I'd only seen my mother twice since she'd sent me to live with one relative then another in New York. I was an orphan, always in a place where I was only half-welcomed, always feeling like I was on my own. Now, that I was right at the beginning of making my mark in my profession, it would be a beautiful thing to have someone like Eli willingly taking this journey with me.

"You don't love him." She stated that as if she knew for sure that were a fact.

I lifted my chin, daring her to say that again.

And she did. "You don't love him. You love his money and I'm telling you, Gal, this will have a no-good ending."

Turning around, I stomped out of Sheila's apartment, determined never to say another word to her again in life. She hadn't walked in my shoes, she didn't know my struggle or my story, so how could she tell me that I didn't love Eli and that he didn't love me?

But the next day, I went straight to Eli's office and was grateful when he was alone. Closing his office door behind me, I didn't even say hello. I just walked right up to his desk and slammed the box with the ring on top of it.

What I really wanted to ask was whether or not he was black-curious. But what came out was, "Do you love me? Eli, do you really love me?"

He didn't even hesitate. "Of course, I do."

With a nod, I said, "Then, yes! I'll marry you."

He stood from his chair, came around his desk and then shocked me when he lifted me off the floor and spun me around the way white guys did to all of the girls in the movies. When he sat me down on my feet, he said, "We're getting married!"

"I know," I said. "And I can't wait."

Then with another one of those movie moves, he got down on one knee and slipped the ring onto my finger and this time when he gave me a gentle kiss, I felt something stir inside of me. Maybe I was getting close to love already.

When we pulled apart, he took my hands and said, "My parents are going to be so happy. My mother will want to plan everything."

I nodded. I was cool with that. I really like Bina Weinstein.

"And my father...."

When he paused, I frowned. Was there a problem with Aaron? I thought he liked me, too.

Eli said, "My father...he's going to ask...I hope you don't mind because it doesn't mean anything...."

"What?" I tried to go over in my head all the things that Aaron could possibly ask me—to meet my mother? Or my father and his wife? Or did he want to see where I lived? Or maybe get me to take extensive medical tests?

Eli stopped my imagination from doing that running thing. "Well, my father is going to want us to sign," he stepped away from me, returned to where he'd been sitting, opened a drawer, and pulled out a folder, "a prenuptial agreement."

I stared at the folder, then looked up at him with the question in my eyes.

He explained. "You know my father, it's always about business. And this is just business."

A prenup? That was kind of shocking. And sudden. It kinda felt like with one hand he was giving me a ring, and with the other hand, he was telling me how he might one day take it away.

"I just wanted to get this out of the way so that we can move full steam ahead." He handed me the folder and I took it because I didn't want it to just drop on the floor. He added, "It's just business, Gwen. You and I are going to be married forever. Just business."

That made me nod because if there was one thing that I knew about the Weinsteins, it was always about business. Isn't that what Eli was teaching me? Isn't that what I loved about him?

"You don't have to sign this now. Our attorney will go over everything with you."

"Okay." And then, I reminded myself: Just business....

Lifting my left hand, I stared at the symbol that I'd accepted from Eli that day. And then just a few months later, in a small ceremony in his parents' Fifth Avenue Penthouse, we promised to love and honor each other and that came really easy for me. I'd never had anyone in my life care about me the way Eli cared. So...what happened?

He gets to take a trip to Africa without getting on a plane. You're exotic and he's black-curious. You're his forbidden fruit...but it will wear off.

I hadn't spoken to Sheila much since that night and it was a good thing. Because I hated told-you-sos. But it was true, and there was nothing that I could do—except do what Bina did. I could accept it and just keep the money.

The notification signal on my cell chimed and I reached over, wondering if Eli was finally contacting me. But the text wasn't from my husband.

Do you have my money?

I wanted to throw this phone across the room, but that would only cost me more. Why was Justin up so early? Was he just roaming the earth, like Satan, searching for where he could make the most trouble?

My first thought was to not respond. The clock hadn't even ticked to seven yet, and this dude was up, extorting me? I tossed the phone onto the side of the bed where Eli should have been, but the moment it hit the mattress, another text came in.

I hope ur not ignoring me. Blogs r always looking 4 a good story.

This time, I did throw my phone across the room, though I tossed it more than giving it a good wind-up. I couldn't believe this. Whenever people were caught doing anything: cheating on tests, robbing banks, cheating on their spouses—they always said it was their first time and no one ever believed them.

So, I knew no one would believe me. I couldn't go to Eli with the story of being so sad and lonely for years and finally, I gave in to one temptation. He would say, "First time, yeah right. Let me call my attorney."

I pushed myself up from the bed, crossed the room, and picked up the phone. Thanks to the hard case, my cell had no crack, no scratch.

For a moment, I thought about telling Justin that I had to wait until tomorrow, since banks weren't open on Sundays, thinking that I'd give myself just a little more time to find a way to get out of this.

But there were two problems with that story—as my Merchandising Manager, he knew that I had cash. And secondly, what would more time buy me besides more grief? I was sure that Justin would not allow me to have Sunday as a day of rest from his blackmail. So, I decided to pay this price.

I texted: *I will have your money in an hour. I'll bring it to your room* and then, I laid the phone on the nightstand.

Another text came in, but I didn't bother to check it. I was going to give Justin this money and to make sure that he didn't come back for more, I had a plan of my own.

I headed into the bathroom; inside the shower, I would work out every single one of the details. Justin might win this battle, but I was going to make sure that if this turned into a war, I'd be the one on the other side claiming victory.

Chapter 27

Gwen

My heart was filled with a mixture of anxiety and downright pissivity as I stuffed the last of the wad of hundred dollar bills into the navy blue duffle bag, grateful that a good part of my business was a cash venture. It was easy enough to get my hands on the twenty-five thousand from where I kept my cash in the safe in the hotel. All of Friday and Saturday nights' receipts were there from the ticket and merchandising sales. Justin may have been the lowest on the scale of low down dirty dogs, but he could sell. Or rather, the way he looked sold a lot of merchandise. It was just a shame that I was returning a good part of what he'd sold back to him.

I zipped the bag and tossed it over my shoulder, then adjusted by cross-body bag, making sure my cell phone was in place. Stomping out my hotel room, I took the stairs down two flights. I'd decided to go to his room, thinking maybe he was dumb enough to have Ted there and then, Ted could turn into a witness for me if I ever needed him.

But when Justin swung open the door, and said, "Just what I like, a woman of her word," I could see that he was alone.

So that part of my plan didn't work. Now, I had to pray that part two would work out for me.

"Come on in," Justin said, swaying his hand as if this was a friendly visit. I took in the white Nike tank top and blue sweat pants he wore and wondered where was his sexy? There was nothing attractive about this man, really, his face was average—I had no idea what I'd been looking at before.

"Here." I tossed the cash into his chest, then stood there as he rushed to his bed like some kid who'd just been given a gift at Christmas.

He unzipped the bag and then this boy from Alabama eyes grew wide. "Wow!" Then, he looked at me with eyes that were filled with glee. "It's all here, right? I can trust you, can't I?"

"It's all there," I repeated, not bothering to hide my attitude.

He laughed, then before I could take a breath, he grabbed my arm and pulled me to him. As soon as I steadied myself, I pushed him away, hitting him harder than I had to.

"Ah, come on, baby." He actually pouted. "Don't be like that. It doesn't have to end like this."

"You stay the hell away from me," I growled.

He chuckled. "You know you want me."

"The only thing I want is for you to take the money and leave me alone." I was so angry I wanted to cry, but I refused to let him see me shed a tear.

"Now, how am I going to do that when I'm opening up in the next show?" He grinned like he believed with everything inside of him that I would give him Donovan's role, or any role.

I stepped closer because I wanted to make sure he didn't miss a syllable of what I was about to say. "Not only are you not going to have a part, but I doubt if there is even going to be a play."

"What? Why?" He acted all innocent, though I didn't

understand this part of his game. I knew he wasn't dumb. "I know you might get some not-so-favorable publicity, but I thought all publicity was good publicity."

I just glared at him.

He shrugged, then looked over at the bag. "Oh well. It is a pity, though. I was looking forward to winning an Oscar." He paused. "Wait, that's what it's called, right? Or," he paused and looked up at the ceiling as if he was trying to put together thoughts in his mind, "do they have awards for plays like the Oscars or BET Awards?"

I looked at him and blinked. I blinked and looked at him. Okay, I had to take back what I thought—he *was* stupid and I was mad at myself for not noticing that before. Why hadn't I noticed there was nothing more to this man than his face and what hung between his legs? Because clearly there was nothing between his ears.

Yet, he had thousands and thousands of dollars that belonged to me.

Waving his hand, he said, "It doesn't even matter. I got this money now." He sat on the bed and placed the bag in his lap. "If you close this one down, just let me know about your next audition, so that I can be all up in there for the lead role."

Right about now, I hated this man. "Is our business done?"

He flipped through a stack of one hundreds, and not even bothering to look up, he said, "For now," as if I were being dismissed.

Before I left, I needed to explain to this dim-wit that this was where his gravy train ended. "Let me give you a clue." I stepped closer to the bed, though he didn't seem to care. His mind was on that money. But soon, I guess, he was able to feel me. So he glanced up.

With my eyes narrowed, I hissed, "That money right there?" I pointed to the bag. "That's...it. No. More. If you try to come at me for more, I'll take my chances with Eli, tell him myself, and then have you arrested for extortion."

He stood, rolled his shoulders back, then laughed...right in my face. "Miss me with that. 'Cause see first, you'd have to prove that I—"

I reached into my bag, pulled out my cell phone and held it up in his face so that he could see that I'd been recording the whole time; and now that the camera was facing him, he was being videoed, too."

"Whoa!" He held up his hands like he was being arrested and backed away. But then, he stopped moving. "You know, all I have to do is grab that cell from you and bust it."

I nodded. "You could. And then, not only would I have you arrested for assault, but you'd still be up on charges for extortion because you won't be able to get the iPad out of my purse that's directly recording to the iPad in my room. I won't have the video, but the audio will be enough."

His glance fell to my bag on my hip. He smiled a little, shook his head a little. "I'm impressed."

"Don't be. Just know, I'm not the one to play with. I messed up," I motioned toward the duffle bag, "and I'm paying the price for that, but that's it. You need to find another way to make your money."

I spun around, and danced out of that room like I was the winner. But once I stepped into the hallway and closed the door behind me, I leaned against the wall, inhaled a couple of gulps of air, fought back, then lost the battle of tears.

My cries didn't come because of Justin; I wouldn't hear from him again. He was a coward, so he wouldn't want to fight my cell phone video and he'd bought my bluff about my iPad, though having that as a back up would have been a great idea.

But I cried because it really did look like this was coming to an end. How could I have a show without Tamara? And if she was gone, would Donovan be far behind? Yeah, he had a contract, but who would want to be caught up in this kind of drama? If I were being honest, I didn't even want to be here.

I pushed myself from the wall and moved toward the elevator, not having the energy to take the stairs. But right before I reached the elevator, I paused, and stared, and then moved closer. To the mirror. So that I could really see my reflection. But then, after a couple of seconds, I jumped back.

Oh, my God! What had happened to me?

I wasn't talking about the way I looked—anyone seeing me would know for sure that I had my life all together. And it wasn't even the puffiness of my eyes from the tears I'd just shed and the insomnia I suffered last night. It was deeper than that—it was inside my eyes, the windows to my soul.

What had happened to my soul?

As I stood there, I thought about all the compromises I'd made: lying to Eli about the last play, being in cahoots with Tamara's agent, setting Tamara and Donovan up...even sleeping with Justin when I had no plans at all of putting him in my play.

And then, there was my biggest compromise. My happiness. Marrying Eli so I wouldn't have to struggle, struggle, struggle.

I got closer to the mirror and saw the lies that I hadn't seen before. I hadn't been a struggler...I'd been a survivor. A victorious survivor. Coming from my situation, I had thrived!

So why was I married to Eli? Why did I stay married to him? My thoughts stopped there. Why? Why stay with a man who didn't even think I was significant enough to let me know if he was still here in Charlotte?

It was his money, of course. I needed his money.

I was a survivor.

I was a thriver.

After a while, though I wasn't sure how long, I turned away from the mirror, I turned away from the elevator and marched back through the hall the way I came. I paused at Justin's door, nodded a bit, then made my way to the stairwell.

Before I got there, I had my cell in my hand. It was Sunday, so I didn't expect an answer. But I left a message because I wanted a call first thing tomorrow.

"Hey, Anthony, it's Gwen Tanner," I paused, "Gwen Tanner," I repeated my maiden name, my professional name to my attorney's voicemail, even though he'd always called me Gwen Tanner Weinstein. "I need to talk to you about a couple of things. Something crazy's happened with my play; it's a mess. But first I need you to handle something else for me. I need you to find me a good divorce attorney. Someone who understands prenups and someone who knows how to go after the money. Call me. First thing."

I tucked my phone into my bag, and then, I trotted up the stairs with a new kind of pep in my step.

Chapter 28

Tamara

My hotel room was bright with the noon sun, no indication of what had happened during the nighttime hours.

"Okay, Maury, thanks so much for getting me out of here. I'll call you when I land in LA."

"Hang in there, kiddo. From what Lewis told me, you should be in the clear. Now, he had to promise that you would return if they had any other questions...."

"I will," I said for what felt like the one hundredth time. Lewis had called me three times in the last two hours, too, stating the same thing. I'd promised him, though I would have told him whatever he needed to hear just so I could be on a plane to Los Angeles.

"Now, are you sure you don't want to wait until tomorrow? Because I can fly there and then fly back with you."

"No, I really want to get out of here and I know I'll be fine." Maury's concern was that there would be paparazzi everywhere, at the hotel, at the airport, probably even waiting for me when I landed in LA. He didn't want me to have to handle the questions about being raped, the questions about a man being dead. But I would just keep my head down, not answering anything anyone asked. Whatever I had to go through would be worth it, as long as I could go home.

"Okay then, just call me when you get to the airport," Maury said before he ended our call.

I stood there, staring at my cell. All of this time I'd been looking for a way out of this play and now I had it, though there was no joy in getting my exit this way. A man was still.....

I shook the thought off before I allowed it to complete. I didn't know how I was going to do it, but I wasn't going to let my mind take me there. Maybe when I got to Los Angeles, I'd have Maury set me up with a psychiatrist. For a couple of visits. I didn't want Randy haunting me, I didn't want my attack to remain always in my mind. I knew I was going to have to find a way to let this—as sad as it was—go.

For a moment, though, I thought about calling Maury back, asking him what he didn't mention—what had Gwen said? Surely, she knew what happened, though she hadn't reached out to me. That surprised me—a little—though it wasn't like we'd become friends.

But I hadn't been friends with Camille either, and look what happened with her. I was definitely going to reach out to her, not today, but when I got back to Los Angeles. Who knows? Maybe we'd become girls. Because no matter how disconnected I'd been with her these past weeks, last night, it almost felt like...I knew her. We'd made a connection and I wanted that bond to remain.

Looking around the hotel room, I adjusted the note for the cleaning staff that rested atop the sweatpants and T-shirt that I'd worn, and then, I faced the last thing I had to do.

I took a breath as I opened the text icon on my phone, then typed: *I'll see you in a little while. Give me another hour.*

Right away, Donovan's text came back: *Ok*. Then a second text followed: with just a red heart.

That made me swallow, that made me sad.

But then, the knock on the door turned me into ice. A second knock. "Ms. Collins."

I melted and breathed, then rushed to the door, though still, I used the peephole before I opened it for the bellman.

"My bags are right here," I said, pointing to the two already set up by the door. "Okay, and your car service just arrived."

"Please tell him to give me a few minutes."

He nodded and then let the door close behind him.

With just my purse on my shoulder, I sat on the bed and glanced down at my phone. At the text that Donovan had sent to me.

I closed my eyes and prayed, prayed that I was doing the right thing. This had to be because I could never be with another woman's husband. He would always be my first real love, my soul love; but I wasn't sure if he was my true love. True love didn't come with this kind of drama, did it? This kind of pain?

And so that meant this chapter with Donovan had to be closed, never to be opened again.

With the deepest of breaths, I dropped the cell phone into my purse and then headed out the room, not looking behind me. When I got into the elevator, I was still pensive about all that had happened, not just last night, but in the weeks that had passed. My mind still felt overwhelmed as I rode down, but then, when the doors parted and I stepped into the lobby, the first person I saw...was Latrice.

Oh, my God! What was she doing here? Had she heard about what happened already? Had Donovan called her?

Her head was down, it looked like she was texting. She hadn't seen me yet, which was my blessing for today. There was no way I wanted to get into any kind of confrontation with her. So it was self preservation that made me duck into the stairwell and walk a half flight up. My plan was to just wait a minute or so, until I was sure she was on the elevator. Then, she'd be Donovan's problem and I'd be on my way to the airport.

But then, the door below opened and it was Latrice's voice that said, "In here."

Inhaling, I took a few more steps up, ready to run all the way to the second floor if she began walking up.

"What's with women and staircases?"

That voice made me pause.

"Y'all sure be spending a lot of time in them."

Justin? Was that Justin, the merchandising guy?

Latrice said, "What are you talking about?"

Justin chuckled. "Nothing that you'd understand." The humor was gone from his voice when he said, "So you got my money?"

My hand flew to my mouth, but not just because I was shocked. Because I wanted to make sure I kept my gasp inside. Latrice huffed, then there were sounds like she was ruffling through something—her purse, maybe?

She said, "I don't understand why you're hitting me up for money when you're blackmailing Gwen."

Now, I had to stop breathing, or else I was going to squeal or do something that would give me and my hiding spot away.

"Come on, cuz, this was all your idea and you said that you'd cover my expenses. The money from Gwen was supposed to be my bonus, remember?"

I pressed my hand hard against my mouth. Cuz? Justin and Latrice? Cousins?

"Yeah," she barked, "but you didn't do a very good job."

"What are you talking about? I did a fantastic job."

"You were supposed to get my husband fired."

"Well, I kinda had my own plan. I was gonna get in the play and after she saw how good I was, I was sure she'd replace Donovan with me."

Latrice chuckled, though she didn't sound like she thought his words were funny. "Really? You thought you could out-act my husband?"

"Please. He ain't all that. Gwen was close to making that switch, but then all of this stuff went down."

"Yeah, right."

"And anyway, why're you complaining? Didn't this all come together nicely? This play is a bust. And all the trouble you've gone through to keep your man from another woman has worked."

"I hate that ho," Latrice growled and I pressed my back into the wall. "She slept with my husband after I warned her!"

I prayed that my sharp inhale didn't carry down the half flight of stairs. How did Latrice know that? If there was one thing I knew for sure, it was that Donovan hadn't told her—had he?

"It doesn't matter," Justin said in a voice that sounded like he was trying to calm her down. "At the end of the day, he's still going home with you."

"It does matter," she shouted so loud, she might as well have been standing in the middle of the lobby. "Because he may be going home with me, but I don't have him. I have his last name, but I don't have his heart."

This time, my gasp was audible and I prayed and prayed and prayed that they hadn't heard me. While they kept talking, I closed my eyes and thought about Latrice's words: *I don't have his heart.*

My mind took me back a few hours ago, to when I was in Lewis's car with my head pressed against Donovan's chest. Listening to the rhythm of his heart, memorizing its beat. The beat that I knew carried on for me.

"Well, to me," Justin's voice brought me back to now, "what's most important is that you have the kid. 'Cause the kid will always be about the money."

"Yeah," there was so much sadness in her tone, "at least I have Don."

"Just as long as he never finds out that kid ain't his, you're good, cuz."

This time, it took both of my hands to keep my gasp inside. I couldn't even breath, which is why I almost missed Latrice's next words.

"What the hell? Don't you ever say that!"

"What? It's true."

"Justin, no one can ever know that."

"What you talkin' 'bout? Everybody in the family knows. You know your mama got a big mouth."

"Whatever. In the family, fine, but never outside of the family. Donovan can never know."

"We got you, cuz. Ain't nobody tellin' that 'cause he's the man with all the money. Just keep collecting those dollars and set some aside," he advised. "Just in case, you know, one day...."

"Stop it, Justin. Just stop it!"

"Okay, okay. Well anyway, I guess this messes up my chances of ever formally meeting my famous cousin."

"Your cousin by marriage. And don't play; it's not like any of us in this dysfunctional family are all that close."

"Yeah, but Donovan Dobbs is still my cousin. He could help me get my career going."

"Look, Justin. We had a deal and you have your ten thousand dollars. This case is closed."

Ten. Thousand. Dollars.

Ten thousand of Donovan's dollars.

Justin said, "I'm just saying. Without a career, I might need some more money from time to time."

There was a pause that was so long, for a moment, I thought the two had left the stairwell. Then, a soft, "Are you blackmailing me?"

"Nah, nah! I wouldn't do that. I'm not a blackmailer. I'm a lover and we're blood. I'm just sayin'...."

"You don't need to say anything else."

"You right. 'Cause what I need to be doing is thanking you. From the moment we mapped out this plan in Atlanta, I'm telling you, this has turned into quite a lucrative enterprise." He laughed.

"So you got the money from Gwen?" Latrice asked.

"Yeah, and more coming from Camille."

Camille? This was getting to be too much. Why had Camille given him money?

Latrice asked the question that was inside my head.

"Don't worry about it," Justin said.

"I'm just sayin'...if you're getting money from Gwen and Camille, why do you need my money?"

"Because that was the deal. My expenses. Remember? And it's not like you can't afford it."

Latrice released an exasperated breath. "Whatever. It's done."

"Yeah, it's done and I'm grateful for you, cuz. Maybe Mama and I'll get a chance to see you if we come to Memphis for Thanksgiving."

"If you're coming, I'll make sure Donovan and I are out of town."

He laughed. "Awwww, come on."

"Don't take it personal. Anyway, you have your money and now, I'm going up to surprise my husband."

"Oh, surprises are never good. You never know what you may walk in on."

"All I know is that he better not be with that heffa. Or else, Randy won't be the only one who died on the job."

She spoke Randy's name with such familiarity it made me wonder—with the tangled web that she and Justin had just revealed, had she sent Randy to my room? Had that been some kind of set-up for me since she wanted me away from Donovan?

"Let me walk out first. Give me a couple of seconds," Latrice said.

"Okay, cuz. Be good. Tell Aunt Nancy I said hey."

The door below squeaked open, then I heard the slam. But I stayed like stone. Then about thirty seconds later, another squeak, another slam. Still, I stayed in place, which wasn't difficult because there was too much going through my head for me to move anywhere. But every thought I had was like a pathway back to Latrice.

Latrice and Justin were cousins.

A plan to separate me from Donovan.

His son, Donovan's son, wasn't his son!

Donovan had left me for a lie.

A lie that he didn't even know.

What did this mean? What should I do?

I let all of those thoughts marinate for more minutes before I made my decision. Tiptoeing down the stairs, I half-expected one or both of them to jump back into the stairwell.

When I got to the door, I peeked through, and it wasn't until I was sure that I saw no familiar faces, that I rushed through the lobby.

I'd already made my decision before I left my hotel room. Donovan Dobbs would always have a part of my heart and a piece of me would always believe that I should have been Donovan's wife. Especially with this news of his son—it should have been me walking down the aisle to meet him at the altar.

But it wasn't my place to mess up his life, wasn't my place to break his heart over his son. He'd never forgive me because the messenger was always blamed. So all I would ever be able to do was pray for that man. And wish him God's best.

My steps slowed as I got closer to the revolving door. Through the glass, I could see the car waiting for me, but at the same time, I saw dozens of men (and two women) with cameras all anticipating, and I wondered if they had been there since the middle of the night. But even as I asked the question, I knew the answer—they had been. Such was the life of the paparazzi, the people who made their money on the misery of others.

I pressed my shoulders back, slid my sunglasses on, then marched out the door to choruses of, "Tamara, Tamara, look this way!"

I didn't do as any of them demanded, I just nodded to the driver, who held the door open for me. But just as I slid into the car, I heard, "Oh, my God, that's Tamara Collins!"

The squealing of the two girls made me glance over my shoulder, made my lips curl, though only a little bit, into a half smile. Then right before I slid into the back seat, one of the young women said, "That should be me rolling in style like that. Did you see her Louis Vuitton bag? Girl, that cost three thousand dollars. I saw it in Vogue."

I disappeared into the back seat and the driver closed the door.

Even though the windows were tinted, the cameras still clicked as if their lenses could cut through glass. But I ignored the cameramen; instead, my glance was on the girls.

They stood shoulder to shoulder with the paparazzi, trying to peer through the darkened window. And though they couldn't see me, I could see clearly—and I could see the envy painted all over their faces.

I guess they hadn't yet heard about what happened last night, though I was sure that not even a rape or a death would change their minds. Everyone looked at my life and saw an actor, being driven around in a Town Car, having roles in plays and movies. They imagined my bank accounts, filled with balances that totaled millions, and the mansion that I lived in with probably two other residences, maybe one in South Beach and another in St. Tropez. They envisioned the parties, the vacations, the gifts given and received.

Their minds filled with images of what was to them my glamorous life, one where my grass was so much greener than theirs would ever be.

If only they knew.

That this green grass came with a high water bill.

And I was proof positive of that.